MARK OF JUSTICE

A Mara Brent Legal Thriller

ROBIN JAMES

1

It was in his eyes. I didn't need to ask who found the body. Deputy Austin Rankin stood apart from the other cops as I approached the barn. Someone had put a paper cup in his hand. He merely picked at the rim but didn't drink from it.

He was fresh-faced with the pale complexion of a true ginger. Three days of searching in the bright, April sun had left his cheeks apple-red. He met my eyes and that's when I knew. They might have been blue, or green, but now they seemed colorless, haunted, sunken into his young face. There would be times in his life where a smell or a sound would bring him back to this particular spring when he was little more than a rookie and had the rotten luck to be the nearest responding unit when Jan Gunderson's eight-year-old Bluetick Coonhound found something Jan knew shouldn't be there. A freshly dug hole in a little-used part of Jan's tree farm just two miles from here. Inside that hole, the horrors would live with Deputy Rankin for the rest of his life, let alone his career.

"Mara!"

"Be right there," I answered back, pulling the end of my cardigan closer around me. I walked up to Rankin.

"You okay?" I asked, putting a motherly hand on his shoulder.

"Yeah," he said, though we both knew it wasn't true. We stood in the shadow of the barn. It loomed over us just like the evil we both knew happened inside of it.

"I ... I knew her," he said. "Haley. My kid brother, Alex. They were in the same class. They were in Spanish club together, I think it was. She was at my house."

"I'm sorry," I said. It seemed like the only thing. It seemed woefully inadequate.

"You coming, Mara?" Lieutenant Sam Cruz stood just outside the shadow. He would walk me through what the lead detective had found so far.

"Get some sleep if you can, Rankin," I said. "You've done all you could do."

He nodded, his breath coming hard, as if he couldn't get enough air. No. It wasn't that. It was the air itself. Thick. Ominous. I wanted to walk out of the shadow and away from this place.

Sam put a hand on my back and guided me toward the barn. I left Austin Rankin behind. I'd see him again. Already, my lawyer brain knew he would make a compelling witness when the time came, if he could keep it together. If we all could.

I walked with Sam toward the barn. At least a dozen vehicles lined the rural highway to the east. The Maumee County sheriffs, the medical examiner, Ohio BCI all had a presence here. Cruz lifted a strand of yellow crime scene tape and guided me in.

I took a breath and held it, feeling a little of what likely afflicted Deputy Rankin. It had all happened here. Everything the killer had done to college student Haley Chambers. Her monster had breathed this air. Calvin Emmons. Now we knew his name too.

"Any word on the actual cause of death yet?" I asked, stalling for time. My feet didn't seem to want to move.

Cruz shook his head, pausing with me. "She was found with her hands bound behind her. Tied together with grocery bags. He put her in the hole feet first. Dug six feet down so she had about half a foot over her head."

"Was she ... do we know if she was alive when he did that?" The thought of it. Being buried alive, bound like that. Helpless.

"Don't know yet. Her shoulder was dislocated. They could see that plain enough when they pulled her out. Also, both of her thumbs were broken. You could tell that on sight too."

Detective Brody Lance stood in front of us. He was new to the detective bureau. Brought in to replace Sam when Sheriff Clancy promoted him to lieutenant. So, a rookie too. Just a different kind than Rankin. Lance slid the heavy wooden barn door open.

Sam took a breath, preparing to speak. This time, I was the one who put a gentle hand on his arm. This was Lance's job now. His case. Old habits die hard.

Lance cleared his throat. He pointed to a taped-off square in the corner of the barn. I stepped over to it. A single hanging light illuminated the space.

"The victim, as you know, was Haley Chambers. Twenty years old. A student at Maumee County Community College," Lance started, running me through the investigation so far. "She lives with her mother and stepfather about three miles north but still here on Kidman Road. She was last seen a week ago on April 2nd. With her boyfriend, Dylan Woodhouse. They just paved that portion of Kidman and Haley liked to rollerblade. Her mother said she left around five o'clock and never came back. The boyfriend said he left her at the end of her driveway a little before six."

"When was she reported missing?" I asked.

"The mother called 9-1-1 just after nine p.m. It was full dark by then and she'd called the boyfriend and a few of Haley's friends. Nobody had seen her. The girl wasn't answering her phone. They went looking for her around seven and turned up nothing. That's when they called it in."

The rest I knew. Haley's family and friends coordinated with the sheriff's department and started searching the soybean fields and surrounding woods along Kidman Road. It went on for days.

"Deputy Rankin received a call from Jan Gunderson out at his tree farm three days ago. One of his dogs kept going out to a spot in his western-most field. Digging. Gunderson finally followed him out there and found a hole with what looked like a foot sticking up. He called it in. Deputy Rankin was first on scene."

I looked out toward the road. Rankin wasn't there anymore. I hoped he'd taken my advice and went home if he could.

Lance took a breath and continued. "One of the search teams found a tee shirt belonging to the victim hooked on a tree in the wooded area behind the boyfriend's house. We questioned the Woodhouse kid. His story checked out initially. After he left the victim's house, he met up with some friends to grab dinner. But he couldn't account for his time from about eight p.m. until ten."

"Two days ago, Dylan Woodhouse was your main person of interest," I said. I'd seen the impassioned pleas from Haley's family on television. The boyfriend's family had stood beside them. "So how did we get here, Detective?" I prayed it was solid. I prayed he hadn't missed any steps that would torpedo this case before it truly got started.

"Yesterday, we got a tip from another search team member. He came forward and said they'd searched the woods behind the boyfriend's house including the area where her shirt was found about an hour before Haley's tee shirt was found. He swore up and down it wasn't there. Our deputies kept detailed logs of who was supposed to be searching where and when. When they started questioning the second search team's members, one of them remembered Cal Emmons was in his group and insisted they go back to the boyfriend's woods. Emmons was adamant. I figured it was worth me asking a couple of questions anyway. His wife told me I'd find him working over there at the garage."

Lance pointed to the west of the barn; the red and white neon lights of a business sign glared. Emmons Garage. They mostly did small engine repairs. I had passed by it a thousand times. A family-owned business that had been in Waynetown for at least fifty years. I'd never met Cal Emmons, but I knew his wife.

"You think Emmons planted it?" I asked.

"It's my working theory," he said. "As soon as I came out here, I noticed that a blue Mercury Sable wagon was parked at a kind of weird angle. Dirt caked on the wheels. I don't know what made me stop, but it's got mismatched tires that fit the description of the ones found leading away from Haley's burial site. Anyway, when I interviewed Emmons initially, he kept changing his story. Bragged about finding the shirt. Then insisted another guy in his group found it. Then he lied about where he was the night Haley Chambers went missing. Said he was out here working in the garage."

It certainly sounded solid. Lance had gotten a search warrant from there and here we were.

"We think he brought her here," Sam said, his voice dropping an octave. "First."

I stepped forward, careful to stay within the boundaries of the tape. Lance led the way. It was an old barn with high, wooden rafters and hay bales in the loft above. It had normal things inside of it. A lawn tractor. Hoses. Garden tools. Two classic cars with the engines torn out.

Lance went ahead of us and opened a door in the back. I might not have noticed it myself. Farm implements hung from it. It would have looked just like any other wall to me. But the door opened to another small, square room.

My pulse raced as I followed Lance inside. There was a wooden bench in the center of the room. Ankle and wrist shackles were bolted at all four corners of the thing.

"We're waiting for labs," Lance said. "But that staining on the bench is blood. We've got hair and nail samples as well."

"He brought her here," I whispered. "He ... tortured her here."

There were plastic bins stacked along one wall, red and green, the kind they sell at Christmas time.

"He had costumes in here," he said. "Maids. Nurse's uniforms, that kind of thing. Duct tape. Plastic grocery bags. Um ... toys."

"You think he kept her here for a while," I said. "Hours maybe?"

"Yes," Lance said simply.

"While they were out searching," I whispered. "My God. While her family and the whole town was out there searching, she was here."

I walked out of the room. I couldn't stand breathing the air in there anymore. My heels sunk into the ground. Panic seized my heart. My shoes would be caked with the dirt from this place. It might never come out.

"She was here," I whispered as we walked back outside. To the east of us, the soybean fields stretched just to the edge of the Emmons's property. Kidman Road ran north and south right through the rural heart of Waynetown. If I kept walking a couple of miles, I would pass right by Haley Chambers's house. Did she know Emmons? Had he stalked her?

"The search teams went through there," I said, pointing to the fields. I felt Sam's steady hand at my back again. "They were calling her name. She would have ... she might have heard them while he ..."

I couldn't let my mind go any further. I would have weeks, months to comb over every aspect of this case. Haley Chambers couldn't cry for help as her monster kept her bound. Help would have come so close. Just a few hundred yards away.

Helpless. Hopeless. Her screams silenced forever. Except through me. As I walked away from the barn where she might have been murdered, I knew I would do whatever I could to give Haley Chambers her voice back. Even as the dirt from her hell clung to my clothes.

2

"Did you know him?" Howard Jordan, the only other full-time assistant prosecutor in the county, sat with his hands folded behind his head in the conference room. He had ten years on me. His hair was too long again, his skin flushed since he'd just run up the stairs.

At Hojo's back, we had a clean whiteboard. I walked up to it with a black marker and poised to write at the very top.

"I knew of him," I said. Then, in bold, black block letters, I wrote his name.

Calvin Emmons.

"His wife was one of my son Will's kindergarten teacher's aides. I met her I think twice. Will liked her."

I tried to remember what I could about Mrs. Emmons. Vickie? Valerie? Something. It wasn't much. She was pretty. Brown hair with blonde streaks and I recalled her wearing false eyelashes every day.

"Are you sitting in on the interrogation?" This from Kenya Spaulding, our boss. She entered the room and took a seat at the end of the table. She wore a pink suit that complemented her dark complexion. Her makeup, flawless. There would be a press conference later today. I didn't plan to attend.

"Waiting on a call from Detective Lance," I said.

Kenya's face hardened. "I don't know if I want to wait on that. Lance's new. Haley Chambers was pretty well known around town. Her disappearance went viral. I just want to be sure Lance knows how important these next couple of days are."

"He knows," I said. "Let's give him a chance." I said the right things, but had the same fears as Kenya.

"He's not all the way new," Hojo offered. "Brody Lance did good work in property crimes. He's ready. Plus, Ritter and Cruz will keep an eye on him."

"I hope so," Kenya said. "Did you have a chance to flyspeck his warrant of Emmons's property?"

"It looks tight," I said, then repeated what I'd heard from Detective Brody Lance. "Lance got tipped off by another searcher that the victim's shirt might have been planted at the boyfriend's house. He ID'd Emmons. The tire tracks leading away from where Haley's body was found matched a 2000 Mercury Sable wagon parked out at Cal Emmons's place. It had a Goodyear snow-type tire on the right front and three Bridgestones on the remaining. Lance made probable cause from there. They're processing all the physical evidence found in the barn. As soon as that comes back ..."

"How long?" Kenya asked.

"Might take a couple of weeks," I said.

"So we don't have enough to charge this guy yet. Lance knows he can't let Cal Emmons out of his sight?"

"He knows." Hojo and I said it together.

"I just can't believe it," Kenya said. She let her shoulders drop and a little of the battle-hardened mask she wore.

"Did you know him?" She asked me the same question as Howard.

"Of him." I answered the same way.

A soft knock on the conference room door drew our attention.

"That'll be Adam Skinner, your new intern," she said. "I think you're going to like him. Professor Bartlett highly recommended him."

"Good," I said. "It's been a couple of years since we had any good interns."

Adam entered the room. I was expecting someone young. Our law school interns usually came to us right after their first year. Early twenties. But Adam looked older. Thirty, perhaps, with a thick head of dark wavy hair and a cleft in his chin to make Joe Namath jealous. He had to duck slightly to clear the door frame as he came in.

"Adam Skinner," Kenya said. "This is Howard Jordan and Mara Brent. You'll be shadowing both of them over the summer. I hope you can handle hitting the ground running. This case might even garner national press."

Adam flashed her a thousand-watt smile. "Looking forward to it," he said. "And thank you again for the opportunity. I can't wait to sink my teeth into a capital murder case."

"That hasn't been decided yet," I said, a little more abruptly than I originally intended. "We don't even have an arrest yet. I cannot stress enough how crucial it will be for discretion. Doesn't matter you're not a lawyer yet. Confidentiality rules applied to you the second you walked into this office. You're not to discuss what you see and hear in this office with anyone. Not your mother, not your significant other, not even your priest, if you have one."

"Of course," he quickly covered. "I didn't mean ..."

"Save it," Kenya intervened. "Sit down. You'll do all right if you listen more than you talk. Mara, what else do we know about the victim and Cal Emmons?"

I grabbed a notepad from the table. I hadn't even had the chance to create a formal file yet.

"Just what I gleaned from a quick internet search," I said.

Adam cleared his throat. "I'm sorry. I don't want to overstep. But I took the liberty of doing some preliminary research. Nothing that isn't publicly available. I just thought with things moving so quickly, you might want ..."

Kenya caught my eye. I detected a smile in hers, but she didn't break. Instead, she waved a hand.

"Go ahead," she said.

"Haley Chambers was pursuing a criminal justice major at MCCC. She'd already been admitted to U.T. Her friends set up a fundraising page to cover some of her funeral costs. She was hoping to pursue a career in law enforcement when she graduated. She'd been working for the D.N.R. as a ranger at one of the state parks."

"What was she doing out on that road by herself?" Hojo asked.

"She was less than a mile from her house," I said. "Her boyfriend dropped her off at the end of her driveway. You know that area. Nothing ever happens out on Kidman Road."

Until the night it did.

"She had mace with her," I said, unable to keep the bitterness out of my voice. "They found a jogger's alarm on her keyring clipped to her shorts."

"She never had the chance to use any of it," Kenya said. "Preliminary autopsy showed injury to the back of her head. He hit her with something. Probably knocked her unconscious before she could put up a fight."

"Yes," I said. "Lance's theory is that she woke up in Emmons's barn. He had her bound."

My stomach churned. I tried hard, but couldn't stop my mind from going to that awful torture room he'd set up. Haley Chambers would have come to chained to that bench, her nightmare just beginning.

"There were signs of sexual assault," Kenya continued. "We're still waiting on DNA. I'll make a call to the county coroner. I don't like Cal Emmons walking around uncharged. He's been tipped off. The wife said he goes on day trips getting parts. No one's seen him yet. I don't like it."

"I don't either," I said. "But until we know, we don't know. I'm more worried about his name being leaked to the press. The last thing we need is a group of vigilantes trying to deal with this."

"Cal Emmons," Adam said, reading from his laptop. "Forty-five years old. He's lived at 41345 Kidman Road for his whole life. He was born there. Emmons Garage was started by his grandfather. Cal took the business over from him twenty years ago. Doesn't look like his own parents were in the picture much. Mother died when he was three. His father left Waynetown when Cal was in his teens. Cal Senior never had any involvement with the family business. Um ... he's got two kids. A son and a daughter. Carter, aged four. Bailey, the daughter, aged seven."

"Good Lord." Kenya whistled. "Where are they now? Do we know?"

"Sam said the wife took the kids and is staying with a sister on the other side of town. He's got a crew watching the house," I answered.

"Good," she said. "They need to get this whole thing locked down quickly. There are way too many moving parts. If the wife takes to social media ..."

"Why would she?" Howard asked. "I mean, seriously. Who in their right mind would broadcast the fact that her husband is wanted for raping, torturing, and killing a twenty-year-old college student?"

"Does he have a record of any kind?" Kenya asked.

"Nothing exciting," I said. "He had a marijuana possession charge about twenty years ago. Plead out. Nothing since except for a couple of speeding tickets. He pays his taxes on time. He's got a five-star rating online for his garage. Raves, actually. Nothing to outwardly indicate this would be our guy."

"What about the boyfriend?" Kenya asked.

"If I may," Adam said. He sat straighter in his seat and adjusted his laptop screen.

"I found some things out about Dylan Woodhouse too. Also a student at MCCC. Local. Lives off Forsythe Road with his parents. They'd been dating a couple of years."

"Any record on him?" Kenya asked.

I looked at Adam. He cast his eyes downward.

"Nothing," I answered. "And his alibi ultimately checked out."

Kenya gripped her pencil so hard I thought it would break. "That's where Lance has already been sloppy. He spent too much time focused on Dylan Woodhouse."

"A day," I said. "Two at the most. And it was a good lead. If that other searcher hadn't been paying attention, maybe we'd still think Dylan had something to do with Hayley's abduction. Lance did what he was supposed to do. I'm not worried. Yet."

"Is he cooperative, the boyfriend?" Kenya asked.

"I haven't heard otherwise," I said. "Plus, I would think at this point he'd be mainly interested in bringing his girlfriend's killer to justice."

"We're sure her family and Woodhouse's family have no idea the investigation has started to focus on Emmons?" Kenya asked.

"Sure as I can be," I said. "We just have to sit tight and let Lance do his job."

I understood Kenya's concern. We couldn't afford any screw-ups. We needed Lance and the sheriff's department to deliver a solid case. For Haley. Her family. And Kenya's own political future.

My phone buzzed. I expected to see Brody Lance's number pop up. The air slipped from my lungs as I saw a different number.

Grantham Elementary.

"I'm sorry," I said. "I have to take this. It's from Will's school."

Kenya smiled at me, but concern filled her eyes too. I quietly stepped out of the room.

"Hi," I said. "This is Mara Brent."

I refrained from asking the urgent question all mothers have when they see the school's caller ID pop up. Is my child okay?

"Hi, Mrs. Brent," the caller said. I recognized his voice as Dan Hampton's, the school principal.

Crap.

"I'm sorry to bother you at work. But I think we're going to need you to come down here. Will's okay. But ... well ... there's been some trouble."

Squeezing my eyes shut, I let out a breath and clicked off the phone.

3

"A fight?"

It was the third time I'd asked but still couldn't believe it was true. When I arrived at Grantham Elementary, I found my nearly eleven-year-old son sitting on a chair outside the office with a wad of tissue up his profusely bleeding nose.

Will had clammed up when I asked him what happened. Every muscle in his body went tense and I recognized it for the bad sign it was. Every one of his boundaries had been crossed. If I so much as put a gentle hand on his head, we'd be in full meltdown territory.

"I'm okay," he said. It was all he would say. Finally, when one of his favorite teacher's aides promised to sit with him, I went in to talk to the principal.

"A fight," I said. "Last time I checked, that takes two people. Will's the only one I see sitting there with a bloody nose. Who did this? What happened?"

Hampton sat perched at the end of his desk. One of the school counselors sat in a chair against the wall.

"We can't get the story out of Will," Hampton said. "It happened as they were coming out of the lunchroom. There was a bit of a pile-up of some students. By the time Mrs. Ray got there, Will was on the bottom of it." He gestured toward the counselor, Mrs. Ray, still seated.

"You're telling me my son got jumped by a bunch of other students? How does that happen? What precipitated it? Don't tell me you can't get the story out of Will. What about the other students? What about the other adults?"

Grantham was a private school ranked for its small student-to-teacher ratio and best-in-the-state support for children with special needs. Will no longer had an aide assigned to him one-on-one but I just couldn't wrap my head around how this could have happened without the adults not seeing anything until Will was at the bottom of a pile.

I started to pace. I wanted nothing more than to peel my son away from this place and get him home safely. He was supposed to feel safe here. This one incident could set him back in ways none of us could fathom yet.

Things had been going so well...

"Perhaps when things calm down," Principal Hampton said, "Will might be more willing to explain what happened."

"What happened is my son was clearly bullied and beaten by another group of kids. He may never tell me what caused it. You're assuming he even knows."

"He's never mentioned any issues he was having with other boys?" Mrs. Ray asked.

"No."

Hampton and Mrs. Ray exchanged a nervous look that curdled my blood. "What aren't you telling me?"

Charleen Ray finally got up from her chair. "Will has been a little more withdrawn lately. He normally sits at a table with about four other boys. For the last couple of weeks, he's been sitting alone. Yesterday, Mr. Bernard, our P.E. teacher sat with him. It seemed to perk him up."

I slapped my thigh. "Why are you just telling me this now? You're saying you've noticed a change in his behavior for weeks? Weeks?"

Just then, the school liaison officer, Deputy Mark Holmes, came to the doorway. "Deputy Holmes," the principal said, a little too brightly. "Have you had a chance to review the security tapes?"

I knew Holmes pretty well. Will looked up to him. He had a good reputation in town and among the other deputies, including Sam Cruz.

"There wasn't much to see," he said. "The uh ... skirmish happened in the north hallway, closest to the broom closet. Mostly out of the range of the cameras. Sorry about that."

"I need to take Will home," I said. "I need to figure out what we're going to do."

"Mara," Hampton said. "I know this is upsetting. I promise you we're going to work with the other students and faculty to try to figure out what set this off. Will needs to know he's safe."

"I know what Will needs," I said, my tone biting. I was angry. Every Mama Bear instinct I had flared. No one in this room could give me the answers I needed.

"If I may," Hampton said, "I'll give you a call later this evening to see how Will's doing."

I didn't answer. My throat felt thick. I left the principal's office and rejoined my son. His nose had stopped bleeding but I didn't like his posture. He kept his back bent, his shoulders sunken in as he fell in step to follow me. I heaved his backpack over my shoulder and started toward the door.

"It's going to be okay," I said. "Let's just get you home."

"I don't want to talk about it," he said.

"I know," I answered. "But at some point soon, I'm going to need you to. You're not in trouble. You know that, right?"

He didn't answer. He just stuffed his hands in his pockets and trudged along beside me. It killed me not to hug him. I knew it was the last thing he needed right now.

I'd parked my car just outside the doors. I would have pulled it into the yard had it got me into the building faster. I hit my key fob and the small, electronic chirp went off, unlocking the doors.

Will had just opened the passenger door when a shout made me freeze.

"You!" she shrieked. "I want to talk to you!"

I turned. It took a moment for my synapses to properly fire. The woman charged forward, her brown hair flying. She batted her false eyelashes at me, her cheeks colored with rage.

"Will," I said. "Just get in the car. Go ahead and turn on the radio."

He did. I put my body between what I thought was Will's line of sight and the woman barreling toward me.

"Mrs. Emmons," I said, bracing myself for the next assault.

I remembered her as a sweet, soft-spoken, pretty woman who had the patience of a saint. Now, deep lines cut through her face. Her eyes were swollen from crying and whatever rage she was about to unleash.

"You have to do something," she said, her voice unnaturally squeaky. I looked behind me. Will was fiddling with the console, probably looking for a podcast. He didn't even seem to register what was happening outside. I gave Valerie Emmons a smile and gestured toward the entrance to a small courtyard where the kids released butterflies every spring.

"They're going to arrest him, aren't they?" Valerie said.

"I can't discuss this with you," I said, keeping my voice even. It occurred to me to play dumb.

"The police are at my house!" she screamed. "Cal had nothing to do with whatever happened to that poor girl. This is insane. He's being framed. Or they're mistaking him for someone else. I'm out of my home. My children are out of their homes!"

"Mrs. Emmons," I said. "This isn't the time or the place. Will's in the car. Even if he wasn't this isn't..."

"This will destroy our lives," she said, starting to cry. "You know me. You know us. We were born in Waynetown. Everyone is going to know about this."

I resisted the urge to tell her they sure would if she insisted on making a scene in a public place. At the same time, it was hard not to feel sorry for her. If the evidence came back how I thought it would, her husband was a cold-blooded killer. I only prayed Haley Chambers had been his only victim. That space, that barn, he'd spent time building it. Getting it just right for whatever...

"I know how this works," she said. "The police aren't the last word. You are. Your office. Mara, you know me. You know my family."

I didn't. Not at all, really.

"I have to go," I said.

"You have to help me," she said. Then, Valerie Emmons lunged at me. She grabbed me by both arms and clutched my shirt in a vice grip that scared me. She was like a drowning woman, about to drag me under.

"Mom!" Will's muffled shout from the car came to me. "Mom!"

I turned. He saw. He pounded on the dashboard.

"Let me go," I said through gritted teeth, then jerked out of Valerie Emmons's grasp. "I told you. Not here. Not now. I'm sorry for what you're going through but it is not appropriate for me to be talking to you right now."

"Will they arrest him?" she said, going meek.

"I can't answer that for you," I said.

"What should I do?" she asked.

I exhaled. "Mrs. Emmons, you should get a lawyer. A good one."

Before she could react, I hurried back to my car, got inside, and locked the door.

4

Will asked me no questions as we drove home. I asked none of him either. I knew what he needed. Quiet. Safety. The comfort of his things. His own bed.

"I don't want to go to school tomorrow," was the only thing he said as we parked in the garage.

"How about we talk about that after dinner?" I said. It would be easy to keep him home. Build a protective bubble around him until I figured out how to handle all of this. But I knew that wouldn't serve him well. Once disrupted, it would be that much harder to get him back into his routine.

He scrambled out of the car and headed for the side door. I was just about to hit the remote on the garage door when another vehicle pulled up. A deputy's cruiser.

"No more," Will said, freezing.

"It's okay," I said. "It's a friend."

Will's shoulders sagged with relief as Sam stepped out from behind the wheel. He gave us a friendly wave.

"It's Lieutenant Cruz," Will said.

"Hi, Sam," I said, meeting him in the driveway. Will stayed on the back step, watching us.

"Heard you had some excitement today," he said and I realized he meant it for Will.

"How did you..."

"Deputy Holmes gave me a call," he said. "I hope you don't mind, I just wanted to make sure everyone was okay out here."

With anyone else, this might have felt intrusive. But the concern in Sam's eyes was genuine and Will had taken a liking to him in recent months. His approval was darn hard to come by.

"He won't tell me what happened," I whispered. "I really appreciate your concern, but I think I just need to get him inside and make things as normal as I can."

Will came down to join us. He didn't say anything. He just stared up at Sam. I could tell by his expression he was working up the courage to ask him a question.

"Mom," Will said. "Can I talk to Lieutenant Cruz alone?"

My jaw dropped. "Uh ... sure." I caught Sam's eyes. He seemed as baffled as me. I wished I had telepathy. I would have asked Sam to see if he could get the truth out of my boy. Instead, I left them to it. I went back into the garage and closed the door behind me.

Ten minutes. That's how long my son spent talking to Sam. There was nowhere in the house I could properly spy. So, I paced in the kitchen, opening and closing cupboards.

Finally, Will came back in. He breezed right past me and headed upstairs. A second later, I heard the bath running.

"What the..."

I went back out the garage door and found Sam leaning against his car. He had a wry smile on his face. I didn't know if that was a good sign or not.

"You gonna tell me what that was all about?" I asked.

Sam shrugged. "Just some guy talk."

My head spun. "That could mean about a dozen things. None of them are necessarily good."

"He's okay," Sam said. "At least I think so."

"Did he tell you what happened at school? Sam, someone hit him. The teachers found him at the bottom of a pile of kids. They ganged up on him."

"He told me a little. Something about a couple of the boys saying something mean to a girl who sits at his lunch table. Will didn't like it. He stood up for her."

I felt a lump in my throat and pride for my quiet, shy little boy.

"So what did he ask you then?"

Sam picked at a nail. "He wanted some pointers."

"Pointers?"

"He wanted to know how to defend himself. He asked me to show him how to throw a proper punch."

I reared back. "Good Lord. Sam ... the school has a zero tolerance policy for fighting. If he..."

"You want him to get his butt kicked again? You want him to be afraid to stand up for himself or other people?"

Angry heat flared through me. "I do not."

"Then the boy needs to know how to throw a punch if the need arises. Don't worry. I made sure he understood it's a last resort. In my experience with bullies, you only ever need to throw the one. They get the message pretty quick after that."

"Sam..." I said, my voice breaking.

He smiled and came to me. "I told you. I think he's okay."

I held back tears. The urge to punch something myself burned through me.

"It's not the only reason I stopped by," he said. "There's been a break in the case against Cal Emmons. Can you clear your schedule for a meeting down at the station first thing in the morning?"

I nodded. I knew I should tell him about my encounter with Valerie Emmons, but I wanted to get back to Will. One crisis at a time.

"Good," he said. "We'll set up in the third floor conference room. There's another witness I think you need to know about."

"I'll be there," I said. "And Sam ... thank you."

He answered by way of a quick wink, then slid back behind the wheel.

5

The next morning, Detectives Gus Ritter and Brody Lance waited for me in the third floor conference room of the sheriff's department. At Kenya's request, I brought my new intern, Adam Skinner, with me. So far, he'd learned fast. He stayed in the background, watched, listened, and took furious notes.

Gus was the most seasoned detective we had in Waynetown. His gruff exterior put most people off. But I'd known him to have a squishy center. He wouldn't sit the entire time we met.

"So where are we?" I asked. Sheriff Clancy quietly let himself in. His presence seemed to unnerve Lance even more. Once again, I worried whether he was in over his head.

"Cal Emmons isn't talking," Lance said. "Picked him up for questioning last night when he resurfaced at home. I had him in an interview room for two hours. He's asserted his rights and shut me down."

"Please tell me you ended the interview at that point," I said, feeling queasy.

"Of course," he said. "He's asking for a public defender. No word yet on who's been appointed."

"That will be my next stop after this," I said. "What about the physical evidence?"

"That's why we called you in," Lance said. "We hit the jackpot this morning. We've got preliminary blood typing that matches the victim. There's a partial shoe impression in the dirt in the corner of the barn. It matches the tennis shoes Haley was wearing."

"So he had her on her feet at one point," I said.

"Looks that way. I'm still waiting on the DNA. I'll hand in my badge if it's not a match. We've got a blood mixture taken from the door handle on the inside of the torture room."

I winced when he said it. I knew I'd never get that room out of my nightmares. Never.

"If it comes back matching both Emmons and Haley Chambers," Clancy said, "this thing is all but over."

"There's more," Ritter said. "Tell her about the carpet fibers."

"Haley had these strange gray carpet fibers sticking to her. The highest concentration was between her fingers. Under one nail. And we found it in her hair on the right side of her head."

"She was lying on it," I said. "I don't remember any carpet in that room."

"It's not from the room," Lance answered. "But it matches the color of the carpet fibers found in the Mercury Sable wagon registered to Cal Emmons. The mismatched tire treads on it match what we found leading to and from the site where the body was recovered on Gunderson's farm. It's definitive now. Like I said, this all came down this morning. Jackpot."

"Holy crap," I said. "Lance, that's huge. You can put Haley in the barn and in that car. Where are you on putting Emmons in the barn with her?"

"Preliminary DNA was inconclusive," he said. "Labs will need a little more time."

"I don't get it," Adam spoke up. I'd almost forgotten he was there. Gus gave him a stern look.

"Sorry," Adam said. "Why can't you arrest Emmons already?"

"They don't have enough for probable cause," I said. "Proving Haley was in the barn doesn't mean she died there. It doesn't even mean Cal Emmons was in there with her. We need more."

"We're close," Lance said. "We're still working out who else might have had access to the barn."

"Good thinking," I said. "But tell them to hurry. If you're right. If it really is Emmons. I don't like him still out there. At the same time, I don't want to be arguing a rush to judgment by this guy's lawyer." I spoke the last bit as much for Adam as I did for Lance.

Gus cleared his throat. A look went between him and Brody Lance. Lance gave him a nod, acquiescing to him picking up the narrative.

"Mara," Gus said. "There's more. As soon as the labs came back this morning, I did some cross-referencing with some cold cases. I worked on a case a little over four years ago. I was part of a task force on unsolved sexual assault cases. Those gray fibers. We found similar ones on a case involving a victim by the name of Dominique Bright."

"I don't remember that case," I said.

"It wasn't a Maumee County case," he said. "Dominique was abducted south of here in Grace County. She was grabbed off the road. Thrown into the back of a car. Her abductor kept her for almost twenty-four hours. Beaten. Raped."

"You're telling me you have identical carpet fibers from both crimes?" I asked. I couldn't help covering my mouth in shock. Four years. Four years. God only knew how many other victims Cal Emmons had tortured or killed.

"Where did he bury her?" I asked.

"That's the thing," Gus said. "He didn't. He took her to a campground off I-75. Middle of the night. Threw her in a pond and tried to drown her. A couple of hikers found her lying still bound half in and half out of the water. The working theory is they spooked him and he had to leave in a hurry."

"She's alive?" I asked.

"Yeah," Gus answered. "Survived with a fractured skull and broken thumbs, but she's okay."

"Can she ID Emmons?" I said, my pulse quickening. I sat straighter in my chair. "We need to get her in."

"Working on it," Gus said. "But this could be the break they need on her abduction case as well. She's uh ... she's been in some trouble with the law herself before and after. I'm working with her probation officer to find her. There's actually a warrant out for her arrest for failing to show up for her last court-ordered drug test."

The skin prickled along my spine. Though this wasn't what I wanted to hear, you have to take your witnesses as you find them.

"The sooner the better," I said. "It might not be a bad idea to have a female detective interview her. And a social worker. If she's been through that level of trauma, this development could make her go to ground all over again. But we need to talk to this Dominique Bright. If there's anything I can do to help on that, you let me know."

"Good thinking," Gus said. "I'd actually like you to be in on any interviews we have with her."

As soon as he said it, Gus's face fell a bit. I knew he didn't want to step on Brody Lance's toes. If he cared that much, it meant he respected Lance as an investigator. That was all the endorsement I needed.

"Works for me," Lance said. I hoped he was smart enough to welcome the help rather than getting into some departmental pissing contest with a senior detective. The thing was, Gus was a legend. If Lance didn't recognize that, I had bigger problems to deal with.

"This is all good news," I said. "Keep me posted. And nobody so much as blinks at Cal Emmons without his lawyer present. Are we clear on that? When you have enough for your arrest warrant, ideally I'd like him to turn himself in."

"Absolutely," Lance said. "He's been released on his own recog, but I've got deputies watching the house and garage. He's not going anywhere without us knowing about it."

"Good," I said. "I had a little run-in myself with Valerie Emmons yesterday."

"Where?" Lance asked.

"She's a teacher at Grantham Elementary. I was there picking up my son and she confronted me in the parking lot."

"You okay?" Clancy and Gus asked me in unison.

"I'm fine. She's of course protesting her husband's innocence. She's in shock. Denial. All the things you'd expect."

"Who witnessed this?" Clancy asked, his expression hard.

"Basically just my son," I said. "Though I don't think he heard very much. He stayed in the car."

"This is gonna get leaked sooner than we'd all like," Clancy said, directing his words to Lance. "You need to put pressure on. We need that DNA back."

"Even without it my warrants will be tight," Lance said.

"I don't want to hear that," I said. "I don't care how rock solid this looks. I already told you, I don't want to deal with any rush to judgment accusations if and when I have you on the stand, Detective. I think we can all agree we're dealing with a potential serial killer here. Gus, was the Bright girl the only other cold case with a similar M.O.?"

"Expanding the net as we speak," he said.

"Did Emmons at least submit to a cheek swab?"

"Not yet," Lance said. "He refused anything like that last night."

"That's something you can get a warrant on now," I said. "Do you need any help getting that in front of Judge Ivey? He's on call today. If you bring me something, I can meet you at the courthouse in an hour."

"Will do," Lance said. "And don't worry. I'm on top of everything here."

I knew he wasn't in an easy position. He had me, Ritter, and the sheriff looking over his shoulder. Too bad. We all knew how important this case was. We all sensed we'd only seen the tip of the iceberg with potential victims.

"Glad to hear it," I said. "Get me that warrant. I'd like you to have your crew with a swab in that creep's face before lunchtime."

"So would I," Lance agreed.

"And I'm with you, Clancy," I said. "We have got to keep a lid on this. No leaks. I don't want to see any of these details posted online or in the news."

"That goes for your office too," Clancy said, eyeing Adam. "You need to make sure you've only got people you trust in the loop on this."

"We understand each other," I said.

With that, the meeting ended. Clancy and Lance hung back while Gus walked me out. I sensed something in his body language so I asked Adam to head back to the office without me. When we were clear of everyone else's ears, I turned to Gus.

"Is Lance up for this?" I asked.

Gus looked me straight in the eye. "He's up for it. If I didn't think so, I would have cornered Clancy and poached the case."

"I'm not convinced you shouldn't," I said. "Yet. He should have had that warrant for Emmons's DNA last night. You wouldn't have made that mistake, Gus."

"Relax," he said. "Have some faith. Nobody wants to make sure we've got the right bastard more than me. I knew that girl."

The statement took me aback.

"You did?"

Gus chewed his lip. "Yeah. Every once in a while I get a crop of booger-nosed interns from Maumee County Community College sent over. She was in a group last year. I remember her because she kept her mouth shut and listened. Most of them can't master that. They ask me too many stupid questions just to hear themselves talk. Or they're on their phones the whole time. She wasn't either. I spent a few minutes talking with her one-on-one. Told her to get out of criminal justice. It's a bullshit degree. Told her to switch to computer science or accounting."

"Well, that's a solid piece of advice," I said.

"She didn't have the chance to take it," he said.

"I'm sorry."

Gus quickly switched gears. "So how's your boy?"

"My boy?" My face fell. Of course, he already knew what happened with Will. He'd have heard it through the grapevine from either Deputy Holmes or Sam. Damn small towns.

"He's okay," I said. "He's studying from home today. My sister-in-law is with him."

"Holmes is a good school officer," he said. "He'll get to the bottom of whatever's going on over at Grantham. He'll keep an eye on Valerie Emmons too. Though I can't imagine she'll be showing up to work much after this."

"I don't know," I said. "She is in complete denial, Gus. It's hard to put myself in her shoes. Her world just got blown up. And she has kids. Little kids. This is just all going to get so much worse very quickly."

"Yeah," he said.

Just then, his phone buzzed. He held up a finger to me as he read the caller ID. Gus turned away from me. I smiled. His answers were short and abrupt, just like anytime I ever got him on the phone.

"Yeah. Where? When? You have her sit tight. On it."

He clicked off and turned to me.

"Good news," he said. "That was a deputy I know down in Allen County, about two hours south. They picked up Dominique Bright on that warrant. They're holding her down there near Lima. Can you clear your afternoon? Lance is going to have his hands full with that DNA warrant and babysitting B.C.I. I'll run it by him, but I don't think he's going to mind if the two of us talk to Dominique today."

It meant a late night. Though I hated leaving Will, I knew the sooner we talked to Dominique Bright, the better.

"I can make that work," I said.

"Be ready in an hour," he said. "I'll pick you up at your office."

"Thanks, Gus," I said. As I said goodbye, my own phone buzzed. I entered the stairwell before answering. This was a call I didn't want anyone else to overhear.

"Mara!" Jason, my ex, practically shouted into the phone.

"Jason, I'm at work. Can whatever this is wait?"

"Our son can't wait," he said. "You want to tell me why I'm hearing second-hand that he got in a fight at school? What the hell, Mara? I should have been the first person they called."

"I'm handling it," I said. I bit the inside of my cheek to keep from shouting what I really wanted to say. He didn't ask me how Will was. He didn't even really ask me what happened. Instead, he immediately made it about him.

"You're handling it? You're not even home. I know my sister's with him right now."

"Exactly," I said. "Our son has a great support system. He's fine. Thanks for asking. And I didn't need you flying off the handle with the school. That only would have upset Will. That's the last thing any of us need. Plus, you're five hundred miles away."

"Don't throw that back at me," he said. "Me being in D.C. was a decision we all made as a family. Just like our agreement on legal custody. You don't get to make decisions about Will without me. Making him stay home from school is the worst thing you could have done. He needs to get right back in there. If somebody's bullying him, he can't cower in his room."

"I can't do this right now," I said. I'd reached the ground floor. I jostled past a few incoming deputies as I made my way outside. "I'm working a murder case. I'll call you tonight. You can talk to Will yourself."

As Jason started to yell, I did something I don't normally do. I hung up on him and silenced my phone. There would be time enough for a fight later. Now, I had to get ready to meet with Dominique Bright.

6

They had her in a small interview room at the Allen County sheriff's department. I saw her first through a two-way mirror. She was pretty. Perhaps too thin, with pale skin, one arm covered in colorful tattoos. She had her hair cut into a shag and dyed a deep shade of maroon. The door opened behind us and a plump, curvy blonde woman walked in.

"I'm Maggie Conroy," she said. "Dominique's been on my caseload for two years. This is the longest I've gone without seeing her."

"You're her probation officer?" I asked.

"Yep. She's got a good heart," Maggie continued. "She tries. For a while anyway. Then she gets hooked up with one loser boyfriend after another and it all goes south. I helped her get a job working for a tattoo parlor about ten miles from here. She's artistic. She's got a real gift."

I looked back at Dominique. She was picking at the skin over her left knuckle.

"I'd like to go in and talk to her," I said. Gus was down the hall, talking to one of the detectives. When he came back, he'd have a copy of Dominique Bright's complete rap sheet, including anything that might have been expunged or happened when she was a juvenile.

"Come on," Maggie said. "I'll introduce you."

"Maggie." I stopped her. "Does Dominique have any idea why we're here?"

"I told her you were from Maumee County and that you think she might have info on another case you're working. I was clear that she's not in trouble for that one."

"Thanks," I said. "Let's go in."

Dominique sat straighter, her eyes darting back and forth as Maggie Conroy led the way. Maggie dropped a file on the table in front of her before she sat down. There would likely be charges relating to her probation violation. Depending on how this went, I might try to leverage that.

"Ms. Bright?" I said. "My name is Mara Brent. I'm an assistant prosecutor for Maumee County. I know you've got a lot on your plate, but I was hoping you'd be willing to talk to me for a few minutes."

Dominique looked over both her shoulders. "Doesn't really seem like I have a choice." She glared at Maggie.

"Let me tell you what I'm working on," I said. "Ms. Bright ... we're about to make an arrest in another case. A murder. A twenty-year-old woman by the name of Haley Chambers went missing in Waynetown two weeks ago. She was found dead last week. She'd been assaulted. There were some ...

similarities in the case to what happened to you four years ago."

Blank stare. No reaction whatsoever.

"Ms. Bright," I said. "There's a good chance we may have caught the man who hurt you. Is there someone we can call for you? A friend? A family member?"

Still no reaction. Just the slight dilation of her pupils.

"I can't help you," she finally said. "I never saw that man. I can't identify him."

I had just the barest facts pertaining to Dominique's case. I was hoping she'd fill in the gaps as we went along. But I knew her abductor had covered her eyes with duct tape. The same had happened to Haley Chambers. In both cases, Cal Emmons, if he truly was our man, had cut the tape off, taking most of Haley's hair with it. Detective Lance theorized it was because he knew the tape could hold his fingerprints.

I hadn't said it. I'd only thought it. But Dominique lifted a hand and absently ran it over the back of her hair. I noticed something else. Her thumbs weren't completely straight. One stayed bent inward at the knuckle as if it hadn't healed properly from a past break.

"There was some physical evidence collected in your case," I said. "Unique carpet fibers from the vehicle this man put you in. Identical carpet fibers were found on my victim, Haley Chambers."

"So," she said. "They make more than one of a certain car. You can't prove anything from that."

Denial. Self-preservation. I don't know what Dominique Bright had done to mentally survive what happened to her, but my questions clearly had the effect of pounding on those walls.

"We also have a match to some tire treads that led away from where you were found. I believe there are other aspects of Haley Chambers's case that mirror what happened to you."

She blinked wildly, fighting back tears.

"He's ... he's alive? He's out there?"

"Dominique," I said. "We can keep you safe."

She shook her head. "No. I gotta get outta here. I can't be here."

She started to rise.

"Dominique, sit," Maggie said. "We have a lot to get through today."

I put a hand on Maggie's arm.

"I can't help you," Dominique said. "I can't have anything to do with any of this. I'm sorry about that Haley girl. But I have nothing to say. You don't know. You have no idea what you've done."

She rose. Running around the desk, she started pounding on the door.

"Dominique," I said. "It's okay. You're safe here. No one is trying to force you into anything."

"You don't know what you're doing!" she said. "You don't know what he's capable of."

"I do," I said. "Believe me. I've seen what this man is capable of. But you're safe now. Please, is there someone we can call for you?"

"There's no one," she shouted. "There's only me."

"I understand..."

"No," she said. "You absolutely don't. What that monster did. He kept me ... He..."

She cowered in the corner, sinking slowly to the ground.

"We need to end this," I said quietly to Maggie. "We need a social worker in here. Can I speak to you outside?"

"We'll be right back, Dominique," Maggie said. "Just breathe, okay? We're going to figure all of this out."

Maggie and I walked back into the observation room. Gus came down the hallway, breathless, just as we did. He had a cell phone to his ear and ended the call.

"She give you anything?" Gus asked.

"Not yet," I said, gesturing to the one-way mirror. Dominique was still in the corner. "I don't like this. We should have had a victim's advocate in there. She's far too fragile for this conversation."

"She's probably in withdrawal to boot," Maggie said. She sat down in the nearest chair and opened her file. She pulled out some newspaper clippings and handed them to me.

"How much do you know about her abduction?"

"I'm just trying to get up to speed on all of this," I answered, taking the clippings.

They told a grisly story. Dominique had been snatched while hitchhiking, struck in the head. She woke up bound with duct tape and garbage bags, then shoved in the back of a moving car. She'd described it then as a station wagon. Her thumbs were broken. Smashed with a hammer. The cops theorized her captor wanted to prevent her from loosening the plastic bags tying her hands or to make it more difficult to wound him in the critical areas of his eyes or groin.

Her captor kept her in the back of the car for hours. He brought her out and held her overnight in a hotel room. The entire time, Dominique had the tape over her eyes. He beat her. He assaulted her throughout the next day. Then, he threw her back in the car and drove her to the campground where she was later found.

Dominique had been able to see under a sliver of the tape that had come loose from her sweat. Never the man's face. But she was able to point out certain landmarks so the police could determine she'd been held at Motel Ten off I-75 just over the line into Grace County.

Her injuries mirrored some of Haley's. The broken thumbs. A cigar burn between her breasts. He'd tried to drown her in a creek at the campground. He knocked her unconscious when he heard the hikers coming. Finally, he cut off all the duct tape, including most of her hair.

Just like Haley.

Except Dominique had lived. "I don't know how good she'll be as a witness," Maggie said. "She's scared to death. This monster threatened to kill her if she ever said anything."

"But she did," I said. "She told the police what she knew."

"She's gotten more fearful in the years since," Maggie said.

"She needs to know she's safe," I said.

"On that," Gus said. "That was Brody Lance. Emmons is in the wind. A crew went out to serve the DNA warrant and he's gone."

"He's what?" I yelled, then quickly lowered my voice to a whisper.

Gus Ritter's whole body registered barely coiled anger. He stood with shaking fists at his side.

"We think the wife had something to do with it," he said. "We had an undercover crew watching the house. She was seen leaving last night. The deputies at the end of the street questioned her. She'd just come to the house to pick up a few things. They're thinking Cal might have been in the trunk of her car but we can't prove it yet."

"Of all the ... you've got to be kidding me," I said.

"I don't like it any more than you do. But for right now he hasn't broken any laws. We hadn't yet served the arrest warrant."

"I told that girl she was safe," I said. "We need to make sure that's true. We don't name Cal Emmons to her just yet. Where's she living right now?"

"She was living with another one of her boyfriends about two miles from here, name of Vincent Meyer. A real dirtbag, that one. But I'll figure all that out," Maggie said.

"I hate to say it, but I think the safest place for her right now is in custody."

"I agree," Gus said.

"Oh, I've got enough to violate her probation," Maggie said. "She did a pee test for me just before you got here. I should have that back within the hour. Dollars to donuts it's going to come back dirty. I know this girl. She went on a bender."

"No," I said. "I know it's not my call, but I don't want to traumatize that girl any more than she already has been. Do you think you can go easy on her on the probation violation?"

Maggie nodded. "Before you got here she swore to me up and down she's broken things off with the dirtbag boyfriend. I don't know if I believe her, but I can at least get her home safe. My paperwork can go to the bottom of the pile, at least for a little while."

"Thanks," I said.

I looked back at the newspaper clippings. Everything fit. Everything was like Haley's abduction. She'd been thrown into the same car. I'd need Gus and Brody Lance to get with the detectives on Dominique's case. No doubt they'd kept more details out of the newspaper. The only difference I could see was the site of the crime. We had no evidence that Dominique Bright had ever stepped foot in Cal Emmons's murder barn out on Kidman Road.

"I think she might have been one of his first," I said, pressing a hand to the glass. Dominique had at least gotten up off the floor. She chewed her thumbnail and walked around the table.

"It got out of hand," I said. "Maybe he just happened to see her. I need the timeline of Dominique's abduction. I need to start figuring out where Cal Emmons was when it happened."

"If that's even still possible," Gus said. "But if there's a way, we'll do it."

"It got out of control for him," I said. "He was out of town. Maybe he built that space in the barn after what happened with Dominique. So he *could* control it the next time."

"Sick bastard," Maggie said. "She's a good kid deep down. Her folks were both junkies. She grew up in foster care. She's just had every bad break a person could have."

"Except for one," I said. "She got away. She lived through what he did to her."

Gus was at my side. "Poor kid," he whispered.

"We have to help her," I said. "We have to make sure that monster pays for what he did to her and to Haley Chambers. We have to prove to her there are still good people in this world. People who will fight for her."

With everything I was, I vowed that day to be one of them.

7

May 11th, nearly six weeks after Haley Chambers disappeared into the twilight, Detective Brody Lance walked into my office with news I'd been waiting to hear.

"The rest of my labs are back," he said, sliding a file folder across my desk. Two minutes ago his email came through with a massive zip file containing everything in that same physical folder.

"All of them?" I asked.

Brody sat in a chair on the other side of my desk. "See for yourself?"

"Give me the highlights," I said.

"Official cause of death is drowning," he said. "The monster held her underwater in the pond at the edge of his property."

"You're sure of that?" I said, picking up the file. Brody had it tabbed. I flipped to the final autopsy report. We'd known asphyxiation was the likely cause of death, but this was far more detailed. I couldn't help but think of the newspaper clippings I'd read about Dominique Bright's abduction. She said her captor had held her underwater until the sound of nearby hikers interrupted him.

"Reasonably sure," he said. "The big news is sand and soil in Haley's mouth and nose match what we found on Emmons's property. And now we've got her hair on some of the branches near that pond. Haley's DNA is all over Emmons's torture room in the barn. Wood splinter under her nails matches the table in there. Bruising on her wrists lines up with the shackles he had bolted to the floor. She was on his property. In that room. In that car. We already had a match on the carpet fibers from his car. Plus the tire treads. She was beaten in that barn. For hours. He took her to that pond while she was still alive, Mara. Otherwise, there wouldn't be water in her lungs. M.E. is certain drowning was the actual cause of death."

"My God," I whispered. I could barely process it all.

"Then he takes her out to Gunderson's farm two miles away. Tries to bury her body in one of his fallow fields. Pulls off all the duct tape he used on her eyes and mouth when he took her from the barn to the pond. Cuts her hair off in the process."

I sat with a hand over my mouth as I listened to Lance and turned page after page.

"But where's *his* DNA?" I asked.

That's when he got quiet.

"Lance," I said. I'd reached the end of the thick report.

"Chemical analysis shows a heavy amount of bleach on the body. We found it all over the room in that barn. He cleaned up after himself. There are several bottles of empty bleach in the garage too. We've got his prints on the barn door and inside the barn where Haley was kept. Hairs matching Emmons's were also in the barn."

I slowly closed the folder. "But you don't have any of Emmons's DNA on Haley Chambers. His defense lawyer will explain away the prints and hair samples. We *know* it was Emmons's property. This would be a heck of a lot tighter if we had his blood or DNA on Haley. Or her DNA on him."

It was a hole. A big one. But not insurmountable.

"We can put her in his barn," Lance said. "We can put her in his car. We can put his car on Gunderson's property driving all the way up to the hole where he buried her, Mara. But no, I don't have Emmons's DNA."

"It's going to have to be enough to arrest him," I said. "This is good work, Lance."

"I'm heading over to Judge Ivey's from here."

Lance handed me another piece of paper. I looked it over. He'd crafted a solid arrest warrant for Calvin Emmons.

"He'll sign it," I said.

I pulled out a file folder of my own. In the two weeks since I met with her, I'd started collecting everything I could about Dominique Bright's case. She hadn't returned a single one of my phone calls. My communications with her probation officer, Maggie Conroy, had been less than encouraging. Dominique was back with the boyfriend Maggie didn't like. Her situation was volatile.

"Have you seen this?" I asked Lance, handing him my file. In it, I'd highlighted and annotated the official police report from the Grace County sheriff's on Dominique's abduction.

Lance scanned it. "I tried talking to Ms. Bright. She hasn't been very forthcoming."

"She's scared to death," I said. "I honestly don't know what kind of witness she'll make. Her P.O. is trying to help me wrangle her."

"You can't put her on the stand," Lance said. "She'll never hold up on cross. Girl hasn't been able to stay clean her entire adult life. There were drugs in her system when those hikers found her after her abduction. I had more luck talking to the Grace County sheriff's deputy assigned to her case. They were worried about her credibility."

"She smoked pot," I said. "And she hadn't smoked in over a week. She was stone cold sober during that abduction. I'm not giving up on her. I'm just worried how she'll take all of this. I got the real sense dredging up the details of her abduction won't do her any good."

"She needs to be told we're about to make an arrest," he said. "I'll get that rolling."

"I'd like to be there when she finds out," I said. "She wouldn't come out and say it directly, but I think a big part of her fear is that Emmons will make good on his threat to kill her if she cooperated with the police."

"She did once," he said. "We'll make her do it again."

"I want to take a light hand with that," I said. "This girl is terrified. Once we name her monster, I'm concerned she'll withdraw even more. She doesn't trust anyone down in Grace County. Her probation officer says she won't step foot in it. She's got a place near Lima. I feel like I can establish some rapport with her. I'd like to be there when she gets the news about Emmons."

Lance gave me a nod, but didn't seem satisfied.

I rose from my desk. "Come on. Let me walk with you over to Judge Ivey's. If there's any change he wants before signing this warrant, we'll make it on the spot."

Just then, Adam popped his head in.

"Sorry, boss," he said, smiling. "Not trying to eavesdrop, but would you mind if I tagged along to the courthouse? I kinda want to see how that's all done."

"Come on in, Adam," I said. "In the future, don't hover. Things are about to get pretty hectic in this case. I could use a second set of ears. You're here for the whole summer."

I made a quick reintroduction between Brody Lance and Adam Skinner. They acknowledged each other then the three of us started down the hall on the way to the courthouse.

"You had any other run-ins with Emmons's wife?" Lance asked as we crossed the street to the county courthouse.

"None," I said. "School lets out in a couple of weeks. She's taken a leave of absence. As far as I know, nobody at Grantham knows exactly what went down on the Emmons farm. As soon as Ivey signs that warrant, you know we won't be able to keep anything else under wraps."

"Oh, there are rumors swirling everywhere," Detective Lance agreed. "And we've had every crackpot in town calling into the tip line."

No sooner had he said it before David Reese, the crime reporter for Channel 8, walked down the courthouse steps.

"Great," I muttered. Reese froze for one second as he saw us. Then, he quickly recovered and grabbed his cell phone.

"Detective Lance, Ms. Brent, I was hoping to catch you on the way in. Can you answer a few questions for me?"

His phone was already recording. He had his camera trained on the three of us. I barely had time to take a breath before he launched into a barrage of questions.

"Are you aware that local business owner Cal Emmons has released a video on social media this morning? He claims the Maumee County sheriff's department has violated his civil rights and made defamatory statements against him. Have you had an opportunity to view that video?"

"He what?" Lance and I said it together.

"Is it true that Mr. Emmons is now the prime suspect in the abduction and murder of Haley Chambers?"

It leaked. I suppose I should have been grateful we'd managed to bottle this up as long as we had. There had been a major law enforcement presence out at Emmons's property. Someone always talks.

"Mr. Emmons claims he is innocent of any wrongdoing."

"This is an active investigation," Lance said before I could. "You know we don't comment on those. As for any recent statements made by Mr. Emmons, I've not seen those. Now if you'll excuse us ..."

"Ms. Brent," Reese said, undeterred. "Is it true your office is pursuing first degree murder charges against Cal Emmons in the Haley Chambers case?"

"I'm with Detective Lance on this one, David," I said. "My office also doesn't comment on active murder investigations. Also, you'll need to run inquiries through our press office, just like always."

We kept walking. Reese put his phone down, but followed. There was no law against it, of course. It was just intrusive.

We got to the elevator and Reese tried to get on with us. Adam brought up the rear. As Reese tried to step across the threshold, Adam made his body as wide as he could and barred Reese's entry.

"Sorry," Adam said. "You'll have to catch the next one."

Reese stood there slack-jawed as the elevator doors closed.

"Nice job," Lance complimented Adam. "Though I wouldn't have minded if you'd given him a shove to go with it."

"I would have," I said. "Let's just try to keep the circus to one ring on this one. Get your warrant signed. Get Emmons in custody. Then we'll hold a press conference."

Adam was on his phone. Before the elevator door opened, he'd pulled up a video of Cal Emmons from an undisclosed location. We stepped out together and watched it.

It was just as David Reese described. Cal sat against a wood-paneled wall with an American flag at his left shoulder. He wore a freshly pressed suit and green tie. His hair was slicked back and his skin tanned. It was the first time I'd really seen what he looked like outside of social media photos. He was plain. Homely even. With a crooked nose and weak chin. Though the hair on the top of his head was thin, he had thick, dark eyebrows and a dimple in his left cheek.

"My name is Calvin Emmons. You all know me. I live at 41345 Kidman Road right here in Waynetown. You've all trusted me to fix your small engines for over twenty years. We're friends. We're neighbors. I'd give the shirt off my back to any one of you. No questions asked. Now, I need your help. People are saying some things about me that just plain aren't true. I'm a good man. A Christian. I've coached your kids in Little League. Your kids go to school with mine. I'm the same guy you all like to shoot the breeze with when you come into my shop. So when you hear some things about me, you'll know they aren't true. Right now, I'm scared. The Maumee County sheriffs are saying some things that make my stomach turn. I swear to you. I'm being railroaded. They've put me out of my home. They've turned my life and my family's lives upside down. Remember what you know. Challenge it. Help me if you can."

Then, the video cut off.

"It's already going viral," Adam said. "Over four thousand views in the last hour."

Just then, Judge Donald Ivey's office door opened. The judge stood there wearing shirtsleeves and a loose tie.

"You got something for me?" he said. In the background, I saw his secretary standing in front of her computer screen. Cal Emmons's video played.

"Get that signed," I said to Lance. "Then for the love of God, get Cal Emmons into custody."

Before Detective Lance could answer, my phone started blowing up.

8

"Have you found any other bodies?"

"Is there any truth to the rumor that Cal Emmons suffered a broken collarbone during his interrogation?"

"Why wasn't the public informed that Mr. Emmons might be considered dangerous?"

"Have the family members of the victim been notified?"

"Is it true that the sheriff's department found two severed heads in the shallow grave where Haley Chambers was buried?"

The questions assaulted me like machine-gun fire. I stood behind the lectern with Kenya, using the thing like a shield. Kenya held up a hand and pulled the microphone forward.

"We need to just all settle down," she said. Beside her, Sheriff Clancy looked ready to spit. He and Kenya shared a calm demeanor before the press. Today was something different.

"Tell them what you did to Cal to get him to confess!" a ragged shout came from the back of the room. It was a woman probably in her mid-seventies. She and about a dozen other people lined the wall wearing black tee shirts emblazoned with #CalisInnocent and railroad tracks right beneath it. I assumed it was the Emmons family. It had only been three days since Judge Ivey issued the arrest warrant for Cal Emmons.

"I hate to sound like a broken record," Clancy said, leaning in so the mic picked up his voice. "But you all know how this goes. This is an ongoing investigation. We are not going to comment on it. Except I'll say we are working closely with the prosecutor's office and Mr. Emmons's defense lawyer. Nobody is being railroaded. And nobody has been mistreated on my watch. You have my word on that."

"Nor mine," Kenya added.

"There is one thing I'd like to say," Clancy said. "There's pretty much no truth to the wild rumors you're hearing, folks. Now, out of respect for the families involved let's all just get a hold of ourselves. I see a lot of supporters and family members of Cal Emmons's out there. That's good. I'm glad you're here. You can do Emmons a favor by telling him he needs to turn himself in. We don't want any drama any more than he does. So do the right thing, man. Let the process work."

A roar went up in the back of the room. Cal's supporters began to chant, "Railroad."

"For crying out loud." Beside me, Sam muttered.

"That's all we have for today," Kenya said. "You can submit your questions through our press office. When we have more to report, I'll let you know."

The double doors at the back of the room flew open. Another crowd of Emmons's supporters in black tee shirts pushed their way in. Clancy spoke into the radio he kept clipped to his belt. Within seconds, a few dozen Maumee County sheriff's deputies moved into tactical positions around the room to try and contain the melee.

"Time to get you out of here." Sam had a hold of my elbow. I grabbed Kenya's hand. We pushed through the crowd and out a side door. Within a few moments, we were safely inside Sheriff Clancy's office.

"This is insane," Kenya said, fuming. Detective Lance pushed in behind her. He was sweating as he shut Clancy's door. Clancy himself was still out there somewhere.

"Lance," Kenya shouted. "Please tell me there's no truth to this broken collarbone nonsense."

"There's none," Lance said. "You've all seen the interview tapes. Nobody laid a hand on Cal Emmons. We barely talked to him. He asked for a lawyer. That was it."

"Who is his defense attorney?" Sam asked. "Has he filed an appearance?"

"Just this morning," I said. I received a copy of it less than an hour ago. "He's going with a court-appointed public defender. Someone I've never heard of. A Peter Reilly."

Adam had squeezed in just after Brody Lance. "I know him," Adam said. "He graduated from UT Law three years ago. He was there during my orientation last year."

"Great," Kenya said. "Emmons has hired a green defense attorney in what I'll probably certify as a capital murder case. That ought to be fun for you, Mara."

It boggled my mind. This case was starting to get statewide attention. That always led to more high profile defense lawyers coming out of the woodwork.

"Let's just get this guy in custody," I said. "This thing is already going sideways. Cal Emmons is controlling the narrative with the press. Lance, this is why I needed eyes on him 24/7. He's been underground for weeks. At this rate, we're going to have a serious problem with a tainted jury pool."

"You're blaming me for this?"

I kept my cool out there. In fact, I rarely lost it in a professional setting ever.

"Yes," I shouted. "The second you got the warrant to search his property, he should have been properly tailed. His wife too. Now he's releasing viral videos from who knows where and convincing half the town you beat him!"

"Mara," Sam said.

"I've had enough," I said. "This has turned into a circus and right now, everyone is letting Cal Emmons be the ring leader. That ends today. Now."

Sam wasn't used to this side of me. I wasn't either. I couldn't stop thinking about Haley Chambers's family. They weren't out there. They were probably watching from home or getting links to Emmons's videos forwarded to them.

"Kenya," I said. "We need to have someone from the Silver Angels with Haley's family. Has anyone bothered to let them know you're about to arrest Cal Emmons?"

"They're already out there," Bill Clancy said as he stepped into his own office. His cheeks were flushed. The din of the crowd outside had dissipated for now.

"We need to get back to the office," Kenya said. "But Mara's right about all of this."

Just then, Brody Lance's phone rang. He lifted it to his ear and said hello. His brow furrowed. "You kidding me with this?" was all he said. After heaving a great sigh, he clicked off.

"Peter Reilly," he said. "The circus is outside. He's got Cal Emmons in the backseat of a car in the north parking lot. He wants the media there when he walks Emmons in."

"No deal!" Sam and Bill Clancy shouted it together.

"It's already happening," Adam said. He'd moved over to the window and peeked through the blinds. Clancy's office overlooked the north parking lot on one side and the courthouse on the other. We all gathered around Adam and looked where he was pointing.

A swarm of people moved toward the building. At the center, I could make out two white males, both in suits. One tall. One short. The shorter man shielded the taller one with a briefcase. As they got closer, the taller man looked up and straight at Clancy's window. We were on the third floor. I didn't think he could possibly see us, but I recognized Cal Emmons from here. He had his thinning brown hair slicked back and trimmed. Those thick brows were unmistakable.

The crowd chanted their support. A few reporters ran to keep up and film everything at Emmons's request.

"Just get that idiot in here," Clancy said. "And get those vultures out."

"By the book, Clancy," Kenya said.

"Oh, don't worry," the sheriff said. "If I have to fingerprint that bastard myself."

"Good," I answered. "Let me know when it's done."

"You wanna talk to Reilly?" Adam asked.

"Not in the slightest," I said. "I have nothing to say."

Assured there would be no more surprises with Emmons, I knew I had to get word to Haley Chambers's family. Her mother, Cindy, was likely fragile. It comforted me to know the Silver Angels would be at her side. They were a victim's advocacy group formed by another assault victim I'd worked with over the years.

I said my terse goodbyes and headed out of the building. One of Clancy's deputies led me out a side door to avoid the crowds.

"Are you heading over to Cindy Chambers's house now?" Kenya asked.

"I'm heading home first," I said. It was past five o'clock already. It meant I would miss another dinner with Will. But I at least wanted to spend a little time with him before I had to go back to work.

With further assurances that Emmons's booking was under control, I headed home. The weight of the day dragged me down and I wanted nothing more than a quiet evening curled up with my son on the couch.

I wouldn't get it. I saw an unfamiliar car pull out of my driveway. Luckily, its driver didn't see me coming. Him, I did recognize. David Reese.

"You came to my house?" I said to myself. My blood boiled as I turned down the driveway. The next surprise waited for me. Jason's car was parked in front of the house.

"Great," I muttered. "Just great."

I pulled into the garage, took a breath for courage, then walked inside.

9

Will was at the dining room table working a puzzle with Kat, my sister-in-law. Jason paced in the foyer. His face was red as he turned to me.

I didn't get a word out before Jason took two strides toward me. He took me by the wrist and pulled me back into the garage.

"What are you doing here?" I asked.

"I came to check on our son," Jason snapped. "What the hell is a reporter doing coming to the house, riling him up?"

"David Reese talked to Will?" I said. "What did he say?"

"He talked to me," Jason said. "But Will knows what's going on. Mara, this isn't good for him. You know how invested Will can get in stuff like this. He practically lived and breathed the facts of your last murder case. I've seen the news. What happened to that Chambers girl is gruesome. He can't be around that."

"He isn't around it," I said. "And it's my job. This has nothing to do with you."

"Will has everything to do with me."

"Jason," I said. "Why are you here? You're not due to get Will for your two weeks until next month."

He clenched his fists. "I wanted to talk to you about that. I think ... especially in light of this latest drama ... Will should spend the whole summer with me. It's not good for him to be around you right now."

I felt like I had whiplash.

"It's not good for my son to be around his mother because she works? Are you kidding me?"

A vein in my temple started to throb. I was tired. Worn out. But the day was far from over.

"Mara. You can't do this by yourself," Jason said, taking a calmer tact.

"I'm not," I said. "Kat's with Will. He likes his life. He likes his home, Jason. The last thing he needs is disruption and you know that as well as anyone."

"I'm taking him," he said. "I've already talked to him about it. Will wants to go. I've got that Congressional trip to London planned in a few weeks. He wants to come along. I want to ask Kat to join us."

I pressed a thumb to my brow. "You what? You're blindsiding me? This isn't our agreement."

"Our agreement is that we work this out together. We are. Right now. It's a good idea. You're just resisting for the sake of resisting. If you calm down for two seconds, you'll see I'm right."

I hated when he told me to calm down. It's why he did it. I had more to say. Before I could, my phone buzzed with a text. I lifted it and knew my long evening was about to get even longer. It was from Kenya.

"There's trouble with Dominique Bright. How fast can you get down to Ransom, Ohio?"

10

By the time I got to the little green ranch house at the corner of Junction and Eighth Street in the worst part of Ransom, Ohio in Allen County, three patrol cars blocked the driveway. All the neighbors were out. Two women in curlers and hair nets scowled at me as I slid out of my car and headed up the sidewalk. I went straight for one of the deputies standing closest to the front door. From here, I could hear screaming from inside the house.

"Officer," I said. "My name is Mara Brent, I'm a Maumee County prosecutor. Would you mind telling me what's going on?"

He eyed me, unimpressed with anything I'd just said. "You lost?"

"No," I said. "But one of the occupants of that house is a material witness in a murder case I've got going. I was hoping I could help sort this out before that blows up in my face."

He shook his head. Just then, the front door opened, and a disheveled guy stumbled out. Drunk. Wild eyes. Hair sticking straight up. He was covered in tattoos and had blood running down his cheek from a cut under his eye. A female deputy followed behind him. She pointed toward the deputy I stood near.

"She's out of her damn mind," the guy shouted.

"Just keep walking, Vinny," the deputy said. I could still hear shouts from inside the house and was fairly certain the voice was Dominique's.

"Is she under arrest?" I read the name badge on my deputy. A. Colby. Colby opened his mouth to answer, but Vinny got to us first.

"She's a psycho," Vinny yelled. "Crazy bi—"

"Zip it." The female deputy cut him off. Her badge read Meyer. It tripped something. Meyer. Vincent Meyer. Was she related to Dominique's loser boyfriend?

"Can someone please tell me what's going on here?" I asked.

Dominique came out of the house then. Her face was swollen from crying. She had bruises on her arm and healed scratches on her face. She jerked her arm away from the other female deputy leading her out of the house.

"He never stops lying!" she yelled to Vinny, her voice ragged and breathy. "He tells me lies about what I see with my own eyes."

Vinny spit on the ground. Deputy Meyer raised a finger. "Do not take the bait, Vinny," she said. "I'm warning you."

"Deputy Meyer," I said; she seemed to be in charge. "Are you making an arrest today?"

"You her lawyer?" Meyer said. She was short, solid, and stood with her hands on her hips.

"I'm a prosecutor in Maumee County. I was just telling Deputy Colby that Ms. Bright is a material witness in a murder case I've got up there. An arrest has been made and I need to talk to her, if you don't mind."

Meyer gestured with her chin. She led me away from the main group and out of Vinny's earshot.

"We got a call a little while ago from one of the neighbors," she said. "Domestic disturbance. When we got here she was starting to throw Vinny's things out of the house. He's my cousin. Not that I'm proud of it. These two go round and round. We were just out here two weeks ago. She was supposed to move out."

"Is he pressing charges?" I asked.

Meyer sighed. "I don't think so."

"Did he hit her?" I asked. "You see she's covered with bruises and healed scratches. Was that from the call two weeks ago?"

"Those aren't new," Deputy Meyer confirmed. "Vinny swears she got them when she tried to give their cat a bath. She backed up his story. Nobody saw anything. Their neighbors just said they heard a lot of screaming and banging. Same as this time. I told Vinny he needed to get her out of here. It's his house. They are one hundred percent toxic to each other."

"So what's going on this time?" I asked.

At that point, Dominique recognized me. Her red face went white and she walked up to me.

"Do you mind?" I said to Meyer.

Meyer stepped aside and made a sweeping gesture with her hand. I thanked her and headed up the walk to Dominique. She sat on the porch step having just lit a cigarette.

"Hey, Dominique," I said. "Do you remember me? I'm Mara Brent."

Her hands shook as she took a drag. "Yeah."

"Can I sit with you for a second?"

She didn't answer, but didn't stop me.

"He cheats on me," she said. "He lies about it. He does it just to hurt me. He never loves them. He just uses them to get me angry. To prove to everybody how he knows I'm crazy. I'm not crazy. They're trash, Vinny! They don't do for you what I do. They have no idea what I have to put up with! He says it's my fault. How can you treat somebody you love like that?"

Vinny charged up the lawn with two deputies running after him. "Whatever she tells you, lady, it's a lie. You ought to do us all a favor and lock her up in the loony bin for good! Psycho. If it weren't for me, you'd be back on the streets earning money on your back."

The deputies pulled Vinny back, lifting him off his feet. Dominique sobbed and hugged her arms around herself. She looked positively terrified and traumatized.

"I'm sorry," I said. "Dominique, is there somewhere else you can stay tonight? A friend? A family member?"

Her tears silently fell. "He's the one who should find someplace else to stay. They won't make him leave though. Vinny's name is on the lease."

"I see," I said. This seemed like the absolute worst time in the world to tell her about Cal Emmons's arrest. I just couldn't risk her hearing it from the internet.

"Can we go inside?" I asked. "Just to talk."

Meyer came back. "He wants you gone," she said to Dominique.

This was turning into an epic disaster. "One second," I said to Dominique. I took Meyer aside.

"Listen," I said. "If you can see your way clear to just let this one go with a warning, I'll make sure to get Dominique away from here for the night. Let them cool off."

"You know how this works," she said. "He's got visible injuries. I have to make a report. But I also know what's going to happen. Vinny's not going to follow through with it. It'll get kicked."

"What a mess," I said. "Look, I'll take Dominique with me. There's a safe house we have in Maumee County. It's run by the Silver Angels. You've heard of them."

"Sure," Meyer said. "That sounds like a good solution. Let me handle it with my cousin."

I had about twenty other questions. Why was she responding to a domestic call involving her own family member? Ransom was half the size of Waynetown or less. I suppose that had at least something to do with it. For now, I just wanted to get Dominique safely away. I'd handled Meyer and Vinny. I just hoped I could get Dominique to agree. I went back to her and laid it out.

"It'll just be for a few days," I said. "Just let things cool down. I'll call your probation officer and clear it with her."

I wasn't even sure I could do that part. It wouldn't surprise me in the least if Vinny had a record himself. If he had any felonies, Dominique was in violation just by associating with him.

"Thank you," she said. My heart broke for her. This girl had had every bad break life could throw her. She also seemed to make every bad choice she could. The next few months might get even rougher once Emmons's trial got underway.

It took about a half an hour, but Meyer stuck to her word and sorted things out with Vinny. Left with my assurances that I'd take care of Dominique, the deputies, Vinny, and finally the neighbors cleared out by the time Dominique emerged with a small overnight bag. I would have liked it better if she'd packed for good. One step at a time.

Finally, I got her in the car. I'd made a couple of phone calls and secured a bed for her tonight at the Silver Angel's safe house.

As soon as I got back on the highway, I steeled myself to deliver the rest of my news. We had a two-hour drive ahead of us. It would be close to midnight by the time I made it home.

"Dominique," I said. "There's another reason why I came out here tonight to talk to you. I was hoping for better circumstances, but word is already out so I wanted you to hear it from me. We've made an arrest in Haley Chambers's murder case. As I told you before, we have pretty strong reasons to believe this man was also responsible for hurting you four years ago."

Dominique went stone still. I realized then I was wrong. This was probably the best place to deliver this news. She was in a moving car with me. She couldn't disappear. And I was getting her to a place where she'd be surrounded by people with the background and empathy to properly care for her.

"I'm sure you have questions," I continued. "I'll answer those I can. There are some things I can't yet discuss because this is still all developing."

She said nothing. For miles and the rest of those two hours, she stared straight ahead. Only a small tremor in her hand revealed her internal turmoil. It wasn't until I pulled down a tree-lined street and came up to an old, beautifully restored blue farmhouse that Dominique turned to me.

"Here?" she asked.

"Here," I said. "Tucked away. It's on ten acres. There's a pond out back. A barn. They keep chickens and ducks and a few horses too. If you're into it, you can even ride."

Two women emerged from the front door. Nicole Silvers and Molly Havens. They co-founded the Silver Angels after Nicole's sister was nearly murdered twenty years ago. I'd helped put her monster behind bars and considered it one of my greatest career achievements. It had come at a terrible price though. But that was a story for another day.

Dominique turned to me. She still hadn't removed her seat belt even though I'd cut the engine. "Calvin Emmons. I saw it on the news a few weeks ago. He posted videos online saying he's being framed."

"You watched them?" I asked. I had been afraid of that.

"Vinny showed me," she said. "I think he thought it would make me feel better."

Vinny. Terrific.

"It's not right what he said about me," she said. "I'm not crazy. He shouldn't cheat on me. He promises, then he does it anyway. I know I shouldn't put up with it. Sometimes when you love someone ... it's just hard to stop. When he's good, he's so good, Mrs. Brent. But then..."

"Let's just get you settled," I said. "I'm sorry you had to watch those videos. But you should know, Calvin Emmons turned himself into the Maumee County sheriff earlier today."

"You're sure it's the guy who killed that Chambers girl?"

"As sure as I can be," I said. "Though he'll have his day in court. The system has to be allowed to work."

"The system," she muttered.

"I can't make you promises," I said. "I can only tell you I'll fight for you. I'll fight for Haley."

"Will he be out?" she asked.

"He'll be arraigned in a few days. Circumstances being what they are, I think it's very unlikely he'll be granted bail pending trial."

"He's ... in jail right now?"

"He is," I said.

"Can I see him?"

I was doubly glad we'd gotten the Silver Angels involved. Nicole had already contacted a social worker who was willing to talk to Dominique if she was amenable. I also wanted to see how she felt about seeing a therapist. Once again, the Angels could help with that.

For now, I pulled up my phone. While I'd waited for Dominique to pack a bag, Brody Lance sent me an update. Emmons had been processed. Lance's text included his booking photo.

I pulled the picture up and turned my phone so Dominique could see it. She hugged her arms around herself, blinking rapidly.

"Calvin Emmons," she whispered.

"Yes."

Nicole and Molly stepped off the porch and slowly made their way to my car.

"He owns a repair shop in Waynetown," I said.

"His eyes look so cold," Dominique said.

"Do you recognize anything about him?" I asked.

Dominique ran her finger over the image. "No," she said. "I never saw his face. I ... I know what he smells like. I'll never forget that."

Unfortunately, smell identification wasn't something I could question her about at trial. We had time though. She'd heard his voice. There might be some small detail I could use to help pin him to Dominique's case too, aside from the physical evidence we'd gathered.

"I want you to be prepared," I said. "He can't hurt you now. You're safe."

She looked at me. "You said you can't make me any promises. No one can. No one is ever safe, Mara. Not even you."

Nicole tapped on the window. Dominique handed me back my phone. She stepped out of the car. I made quick introductions. Molly and Nicole were kind, gentle, welcoming.

"We're glad you're here, Dominique," Molly said. "You're among friends now. We have a room set up for you. It overlooks the pasture. Would you like to see it?"

Molly took Dominique's bag. Dominique went with her willingly enough. Though she walked as if she were in a sort of trance. She let Molly put a hand on her back as she led her up the porch and into the house.

"She's scared," Nicole said. "But you brought her to the right place."

"Thank you," I said. "I just told her about Cal Emmons's arrest. I think she might be in for a rough couple of nights. I don't want her back in Ransom. The more distance she can put between herself and her current boyfriend, the better."

"We'll take it from here," Nicole said. "Now, if you don't mind me saying so, you look like hell. Why don't you go home and get some rest? We need you at your best."

Nicole's kindness always affected me. At the same time, her words had bite. She relied on me. They all did. It would be up to me to make sure Cal Emmons never hurt another woman again. The weight of the task settled over me as I left Dominique in the care of the Silver Angels.

11

June 24th. Nine a.m. Weeks after Calvin Emmons's grand jury indictment, I stood in Common Pleas Judge Vivian Saul's courtroom ready for Haley Chambers's monster to enter a plea.

He had a fan club. The town dubbed them "The Railroaders." As in, he wanted the public to believe the entire Maumee County criminal justice system had railroaded him. I had to find a way to ignore it. They didn't know the evidence.

Peter Reilly came in first as I stood at the prosecution table. He had on a suit that looked so new I checked for tags. Coal black with a bright red tie. He was twenty-nine years old.

"Ms. Brent," he said, coming straight for me to shake my hand. Reilly had a firm handshake, straight teeth, but a deer-in-the-headlights look that wouldn't serve him well in front of a jury.

"Mr. Reilly," I said. Peter reached over and shook Adam's hand next. So far, Adam had proven himself a capable intern. Detail-oriented, calm, with an affable sense of humor. Plus, he was good-looking. If he stuck around for the fall term, I might be able to use him at trial.

Two deputy sheriffs brought Cal Emmons into the courtroom. He wore a jailhouse jumpsuit and ankle chains. Reilly protested, but since the arraignment and bail hearing didn't take place in front of a jury, he lost that argument.

My heart skipped a bit as Emmons walked by my table. It was the first time I'd been in the same room with him as defendants don't participate in grand jury hearings.

He was big. Six foot one probably. Broad through the chest. The sleeves of his jumper just covered his elbows so I got a good look at his forearms. Well-muscled, covered in dark hair. He kept his cuffed hands folded in front of him but he was long-fingered with large palms. I couldn't stop myself from imagining him holding Haley Chambers underwater until she drowned. If I closed my eyes, I could see him pressing the lit end of his cigar against Dominique Bright's chest.

"All rise!" Judge Saul's bailiff called the court to order. Emmons whispered something to Reilly. Reilly didn't react.

Vivian Saul took the bench. She wore her dark hair in a tightly cropped style that matched her personality. All business, she quickly reviewed the file in front of her and called the case.

"Mr. Emmons," she said. "You have multiple charges against you. Kidnapping. Aggravated sexual assault. First degree murder. Abuse of a corpse. Obstruction of justice. Do you understand these charges?"

Cal leaned far over the lectern, practically swallowing the microphone. "Yes, Your Honor."

"And how do you plead?"

Cal straightened. He looked over his shoulders at his supporters.

"We love you, Cal!" someone shouted.

Judge Saul banged her gavel. "We'll have order here today. Your presence in this courtroom is a privilege, not a right. Act accordingly. Mr. Emmons, you may enter your plea."

Cal stood rod straight. "Your Honor, I am one hundred percent innocent. I did not commit these crimes. I am..."

"Not guilty will suffice," she said. "So entered. I'll hear arguments on bail. Ms. Brent?"

"Your Honor, we are requesting the defendant be denied bail. I won't rehash every argument in my written brief as I know the court has read it. But due to the brutal nature of the crime and the defendant's conduct since the first search warrant was served, I think he's shown himself to be a substantial flight risk. The state will be certifying this as a capital case. Should Mr. Emmons be convicted, we'll be seeking the death penalty. We request he remain in the county jail pending the outcome of this trial."

A murmur rose behind me from Emmons's supporters. I heard a female voice burst into tears. It might have been Cal's mother. So far, his wife Valerie hadn't shown up for court.

"Mr. Reilly?" Judge Saul said.

"Your Honor, we of course strenuously object to the state's request. We ask for reasonable bail and that the defendant be allowed to return home during these proceedings. He has family roots. His business is here. His children are here in Waynetown. He isn't going anywhere."

"Except he's already disappeared once," Judge Saul said, clasping her hands together; she rested them on the bench with a thud. "I agree with the state. Bail is denied. The defendant will remain in custody pending the outcome of this trial. You'll get a formal scheduling order by the end of the week but I'm looking at mid-October as my earliest available trial date. That is all."

She banged her gavel. The crowd at the back started yelling. The crying woman erupted in a wail. Cal Emmons stayed still as a statue as the deputies came around to his side and nudged him to follow them.

"Thank God," Adam whispered beside me. "I mean, I didn't think she'd let him out on bail, but..."

"But you never know," I said. Relief washed over me. Finally, I'd have something good to tell Dominique Bright and Haley Chambers's family.

"This is wrong!" Cal Emmons said. The hairs went up on the back of my neck. I felt his breath on my face. I looked up. He was there, in my face, just inches away. I knew in my heart his face was the very last thing Haley Chambers ever saw.

12

Emmons stared at me. Time slowed. The whites of his eyes had gone red, making the green stand out in contrast.

She couldn't fight. He was too big. He pushed her down and let the water fill her lungs. She might have welcomed it after everything else he'd done to her.

"Do the right thing," he said. His voice snapped me out of the nightmare I imagined. Haley's nightmare. Dominique's.

"Cal," Peter Reilly said. "Enough."

"You should listen to your lawyer," I said, stuffing my files in my briefcase.

"I'm not afraid of you," he said. "I know what your office does. You don't care about justice."

"That's enough, Emmons," Deputy Monroe said. He put a strong arm on Cal's back and started to push him forward.

"I'll be a millionaire after this," Cal said, laughing.

"You might be dead after this," I said, shocking even myself. It wasn't like me. I scanned the room, grateful civilians weren't allowed in here with cell phones. But someone else might have heard me anyway.

He didn't break his stare. Cold. Hard. I don't know why I took the bait. I don't know why I didn't just scoot on past him and walk away.

Cal smiled. Sick. Smarmy. I got a good look at his nicotine-stained teeth. Perhaps from a lifetime of smoking cigars. That's when I shivered. That's when I broke his stare.

Cal gave a little grunt as the deputy tried to shove him again.

"You're not going to make your career off me, lady," he said. "I've got your number."

"Is that a threat?" I said. Something snapped inside of me. I thought of Dominique. Of Haley. In the back of my mind, I knew there were others. Maybe he'd killed before. Maybe Haley was the first. But I knew in my soul that if he hadn't been caught this time, he would have brought another girl to that barn.

"Mara," Adam said beside me.

"You're a liar!" A shriek came from the gallery. "You're all liars. You won't take my boy. You won't get away with this!"

She burst through the crowd, wild-eyed, gray hair flying. "My baby! My baby!"

Cal Emmons's mother launched herself at the deputy guarding her son. His partner got out in front before she got to him. Chaos erupted in the courtroom as the deputy body-blocked her and got her to the ground.

"Don't you hurt her!" Cal yelled. "Somebody get their phone out. Make sure everyone sees."

I felt a strong grip on my arm. Adam pulled me away from Emmons. He was no threat though. The other deputy had him well in hand. Three more came from the back of the courtroom.

"Let's get out of here," Adam shouted at me. Within seconds, they had Emmons's mother in cuffs. She spat at the deputies and screamed obscenities. They got Emmons out a side door. The rest of the deputies controlled the crowd as we made our way out.

I was sweating. Heart racing. By the time we made it to the parking lot, I saw a news truck parked out front. No doubt one of the Railroaders had done just what Cal wanted and recorded the whole thing. Someone probably snuck a cell phone in anyway. It happened all the time. There would be another viral video within the hour.

I said nothing as Adam and I walked back to the office. Kenya was waiting in the conference room, a laptop pulled up. On screen, the video from inside the courtroom was already playing. It had only been fifteen minutes.

"You okay?" Kenya asked when she saw me.

"Never better."

Kenya gave me a stern look.

"He's showboating," I said.

"He's winning," Kenya responded. "What did he say to you? Or more to the point, what did you say to him?"

"Doesn't matter," I said.

"Adam," Kenya barked. "I need you to give us the room."

Adam gave Kenya a tight-lipped nod then disappeared down the hallway.

"Calm down," I said. "We got what we wanted today. Saul denied bail. It's good news. I need to get a call to Haley's mother and to Dominique Bright. Maybe they'll both sleep better tonight."

"You sure you're okay?" she asked.

I stopped. "Yes. I'm fine. Why do you keep asking me that?"

Kenya tilted the laptop so I could see the screen. She played back the video from inside the courtroom. I saw Cal leaning in to say something to me. Adam had a hand on my arm. Kenya froze the frame as the camera caught my face.

I barely recognized the person staring back at me on screen. Clenched jaw, narrowed eyes in fury.

"He's already getting to you," Kenya said. "It's not like you to lose your cool."

"I didn't lose my cool," I said. Though even as my words hung in the air, my pulse still hammered between my ears.

"You can't let this guy get under your skin again," Kenya said. "I need you at the top of your game."

"I am," I said. "That doesn't mean I can't hate him. This guy's the devil. And I'm going to make sure the whole world knows it."

Kenya straightened. We'd known each other for over ten years. She'd seen me at my best. And she'd seen me at my worst. I could tell what she was thinking just by the set of her jaw. Right now, she was worried. Deeply worried.

"I've got this," I said. "Promise."

"Fine," she said. "It's just ... I've got a really bad feeling about this guy. It feels like we're already losing control."

It was a diplomatic use of the word "we." I knew what she really meant. It was me. She worried I'd lost some control today and what that might cost down the road. She was wrong.

"You'll tell me if you need something?" Kenya asked. "Swear it."

"I swear," I said.

She didn't look convinced.

"Kenya, I swear. I'm not rattled. I'm not too close to this. I'm not any of the things you're worried about. This guy is going down. He has to. We're going to win."

I had more to say but never got the chance. Caro, our office administrator, came to the conference room door.

"Guys," she said. "I don't mean to interrupt, but we've got a situation. Those Railroader kooks are out in force. They're staging a protest march. Mara ... they're heading for your house."

13

Adam drove. Kenya worried the local reporters would recognize my car. I felt sick, physically sick when we turned down my street.

It wasn't a huge crowd, maybe twenty people carrying Railroader signs. But they stood at the end of my winding driveway shouting for Cal Emmons's release.

"Stay in the car, Mara," Adam said. "In fact, we should just keep on driving."

"My son is inside," I said, voice cracking. "We have security cameras. He'll have heard them go off. He's probably watching all of this on his tablet right now."

A quick siren blast behind us made me jump. Adam pulled up and parked just a few yards from the protesters. A deputy patrol car pulled in right behind. Sam and two uniformed officers got out.

As much as it killed me to sit there and do nothing, I knew Adam was right. If I got out, I might get swarmed. Then Will would see that on the security feed too.

Sam saw me and made a downward gesture with his hands. He mouthed "stay put."

I did.

Sam and the deputies walked up to the protesters and had words I couldn't hear. I knew the law though. As long as they stayed in the public roadway, there was little Sam could do. Now, if they started marching down my actual driveway? That was something else again.

Whatever Sam said made the group move away from the end of the driveway. They split into two groups, bracketing the entrance to my home. I could get through. I could get out. But they might stay there anyway.

"I don't get it," Adam said. "This guy is a murderer. A rapist. The physical evidence is rock solid. Do you think it will matter? I mean, once everything comes out at trial?"

"I don't know," I said. "Right now I don't care. I need to get to my kid."

Sam walked up to the car. I rolled down my window. "You okay?"

"I need people to quit asking me that. And I need to get to Will."

Sam gave Adam a hard look. "Follow me in," he said. "Don't get out of the car."

Sam went back to the patrol car, leaving the deputies up by the road to stand guard. He pulled out in front of Adam and we followed him up my driveway.

I didn't make eye contact with anyone. I didn't want them to see any emotion on my face. They shouted a few choice words at me but I ignored it all. Or tried to.

Adam and Sam parked in front while I barely waited for the car to come to a complete stop. I punched in my garage code and flew inside.

Just as I suspected, Will sat at the kitchen table, his eyes glued to his tablet. Kat stood behind him, worry carving deep lines into her face.

"I'm sorry about all of that," I said to Will. "There are some people who just want to have their voices heard on a case I'm working on. It has nothing to do with you. It really has nothing to do with me personally either."

"They're loud," Will said.

"I know." I went to him. "They won't be there forever."

"Can't they be arrested?" Kat asked. "This is your home."

"They have a constitutional right to gather and protest," Will said. "As long as they stay on the public roadway and don't block traffic, they aren't breaking the law."

Adam and Sam walked in just in time to hear my almost eleven-year-old son's legal analysis.

"Who are you?" Will asked, using a sharp tone.

"This is Adam," I said. "He works with me. He was just doing me a favor and dropping me off. Adam, this is my son, Will."

Adam waved; Will barely looked up at him. I knew this was too many out-of-the-ordinary things at once.

Giving him a polite smile, I gestured to Adam to follow me into the garage.

"Thank you," I said. "I think we're okay now. This is a lot for Will to process. Why don't you go ahead and take off and I'll see you at the office tomorrow."

"What about your car?" Adam asked. "I can pick you up in the morning, if you'd like."

"I'll have my sister-in-law drive me in after we drop my son off at his friend's. Thank you though. For everything."

"You sure there's nothing I can do?" Adam asked. He reached for me then, running his hand down my arm. He let it linger just above my elbow.

I froze. It was an innocent gesture, sort of. But Adam's gaze took on an intensity that felt overfamiliar.

"It's been a long day," I said quickly, taking a step back and out of Adam's reach. My brain was fried. Adam was just overly concerned, perhaps. And I was just plain tired.

"I'll see you tomorrow," I said. When I turned to go back into the house, both Sam and Kat were staring at me. I closed the garage door.

"How was your day?" I asked Will. Kat had succeeded in getting him to put the tablet down. I took it from him. So far, the protestors had stayed off my driveway. I watched as Adam drove to the end of it. They waved signs at him but otherwise let him pass unaccosted. When his car drove out of view, I put the tablet down.

This time, Sam gestured for me to follow him into the garage. I did.

"You sure there's nothing we can do about that?" I asked.

"I'm going to make some calls," Sam said.

I'd kept my temper in check until this very moment. "Emmons's wife was one of Will's teachers, for crying out loud. She knows him. And she knows having those people out there is disruptive to him. As angry as she is about what's going on with her husband, I just cannot fathom why she wouldn't say something to keep them from coming here. Protest around my office, I don't care. But my home?"

"Mara," Sam said. "Give me a little time. I promise you, by the time Will goes to bed tonight, those people will be gone."

"Thank you," I said, feeling my rage subside. "You're a good friend, Sam."

He got quiet. Then, "Yeah. I am, Mara. If you need anything. I don't care when. Just call. I could have driven you home today."

His statement took me aback. Was that anger?

"You shouldn't have come flying over here without an escort," Sam said, perhaps reading something on my face. He was right, of course.

"At the end of the day," I said. "I care about one thing. That little guy in there." I pointed with my thumb over my shoulder.

"I'm going to keep a couple of deputies stationed at the end of your driveway. Those people out there, they may be misguided, but I know most of them. They have jobs. Families to go home to. They might think Cal Emmons is some great guy, but they aren't going to jeopardize their own lives for him. This will die down. In the meantime, I want you to feel safe. More importantly, I want Will to feel safe."

"He likes you," I said. "That's a rare thing with him."

Sam smiled. "Yeah. That's kind of why I like him too. He uh ... sure didn't seem to like your new buddy today."

I narrowed my eyes. "Adam? He's not my new buddy. He's my intern. But you already knew that. Don't be cute."

"Hmm. Well, are you sure you've got things under control there?"

"In what way?"

Sam held an expression of concern for a few seconds, then his face split into a smile. "Nothing. Nothing at all. I can head out. I mean it though. Give me a call if you need something, no matter what or when. This will all calm down soon enough."

My phone started ringing from the kitchen. Jason's ringtone. Great.

"You need to get that?" Sam asked.

"It's my ex," I said. "I swear that man has spies everywhere. My luck, he probably already knows about what's going on out there."

"Oh geez. Mara, I'm sorry. Is this whole thing going to cause you trouble with that?"

I waved him off, not entirely sure whether I was doing it for his benefit, or to convince myself. "He's just worried about

Will," I said. "So am I. With what happened at school a few weeks ago, Jason's just been hypersensitive to everything. It'll blow over."

"Will talk to you anymore about what happened?" Sam asked.

"No," I said. "And thankfully he's on summer break now. He'll be leaving for D.C. to spend a few weeks with his father. It'll all be fine."

"Okay," Sam said, but he didn't sound convinced.

"Really, I've got this all handled. If you really think you can work your magic and get those people to move somewhere else ... anywhere else... I'd appreciate it. Just promise me you won't do anything that'll bite either of us in the behind."

Sam smiled. "Wouldn't dream of it. I'll let you get back to your family. But don't forget what I said. I'm here if you need me."

I thanked Sam again and walked into the house. Jason's first call had gone to voicemail. Before I could even pick up the phone, he called back. I squeezed my eyes shut, steeling myself for the next fire I would have to put out.

❧ 14 ❧

Cindy Chambers looked exactly like her daughter Haley. Big brown eyes framed with thick, naturally arched brows. She had the same dimples in her cheeks. I imagined it added to the dazzle of her smile. Today, eleven weeks before I would try her daughter's killer, Cindy Chambers's dimples showed as she grimaced and tried to hold back tears.

"Thanks for seeing me today," I said. Cindy lived with her second husband, Rob, the man who'd adopted Haley when she was seven years old. Since then, they'd had two more children. Twin boys. Conner and Zack. They'd just turned fifteen. They sat on the porch when I pulled up, their identical faces haunted and aged.

"Can I get you some coffee or tea? I think I might have some bottled water somewhere," Cindy said.

"No, thank you. Please don't put yourself out. I just need a quiet place where we can talk."

"Rob's at work," Cindy said quickly. "He had to go back. He took a leave of absence after Haley ... after we lost her. But he could only get twelve weeks. I don't know what we're going to do in October when the trial starts. He might have to quit. And then I don't know..."

"Let's just do this one step at a time," I offered.

Cindy looked unsure. As if she'd forgotten how to navigate her own house. She took a step toward the living room, stopped, then headed for the kitchen. One of the boys came inside and leaned against the wall, watching her. I wondered then, if that was something their father told them to do. A condition of his going back to work, perhaps.

I took the lead. Finding a sympathetic smile, I gently pulled out a kitchen chair. Cindy seemed relieved. She sat, folding her hands in her lap. I sat opposite her.

All the mundane, polite questions people ask in times like this seemed pointless. I couldn't ask her how she was holding up. That was obvious. How could anyone "hold up" after something like this?

"Cindy," I said. "Things are moving along. Judge Saul has denied Mr. Reilly's latest motion to suppress. I don't anticipate any surprises that might delay the trial. As of now, we're set to start October 13th."

"He'll have to quit," she whispered. "I just don't see how Rob can get any more time off. We have to be there, right? For Haley?"

"You have to do what you need to and what you can handle," I said. "You don't have to sit in the courtroom every day."

She looked up. "I do. I have to."

"Then I'll make sure you're never alone. Your case worker with the Silver Angels is Diane Logan, right? With your permission, I can contact her and give her all the dates you need to know."

She nodded. "She's been very nice."

"Can I be there?" her son said. He'd been so quiet, I hadn't even seen him come into the kitchen.

"Go back outside with your brother, Connor," Cindy said.

"No," he answered. It wasn't a tone of defiance, just a simple declaration. He would not leave his mother's side.

"The trial will take place during the school day," I said. "I understand you and your brother are entering your freshman year?"

Connor shook his head. "We're staying home. We've decided to home school this year."

Cindy got up suddenly. She moved soundlessly, like a ghost. Her fingers trailed over the backs of the chairs as she walked toward the front of the house and out the door.

I moved to follow her but Connor came in and sat in her place.

"What do you need from her?" he asked.

I could see the front yard through the bay window in the living room. Cindy kept on walking, disappearing down the sidewalk. Her other son, Zack, rose and followed her.

"You can talk to me," Connor said. "My mom is on a lot of medication for her nerves."

I looked at the boy closely. Fifteen. He was just fifteen. He held my gaze, challenging me.

"Is it just the three of you here during the day?"

"My dad drives a truck," he said. "She says he might have to quit work but we can't afford that. Zack and I are picking up work doing lawn care and moving stuff for people. Between the two of us we make enough to pay some bills, but there's still the mortgage."

"There's help, Connor," I said. "Let me talk to Diane at the Silver Angels and..."

"It won't do any good," Connor said. "They're too proud to ask for help. Our neighbors put up one of those fundraising pages. It got flooded with comments from those Railroader people."

"I see..." My heart twisted. This boy and his brother were holding the family together. They were babies. Just a handful of years older than Will. They hadn't just lost their sister that day. Their parents were gone from them in a different way.

"Will you let me see if I can do something?" I asked.

He rose and went to a pile of papers on the kitchen counter. He brought one back and handed it to me. It was the mortgage statement from this month. It was two weeks past due.

"There's nothing left in the bank account until my dad gets paid again. That's not for a few weeks. Will we lose the house? I mean, you're a lawyer, right?"

I put a hand over Connor's. "Not yet," I said. How much had Cindy and Rob Chambers kept from Diane and the Silver

Angels? I knew they had a fund set up to handle issues just like this.

"You know they said my dad killed Haley," Connor said. "And Dylan, her boyfriend. There was even a comment on one of the online forums asking if Zack or I had something to do with it."

"Oh Connor, you don't deserve any of this. Have you or your parents told this to Detective Lance? There are things we can do. Court papers we can file."

"A restraining order," he said. "I don't think that will help. They've already said it. People are already whispering about it at school. That's why we aren't going back this year."

"I'll do what I can," I said. "And I'm sorry that happened to you. This ... I know this might seem strange for me to say but I'm going to say it anyway. I'm proud of you and your brother. You've had to grow up very quickly. It's not fair to you."

"She blames herself," Connor said. "My mom and Haley got in a fight the night before she went missing. Haley hit a mailbox with her car a few days before that and didn't tell anybody. My dad was really pissed. They took the keys away from her for a week. My mom didn't want to but my dad said she's always too soft on Haley. That she has to learn and that cars are no joke. My mom thinks if she hadn't done that ... if she hadn't taken the keys, Haley wouldn't have been out rollerblading that night. She would have been driving her car like normal and that Emmons guy wouldn't have had the chance to take her."

"It wasn't her fault," I said.

"She blames my dad too. They don't talk to each other anymore. Ever. Nobody will say anything, but Zack and I know what's going on. They won't stay married. My dad is going to wait until after the trial, but then they're going to get a divorce. We'll have to figure out who to live with."

"Connor, that's a long way away," I said. "Your parents are grieving. Things are raw."

"No," he said. "They were going to get a divorce even before all of this happened. They just hadn't worked up the nerve to tell us."

This poor family. It was just all so awful. I felt helpless to make any of it better.

"Will you call me first?"

I jumped. Cindy Chambers leaned against the wall. I never even heard the front door open again.

"I may," I said. "We can go over your testimony again if you'd like. I have to establish a timeline and your story is a big part of that."

"I don't need to go over it again," she said. "I'll be ready. And the boys ... if they need to be there."

"We do," Connor said. His voice was joined by that of his brother. Zack came into the kitchen.

"It will help," I said. "The jury needs to get to know Haley."

"I want that," Cindy said. For the first time since I walked in, I saw a spark of light in her eyes. "If I think of it like that, it won't be so hard."

"We'll be there," Connor said. "Don't worry, Mom. We can handle it together."

I left them then. The twins gathered around their mother. I heard Connor making plans for dinner. He wanted to grill some burgers. Cindy said she thought that sounded good.

Fifteen. They were just fifteen. Collateral damage. You hear about the murder victims. You grieve for their lost potential. But their pain is over. It's the living who suffer for the rest of their lives. Days like this, I hated my job. Hated that no matter what happened at trial, I could not ease the Chambers family's pain. Justice felt like an illusion. A false promise. As I sat in the car, staring at the dirt road leaving away from the Chambers's house, a new thought hit me straight in the chest. No matter what happened with Cal Emmons. Maybe it was time to find another job.

15

As summer waned and turned into fall, Cal Emmons's trial date loomed. One by one, Judge Saul rejected Peter Reilly's various motions to suppress. He tried to claim Emmons hadn't been properly read his rights. He tried to claim Lance exceeded the scope of his warrant when searching the barn. It was ludicrous. All of it. Each time we appeared in court, Reilly looked more scared and skinnier than the time before. He might lose this case before the trial even started.

Will celebrated his eleventh birthday with a small party at the house. Jason flew in. We pretended everything was fine between us for Will's sake. Jason had a new girlfriend. Her name was Jennifer. She was a congressional aide for a senior colleague on the other side of the aisle. Blonde. Bubbly. I hated her. But she seemed nice to Will so in the end, that's all I cared about.

We'd reached a compromise. Will would spend the whole month of August with Jason. Additionally, the trial was scheduled for Will's mid-semester break in mid-October. He'd have a week off school and when Jason first suggested he spend it with him, I wanted to object. It wasn't our routine. It wasn't part of our custody agreement. The thing was, Jason was right. It might be better for Will in the end. So I agreed with the proviso that Will would spend all of Christmas with me. He'd go back to D.C. for the first week of the New Year before school started back up again.

Now, I sat in the war room, staring at my whiteboards. Adam had magnetized the head shots of all my witnesses so I could move them around as I figured out which order I wanted to call them in.

"If you start with Cindy Chambers, that might have the biggest emotional impact," Adam said. "Is that the thinking?"

"It's one of them," I said. This was the dance. The faces of my witnesses shifted around in my mind. It was like locking puzzle pieces into place. In every single trial, my job was to tell the jury a story. Lead them through the complex web of scientific evidence, weaknesses and all, until they understood the defendant's guilt beyond a reasonable doubt.

"I'm worried about Lance," Kenya said. She sat at the table, looking up at the board. "He can be shaky on cross. Comes across like he's got a chip on his shoulder a lot."

"I think he'll be fine," I said. "He did good work on this case. He frustrates me too. And I'd be a lot more nervous if Saul hadn't already shot down Reilly's best arguments in pre-trial motions. Everything he found in that barn is getting in."

"He should have taken our offer," Kenya said. "A guilty plea for taking the death penalty off the table."

"He can't take it if his client won't agree," I said.

"Then Emmons is a fool as well as a psychopath," Adam said. "These images are gonna bury him."

Adam had a blow-up of the torture bench in Emmons's barn. The B.C.I. photographer shot it from above. A single light shone down on it. The shadows around the thing were even more sinister than the bench with bolted shackles.

"Kenya, can you make sure Diane with the Silver Angels is on board for every minute of this thing? Cindy Chambers is hellbent on staying through the whole trial. As far as I'm aware, she's never seen these pictures. I don't think she should. I know I can't stop her if she truly has a mind. But I'm worried it'll kill her. She's also planning on bringing both her sons to trial with her."

"God," Kenya gasped. "We can't let that happen."

"I don't mean to sound callous," Adam said. "But that'll have an impact on the jury. I mean, just knowing Haley's mother is seeing all of this too."

"I will not do that for show," I said, my tone harsh. "I don't care what kind of points that scores. I want Cindy Chambers and those kids far away when we get into the barn evidence. Adam, you know this stuff as well as I do. So I'm going to rely on you to get her out at the right time. Are we clear?"

He reared his head back as if I'd slapped him. Anger boiled through me.

"Are we clear?" I said again.

"Mara," he said. "I should be in the courtroom with you every second. I know where you're going with your direct exams. You need me."

"I need you to do what I ask," I said.

"I'll let you hammer it all out," Kenya said. "For the record, Mara's right, Adam. Regardless of what Cindy Chambers thinks she needs, this is the right call. You do what Mara says. It's what you're here for."

She left the room. Adam exhaled sharply. He shifted his weight in his seat.

"What?" I asked. "You got something on your mind?"

"No," he said. "It's just ... I think I can be more useful to you than just babysitting witnesses, Mara."

"If I have to sit there and worry about Cindy Chambers and her kids, that's no good. So you take that off my plate."

"Is that how this is going to go?" he asked.

"What do you mean?"

"I mean, are you going to bench me? Shove me out in the hallway to sit at the kiddie table with a couple of fifteen-year-old boys?"

There was a bite to his question. I let out an exasperated sigh.

"I don't have time for this. Your job is to get what I need during trial. This is what I need. We're done here."

Adam's face fell. He rose from his seat and came to me.

"I'm worried about you," he said.

"What?"

He got too close. He put a hand on my arm. "When's the last time you ate something? Come on. Let me take you out to dinner. It's Friday night. We've got the weekend to plan. You look tense."

I felt my eyes bulge. Adam's eyes were hooded.

"Adam," I said. "It's past five. You're off the clock. Thanks for your help today. Are we clear on what I'll need from you Monday and when?"

"Mara ..."

"Goodnight, Adam," I said. I brushed past him and gathered the files I wanted to take home. I'd run through my direct exam of Brody Lance and Cindy Chambers a thousand times. I knew it in my sleep. Right now, I could not deal with the inappropriate, moony-eyed gaze of an intern on a power trip.

I left Adam staring after me as I left the building and drove home.

The lights were on in the kitchen when I pulled into the driveway. Mercifully, the Railroader protesters had long since given up standing vigil on my street. They'd be out in force at the courthouse tomorrow. Saul had already ordered them to stay out of the building. If she caught wind of them harassing the potential jury pool, that would be a whole other battle to fight.

I found Kat in the kitchen, pouring herself a glass of wine. She had a second glass ready to go.

"Oh, I love you." I smiled, setting my briefcase in the hall.

She poured me a glass and slid it across the bar. "I love you too. You look like hell. When's the last time you ate?"

"Why do people keep asking me that?" I took the wine.

"There's leftover pizza in the fridge. Luigi's."

"Heaven," I said. I grabbed a cold slice of pepperoni.

"Will's just putting his PJs on," she said. "You up for watching a documentary with him before bedtime?"

"I've been looking forward to it."

"Listen," Kat said. "I know you've got a full plate. I debated saying anything at all. But I think there's been some drama in Will's friend group. I overheard them talking on their headsets. Will was pretty upset. He wouldn't give me any details."

"Great," I said, my blood boiling. "Did this have anything to do with the bullies he dealt with last spring?"

Kat shrugged. "He wouldn't say. But I think so. I think he's glad he's going to D.C. to be with his dad for a while. I'm sorry, I hope that doesn't make you feel bad."

"Thank you," I said. "But don't think you have to shield me from anything or sugarcoat it. I *want* Will to have a good relationship with Jason. They love each other."

As I said it, Will came downstairs. His hair was still wet from his bath. He went straight for the big couch in the living room and turned on the TV.

Smiling, I grabbed my wine glass and went to join him. Will was quiet. Sometimes, this was his way. He squeezed in close beside me, resting his head on my shoulder.

"You wanna talk about it?" I asked him.

Will put a hand on my knee, squeezing it. Today, it seemed, it was the closest he could get to a hug. It was gold to me.

"You wanna talk about your day?"

I smiled. "Fair point, young man. No. I do not."

We sat in silence for a few moments. He'd picked a nature documentary about killer whales. We watched for an hour before either of us said anything.

"I'm going to miss you when you're in D.C.," I whispered, kissing his head. "But you'll have fun with your dad. And Aunt Kat is flying with you. That's always fun."

"He upgraded us to first class," Will said.

"Wow."

"Yeah. But will you call me every night and let me know how your day went?"

I felt a lump in my throat. It was the exact question I meant to ask him.

"Yes," I whispered, kissing him again. "That's a promise." As Will snuggled against me, I knew I was headed for the hardest few weeks of my life.

16

October 14th, Thursday ...

Twelve jurors. Men and women. Some young. Some old. Some in between. It had taken us the entire first day of trial to narrow them down from a pool of over a hundred. Too many had heard about the case from the news. Dozens had watched Cal Emmons's viral videos or been told about them. Quite a few knew Haley Chambers's family. But now, on the second morning of our scheduled trial, we had them seated.

"Are you ready to proceed, Ms. Brent?" Judge Saul asked me. She sat with her hands folded, patience wearing thin. Three times Peter Reilly had tried to renew motions she'd already ruled on pre-trial.

"I am, Your Honor," I said. Behind me, Cindy Chambers sat, along with her sons and husband Rob. The trucking company where he worked agreed to give him two weeks' paid leave while the trial went on. I knew Nicole Silvers had something to do with that. She knew how to work the P.R. angle and the

Silver Angels had increasing clout. They'd opened two more chapters. One in mid-Michigan. The other near Chicago.

"Ladies and gentlemen of the jury," I started. All eyes stayed focused on me. "I wish you could meet Haley Chambers. Her friends will tell you she had an infectious laugh. The kind you could hear in a crowd and she couldn't stop snorting. We all know people like that, don't we?

"When Haley was twelve years old, she and her mother were at a gas station. Haley wanted some candy and her mother sent her in to get it while she finished pumping gas. That day, a man came in holding a gun. He tried to rob the cashier while Haley hid in a corner by the freezer. There was a woman there that day. A stranger. She held a finger to her lips and told Haley to be quiet. To be brave. She was an off-duty police officer. A member of the Maumee County sheriff's department. Her name was Kelly LaChance. That day, Deputy LaChance changed two lives. She drew her gun and stopped the would-be robber from hurting anyone. And she inspired twelve-year-old Haley Chambers to pursue a career in law enforcement.

"Haley wanted to save people. To help those who needed a voice. She was working on her degree in criminal justice, getting straight As. When she finished, Haley would have taken the civil service test to get into the police academy. She wanted to work right here in Waynetown. She wanted to serve you.

"As we all know, that never happened. Instead, Haley's life was cut short. No ... that's not true. It would be easier for all of us if it had been short. It wasn't. I wish I could spare the people in this room from the details of what happened to

Haley. I wish I could spare her mother. Her family. Her friends. But I can't. Because it is our job to bear witness.

"Haley was going home. She'd been studying for a tough exam in an accounting class. It was April 2nd. Unseasonably warm. They'd just finished paving Kidman Road and Haley liked to rollerblade. She said goodbye to her boyfriend. She texted her mother she'd be home soon. They were waiting for her. They were planning a big family dinner and Haley needed to help.

"She never made it. Instead, she met Calvin Emmons, the defendant. The evidence will show that Cal approached Haley while she skated. He was driving alongside her. He slowed down. He might have asked her for directions. We don't know. What we do know is that he side-swiped Haley. She was knocked into a ditch. Bruised. Bleeding. The fall broke her collarbone and knocked her unconscious.

"Haley never saw daylight again. Not as a carefree woman. No. The evidence will show without a trace of a doubt that Haley woke up to a nightmare. Shackled to a bench in a dark, dingy barn. We know she was tortured for hours. Her bones systematically broken. Bruised. Bleeding. Scared. Alone. In agony.

"She could not escape. Her screams went unheard. There was no one there to help her.

"The defendant took his time with her. Beat her. Broke her thumbs, her right wrist. She was whipped. She was cut. She was burned. And she was raped. All of this happened while she was alive. While she was conscious.

"But Haley didn't die in that barn. The evidence will show that the defendant took Haley from that barn. He threw her in the back of his car while she was still bound with duct tape. It was over her eyes, her mouth.

"Haley died of drowning. The defendant took her to a pond at the back of his property. He waited until Haley was awake again. Then, he submerged her in four inches of water and held her down. She could not scream. With her wrist, thumbs, and collarbone broken, she likely couldn't even fight.

"She died in that fetid water. Alone and terrified. Then, the evidence will show the defendant took her body to Gunderson's Christmas tree farm and buried her in a shallow grave.

"He thought he wouldn't get caught. He thought he would get away with it. There were other shallow holes out at Gunderson's farm. Ones Mr. Gunderson knew nothing about. Perhaps the defendant did.

"Haley couldn't fight back. The defendant broke her body. Perhaps her spirit. He took her voice then finally, her life. So today, during this trial, I will give Haley Chambers her voice back. Because, believe me, she can still speak.

"She'll speak to you through her blood, her hair, her skin. She'll speak to you in the mountain of physical evidence left behind. What happened to Haley was brutal, ugly, horrific, unspeakable. Except we will speak it. We will hear it. We owe that to Haley. She's left a trail to her killer in every fiber of her being. You must follow it. I will take you there. At the end of that trail, you'll hear Haley's voice loud and clear. You'll know exactly what she was trying to tell you. Because even in death, even in her suffering, Haley was doing what she meant to dedicate her life to. She was trying to bring a killer to justice.

We couldn't help her in time to save her life. But we can help her now. Thank you."

I hadn't chanced a look at Cindy Chambers during my entire opening statement. To be truthful, I didn't think I'd be able to get through it if I had. She sat motionless, her back rod straight. A single tear fell from her right eye. Though I hadn't looked at her, a few members of the jury had. Rob Chambers sat beside his wife, his whole body quaking with rage.

He's going to kill him, I thought. If that jury didn't deliver the right verdict, I knew Rob might try to deliver one of his own. I made a mental note to say something to Sam. I wanted a deputy keeping an eye out.

"Mr. Reilly," Judge Saul said.

Peter Reilly had a certain appeal, I'll give him that. He wore a crisp blue suit and had a confident stride. He paused and looked back at the Chambers family, with sympathy in his eyes. It was a nice touch.

For his part, Cal Emmons appeared to be on his best behavior. He too wore a new, black suit. He'd shaved the scruff around his face and ditched his collar-length hair in favor of a close-cropped cut.

Normal. Respectable. The man you took your mower or your boat engine to when you needed it fixed. Valerie Emmons came to court today wearing a blue cardigan over a white blouse. Besides Cindy Chambers, she was the only one in the courtroom crying. Emmons's mother had been barred from the courtroom as a result of her assault on a deputy during the bail hearing.

"Ladies and gentlemen," Peter started. "Thank you for being here today. That was rough. Hearing about Haley's last moments was hard to get through. It's going to get harder. It's awful, just awful."

Peter shook his head and stepped away from the lectern. He pursed his lips, took a few more steps, stopped, turned, then headed back to the lectern. It was as if he meant to say something else then changed his mind. "Look," he said. "Nobody, not even I, will deny the tragedy that befell that girl. She didn't deserve it. Everything my colleague, Ms. Brent, said was absolutely right in terms of the horror of it all. Only, my client isn't responsible for Haley Chambers's death. He just flat out didn't kill her.

"Ms. Brent has said a lot of stuff. She's made a lot of promises about what she thinks the evidence will show. I need you to remember that word. Promise. She promised to tie my client to the so-called evidence in this case. It's her job—her legal burden—to deliver on that promise.

"I'm here to tell you she can't do it. Much as we'd all love some neat little package tied up with a bow, delivering Cal Emmons to you as some monster, it won't happen. When the prosecution is done with its case, you're going to find not a single piece of their physical evidence can be tied to Cal Emmons conclusively. Not even theoretically. They just don't have the goods, ladies and gentlemen.

"Somebody hurt that girl. Somebody killed her. But it wasn't Cal Emmons. Every second that we spend pointing fingers at Cal is another second that someone else is out there. They're watching. Waiting. They're probably laughing at all of us. When the dust settles, my biggest fear is that the real killer will grow bolder. That there'll be another girl like Haley

Chambers. She has no idea what nightmare is about to befall her. It'll be up to us to make sure the right person is held accountable for what happened to Haley. That's the state's job. It's the Maumee County sheriff's job. You're going to see, by the stunning lack of evidence in this case, that they've failed at that. Spectacularly. And the sad thing is, Haley will pay for that. Cal Emmons will pay for that in the time he's had to sit in jail falsely accused. And that innocent, unsuspecting girl out there will pay for it. And that's the biggest tragedy of all. Thank you."

"Oh boy," Adam whispered beside me.

I didn't move. Barely blinked.

"All right," Judge Saul said. "It's almost ten. Ms. Brent, is the state ready to call its first witness?"

I cleared my throat. "We are indeed, Your Honor. The state calls Dylan Woodhouse to the stand."

17

Dylan Woodhouse wore his father's suit today. It fit him through the shoulders but the sleeves fell over the big knuckle on his thumbs as he sat down. The bailiff helped him adjust the microphone. His face thin and hollowed out with grief, Dylan looked a decade younger than his twenty-two years.

"Dylan," I said. "Will you tell the jury how you knew Haley Chambers?"

He closed his eyes slowly, not opening them even when he first spoke. "Haley was my girlfriend."

Was. Not is. It had taken him a long time to get here, but I believed Dylan had begun the slow process of climbing out of the dark, emotional hole he'd been left in the night of April 2nd.

"How did you meet?"

"We took a class together at Maumee County Community College. Sociology. She was pretty and always knew the answers when our professor called on her. I had to miss a week of class in the middle of the semester. When I came back, I asked her if she'd mind sharing her notes. She said yes. We got to talking. We kept texting. I asked her out. She said yes to that too. That was two years ago."

"Tell me about Haley," I asked. "What did you like about her?"

Dylan finally opened his eyes. "She was serious. You just always knew where you stood with her. She wasn't like a lot of other girls I dated. Not flighty or emotional. If she was mad at me for something, she'd say so. And she'd tell me why. I might not always agree with her, but I knew where her head was. She was, you know, organized. She helped me keep my act together. And she didn't have to talk all the time. We could just be ... you know ... quiet together. I loved her. I still love her."

I let his answers sit. He'd told me all this before when I interviewed him pre-trial. With his hair a bit too long and that ill-fitting suit, I knew Dylan was having a very difficult time keeping his act together on his own.

"What were you studying when you went to MCCC?" I asked.

"I'm ... I was going into education. I wanted to be a high school science teacher. I was about to transfer my credits and go to Miami of Ohio."

"Was going to?" I asked.

"I haven't been back to school since Haley died," he said. "It's hard to focus."

"I see. Dylan, will you tell me about the last time you saw Haley?"

"April 2nd," he said, in a strong, clear voice.

"What happened that day?"

"It was the week before exams. Haley and I didn't have any other classes together, but we always studied together. It's loud sometimes at my house. So Haley and I would hang out at her place. We were studying in her den. I mean, her brothers were around but Connor and Zack are really respectful. They're more like my brothers. Or ... were."

This was the hard part. "What time did you get to Haley's house?"

"About three o'clock. I work at the Farm Supply Store in town. I got off at two, went home, took a shower, changed, then headed over to Haley's. We studied for two hours, until about five. Then Haley wanted a break. Her mom had company coming over for dinner. Her aunt and cousins. She was going to help cook dinner but she and her mom weren't getting along. She just wanted to leave the house for a little bit. Haley has ... had these rollerblades. They just paved Kidman Street so it's really smooth. I went out with her."

"You rollerbladed?"

"No, I jogged alongside her for a while."

"How long is a while?"

"It was before six when Haley wanted to head back so she could help cook dinner. So I ran back with her. She lives up a winding, quarter-mile drive. I'd parked my car at the end of it because I knew some of her family were coming over and I didn't want to get blocked in. When we got to my car, I said goodbye and I left. Haley was just supposed to skate down her driveway. I never saw her again. She never got there."

"She never made it home?" I asked.

"No," Dylan said. "I kissed her goodbye, told her I'd text her later. She was going to be busy with family stuff all weekend so I was going to pick her up Monday and drive her to class. I never heard from her again."

"What happened next?" I asked.

"I went and had dinner with a couple of my friends. Joe Pratt and George Irwin. We met at the Press Box bar, had a few drinks. Only two. I was driving my own car. Joe and George wanted to stay longer. There were girls they were hoping to hook up with. I just went home."

"What time was that?"

"It was a little after eleven when I left the bar. I drove home. My parents were already in bed so I went around and locked up the house. Turned on the TV. Just normal stuff. I wasn't tired enough to go to bed yet. So I went to text Haley and realized my phone died. As soon as I plugged it in, I saw a bunch of missed calls from Haley's mom. I called her back. That's when I found out Haley was missing."

"What did you do then?"

"I tried calling her. I called some of her friends. I pretty much freaked out. At the time, I wasn't really clear what happened. I didn't realize Haley never actually came back from when she went rollerblading. In the confusion, I just thought she went out again and didn't come back."

"What did you do then, Dylan?" I asked.

"I think it was close to midnight. Nobody had heard from Haley, so I went over to her house. Her mom was out of her mind, crying. Screaming. She lost it when she saw me. Flew at me. Grabbed me by the shirt. I couldn't even really understand what was going on. Her dad ... her stepdad, I mean. He pulled her off me. Haley's uncle, her mom's brother, Tony, came out. He took me aside and told me what was going on. Or ... rather, I got a word in and was able to ask what they knew. That's when it first dawned on me she'd never made it down the driveway."

"Dylan," I said. "Did Haley tell you where she was going?"

"She told me she was gonna skate for a little while longer. I told her she should stick to the driveway. It was still getting dark kind of soon by then."

"Objection!" Reilly stood up. I'd almost forgotten he was there. "Your Honor, anything this witness said or was told by Ms. Chambers is self-serving hearsay."

"Your Honor," I said. "That's an overly broad objection."

"I agree," Judge Saul said. "That being said, I'll sustain the objection in part. Mr. Woodhouse, stick to what you did, not what was said."

Dylan looked a little confused, but nodded.

"Dylan," I said. "What happened next, at Haley's house, I mean?"

"I told her parents everything I just told you. I hadn't seen her since I left. I was under the impression she was just going to go back home. Like I said, I told her to just stick to the driveway. People fly down Kidman Road. If I'd known she was going to keep going on the road after I left, I would have stayed. I swear to God, I would have stayed. I wanted to see her home. I always see her home."

He choked on the air he breathed. Dylan Woodhouse crumpled in on himself. I waited a moment, about to ask for a recess, but Dylan straightened. His eyes cleared.

"Did you ever go back home?" I asked.

"I stayed at Haley's house until about six in the morning. We called everyone. I drove up and down her road and looked with her stepdad and uncles. We called out for her. She was nowhere. It was dark. I knew. I just knew in my gut something really bad had happened. I think it was about that time the police finally showed up. They wouldn't do anything. Not until Haley had been gone a while. I don't know. I talked to Detective Lance. I told him everything I told you all here today."

"Then what happened?" I asked.

"He took me to the police station. They put me in a room. They asked me all of this over and over. They wanted to see my cell phone. I gave it to them. I would have given them anything. Done anything. I know they were trying to figure out if I knew where she was. If I did something, but they let me go. They talked to my friends George and Joe, the guys I went out with that night. They spoke to my parents."

"Did you ever speak to the police again?" I asked.

"Yeah. I was part of the search party that got organized. Joe and George and me, we were all on a team together. We searched the fields on either side of Kidman Road. This went on for days. And then ... the cops came to my house again. They said they'd found the shirt Haley was wearing on a branch in the woods behind my house. I have no idea how it got there. For a little while, I knew they thought I was lying. But then ... they knew I was telling the truth."

"Objection," Reilly said.

"Sustained," Judge Saul admonished.

Dylan wept. He kept his head up, his eyes straight forward, but he wept.

"Dylan, thank you," I said. "I have nothing further."

Dylan wasn't a perfect witness. But he was critical in establishing the timeline of Haley's disappearance. The poor kid had been blamed by armchair detectives and keyboard warriors for leaving Haley alone when he did. Then later, he'd become a victim of Cal Emmons in another way.

"Mr. Reilly, your witness," I said.

Reilly stood up. "Dylan," he said sharply. "I need to get this straight. You claim you left Haley Chambers at roughly six p.m. the evening of April 2nd, is that right?"

"That's right," he said. "A little before that, actually. It was probably closer to five thirty, five forty-five."

"And you claim you met your friends at the Press Box for dinner and drinks?"

"I don't claim it," he said. "It happened. Ask George and Joe. I was there. Don't try making it sound like it didn't happen."

"But you claim you left by eleven, is that right?"

"That's around when I left, yes," he answered.

"But isn't it true there is no cell phone data from you from six o'clock until almost midnight?"

"I said my battery was dead. I already answered that."

Adam shifted in his seat beside me. If he was nervous, I wasn't. Reilly was doing exactly as I hoped. He centered his opening statement on the police having pinned this murder on the wrong guy. But I knew better. The more Reilly dug, the bigger his hole would get.

"So you claim you left the Press Box at eleven. And you didn't realize your cell phone was off until closer to midnight when you plugged it in and saw all those missed calls."

"That's right," he said.

"Did you and Haley ever have arguments?" Reilly asked.

Dylan had stopped crying. He was calm. Perhaps even a little angry. I had prepared him for this.

"We argued sometimes, yes," he said. "Just like all couples."

"Isn't it true you were arguing the night of April 2nd?" Reilly asked.

"I don't remember arguing that night," Dylan said.

"You don't remember, or it didn't happen?"

"I don't remember. I know we were both stressed about exams. I don't remember having an argument though."

"So if someone saw you arguing with Haley on the side of the road, they'd be lying?"

Adam wrote a note. "What someone?"

I wrote back, "He's bluffing." I hoped. At the same time, it didn't matter. None of this would explain away the mountain of physical evidence we had.

"You admit that the shirt Haley Chambers was wearing the night she disappeared somehow ended up in your backyard, isn't that true?" Reilly asked. There went another shovelful of dirt from the metaphorical hole Peter Reilly dug for himself.

"I was told the shirt was found in the woods behind my house. I don't know how it got there. I know I didn't put it there. And I know Haley was wearing it the last time I saw her. I suppose you'll have to ask your client how it got there."

"Objection!" Reilly shouted.

"You're objecting to your own question?" Judge Saul answered before I could.

"I'm objecting to the witness making statements outside the scope of my questions," Reilly said.

"Your Honor," I said. "He asked a question. He got an answer. The fact that counsel doesn't like the answer isn't the fault of the witness."

"Mr. Woodhouse, please refrain from editorializing. Just stick to the facts. Beyond that, I agree with Ms. Brent," the judge said.

Reilly fumbled with his notes. He was flustered. The man was off to an awkward start, but I knew he wasn't stupid. At least ... I thought he wasn't stupid.

"You know," Reilly said. "I don't believe I have any other questions for this witness."

"You don't believe?" Judge Saul asked.

"I don't have any further questions," Reilly answered, sheepishly.

"None from me, Your Honor," I said.

"All right," Judge Saul said. "Are you ready to call your next witness?"

"I am," I answered. "The state calls Detective Brody Lance."

Judge Saul raised a hand. "All right. Then let's break for lunch then we'll put the detective on the stand. The jury is excused."

I waited. Once the jury left the room, Judge Saul called us to the bench.

"Mr. Reilly," she said. "I don't normally do this. But I have to tell you, I'm concerned. This is a capital murder case and you seem to be struggling."

"I'm fine," Reilly snapped. I chanced a look at Cal Emmons. He wasn't even watching. He had his head turned and whispered something to his wife.

"I hope so," Judge Saul said.

I couldn't believe it. In all my years trying criminal cases, I'd never seen a judge borderline offer a lifeline to a defense attorney like that. I knew better than to get cocky about it. Things that seem too good to be true, usually aren't. And I was about to call my most crucial witness.

18

Twenty minutes into Brody Lance's testimony, I noticed the first sign of trouble. Lance had a bad habit of fiddling with the buttons on the cuffs of his suit jacket. The first time he did it, it looked like he was trying to unbutton them. After that, he settled on pressing his thumb against the small, black disks, one by one. Maybe nobody else noticed. It happened mostly beneath the small ledge of the witness box. But to the jury, it produced an odd shoulder movement.

He was nervous. It could kill us.

"Detective Lance," I said, "When did you begin to suspect Haley Chambers's case was more than just a runaway?"

"After talking to the boyfriend, Dylan Woodhouse," he said. "He was adamant that Haley had promised to head back home after he left her near her own driveway. We had also spoken with several of her friends and her family. She was expected back at her family's barbeque. Her mother showed me a text from about twenty minutes before Dylan Woodhouse said he left her. The text indicated she was on her way home. She offered to help prepare some of the food for the occasion. There was nothing to indicate this girl was planning to run off and not tell anyone. None of her friends reported any suspicion of drug use."

"Was that your first thought?"

"Unfortunately, it always is," he said. "In most cases like this, where you have a missing teen or young person, we have to rule out drug involvement. Like I said, we had no indication of that from her friends or family. Then, by about two o'clock the morning of April 3rd, our initial cell phone data came back. Haley's phone pinged a tower about a mile down the road. One of my officers found it in a ditch."

"I see," I said. "What did you do next?"

"Well, at that point, it became pretty obvious we were dealing with foul play. I brought the boyfriend, Dylan Woodhouse, in for questioning. The phone was found, like I said, only about a mile from Haley's house on Kidman Road. It was pretty badly damaged. The screen was cracked. Neither Woodhouse nor Haley's mother remembered it in that condition earlier in the day."

"What did you do next?" I asked, keeping to as open-ended a line of questioning as I could.

"Some of Woodhouse's answers caused me concern. He was unable to account for his whereabouts for about an hour's window of time from eleven p.m. to midnight. I was able to quickly ascertain that he was, indeed, at the Press Box bar from about six thirty to just before eleven. His friends confirmed that; later we ran his credit card and there was a charge at 10:42 p.m."

"So it's fair to say that Dylan Woodhouse was your initial person of interest?"

"Absolutely," he said. "The problem was, Haley Chambers was already missing by six p.m. that night. Dylan had an alibi then."

"Did the focus of your investigation change?"

"It did," he said. "We organized a search party for Haley. The area along Kidman Road where Haley's phone was found and leading up to her house is surrounded by soybean fields. There's miles of it. We had hundreds of friends and neighbors and just good Samaritans in Waynetown and countywide wanting to help. So, I authorized the search. We had twelve teams of three people searching all through those fields and about a ten-mile radius around where Haley was last seen for several days. Each of those teams reported to one of our deputies. We had a spreadsheet and a grid map to cut down on overlap. Plus, I wanted to protect the integrity of any potential crime scene in the event Haley was found."

"What did they find, Detective?" I asked.

"Two things happened in pretty close proximity. A few days after the search teams started, we got a tip from a worker at Jan Gunderson's tree farm. It's about four miles from our main search site. That worker noticed three mounds of dirt dug in a place where they shouldn't be. In a fallow section of Jan's fields. He's got a dog out there, a Coonhound. They said he was acting strange, whining, heading back to that spot. So I sent a crew out there. This was four days after Haley disappeared, on April 6th."

I moved to introduce the photos from the Gunderson farm dig site. Lance went through them. Three ominous mounds of freshly turned earth at the edge of the tree field.

"Then what happened?" I asked.

"Deputy Rankin was the first on scene. When he approached the scene, he reported seeing what appeared to be a human foot sticking out of an area of displaced earth."

I pulled a photograph up. You could see red-painted toenails sticking up in the brown dirt.

"Detective, is this a true and accurate representation of what you saw when you arrived on scene?"

"Yes."

"What did you find in that hole, Detective?" I asked.

"We found human female remains matching the description of Haley Chambers. She was naked with visible injuries. Her hair had been chopped off."

For the next half an hour, I walked Detective Lance through the grisly crime scene photos. Haley had been found buried upside down. She'd been in that hole for at least three days. The jury took in each image, bracing themselves for the next. So did I. I'd seen them all a thousand times over the last six months. It didn't matter. It never got easier. This was a human being. A daughter. A sister. A girlfriend. A friend. To be discarded like that.

The burn to her chest was evident, though I would have the medical examiner explain all of that to the jury later. Her broken bones spoke for themselves. Haley's left shoulder angled violently downward. Her thumbs bent at wrong angles at each knuckle. With every brutal photograph the jury saw, I delivered on the promise I made during my opening statement. Though Haley Chambers could no longer speak, her broken, battered body gave her a voice.

"Detective," I said. "Earlier you mentioned that two significant things happened at roughly the same time that changed the course of your investigation. You indicated one was the discovery of Haley's body. What was the other one?"

"Yes," Lance said. He, too, was still shaken by the photographs. "As I said, we had organized search teams looking for her. One of those teams found an athletic-type shirt that matched the description of one Haley'd last been wearing."

"Where was this shirt located?" I asked.

"It was in a wooded area just behind Dylan Woodhouse's residence."

I showed the jury a picture of the shirt. It had been a bright-pink, dri-fit, vee-neck tee shirt. It was covered with dirt and a visible bloodstain near the bottom front hem.

"What happened next, Detective?" I asked.

"At that point, Dylan Woodhouse was still looking like the prime suspect in the case. I'll be honest though, something just didn't feel right about how that shirt was found. I interviewed the team of three who located it. They were Tom Steele, Phil Majewski, and the defendant, Calvin Emmons."

"Who actually found the shirt? Who spotted it?" I asked.

"Mr. Emmons did. Mr. Majewski indicated that Mr. Emmons pointed to it from some distance. Mr. Steele was closest to it so technically he happened upon it first. He immediately called Deputy Laurie Garvin. She was who that team reported to."

I showed the shirt as it was found, hanging off a bush near the back of the Woodhouse property.

"Did you question the defendant?" I asked.

"I did," he answered. "He told me he and his team were just about to leave that area of the woods when the pink shirt caught his eye. It was dusk but that bright color stuck out against the foliage."

"That's all he said?"

"That was it."

"Then what did you do?"

"Well, the next morning, Deputy Garvin came to my office along with Deputy Jordan Smythe. Smythe was in charge of another search party team consisting of Henry Gunderson, Nathan Overmeyer, and Braden Hughey. Mr. Hughey had some concerns about the other team's discovery of that shirt. It turns out, the Emmons team wasn't assigned to search the area behind the Woodhouse property. They were supposed to be on a stretch of Kidman Road. We had records, Deputy Smythe had no reports of that shirt being seen by Hughey's team. So, I questioned Hughey."

"How did that go?"

"Hughey confirmed Deputy Smythe's concerns. So, I went to Phil Majewski's house and questioned him further."

"What did you find out?"

"Majewski seemed frazzled. He said he hadn't slept all night. He said he was going to call me that morning of his own volition."

"Objection," Reilly said. "Mr. Majewski is available to testify for himself. This is hearsay testimony."

"Your Honor," I said. "The purpose of this line of questioning is to establish what Detective Lance did and why. He is allowed to testify as to how the investigation unfolded."

"Overruled. You may answer, Detective."

"Mr. Majewski said it was Mr. Emmons who insisted their party search the Woodhouse property. He was adamant. Majewski said he protested and tried to get him to follow the protocol, but that Emmons could be a very forceful guy. They were all tired and stressed out looking for Haley. So they went."

"What did you do next?"

"At that point, I decided I needed to question Mr. Emmons again. I went to his residence. This was the afternoon of April 8th. When I arrived, his wife informed me Mr. Emmons was working in the garage on the property. I drove back there. I didn't immediately see Mr. Emmons. However, I noticed a blue Mercury Sable wagon parked alongside the building. I don't know what made me look—instinct, I guess. At any rate, the vehicle was parked in the public parking lot of Emmons Repairs. As I looked closer, I noticed it had two different makes of tires on it. I also noticed from the window, it had gray carpeting. I knew that a significant amount of gray fibers had been found on Haley's body. We had also taken impressions of tire tracks leading away from the area where her body was found. They were unique in that the make of the tires were mismatched."

"What did you do then?" I asked.

"I became concerned that Mr. Emmons may have tampered with evidence and provided a false statement when I questioned him earlier. The car parked at the garage, at least on visible inspection, appeared to match some of the features of the tire treads we found leading away from where Haley's body was found. So, I left. I went back to the office and got a search warrant for Cal Emmons's premises, garage, and that vehicle. I ran the plates on it and knew it was registered to Mr. Emmons."

Reilly objected again. He'd been arguing for months that Lance's visual inspection of that Mercury Sable violated Cal Emmons's rights. He was wrong. Maybe if the car had been parked in a private lot or inside the garage. But it wasn't. It was in the public parking lot. I introduced the pictures of where Lance found it. Again, like she had in pre-trial, Judge Saul denied the objections.

The evidence from the barn was coming in.

The gravesite was haunting enough. But as the jury got their first look at what was inside Cal Emmons's barn I knew it would stay with them forever, just like it would me.

The blood. The shackles. The whips and chains. Hair samples. Carpet samples. Everything Haley Chambers left behind. They saw it all. They heard it all.

At the end of it, even Detective Lance had tears in his eyes. Finally, I turned. Cindy Chambers was gone. With my focus on Lance, I didn't know how much of his testimony she'd seen and heard. I hoped none. Adam had done his job and ushered her out at the right time. But Rob Chambers now sat on the bench behind Adam. His eyes were cold and blank as he stared at Cal Emmons.

Emmons slumped in his chair. Sweat poured from his brow. He looked physically ill. Was it an act? I might never know.

"Thank you, Detective," I said. "I have no further questions."

Slowly, Peter Reilly rose. His fingers trembled as he picked up his notes and passed me on the way to the lectern.

19

"Detective Lance," Reilly started. "Could you remind me how long you've been a homicide detective?"

"Eight months," he said.

"Wow. A whole eight months ..."

"Objection," I said. "Is defense counsel going to ask questions or editorialize?"

Reilly pursed his lips in anger. He stood with both fists clenched on top of the lectern.

"Ask your questions, Mr. Reilly," Judge Saul said. "Save your arguments for closing."

"Eight months," Reilly repeated. "And before that you handled property crimes. Stolen cars. Petty larceny, that kind of thing?"

"Sure," Lance said, unrattled.

"Isn't it true that the Chambers matter is the first murder case you've handled all by yourself?"

"No," he said. "I take issue with your characterization that I've done this solo. I have an entire team working this case with me. Field ops, B.C.I., computer forensics, the medical examiner's office. The list is long."

"But this is your show as lead detective, isn't it? You direct the course of the investigation?"

"Yes, to the last part of your question. I take issue with your characterization and the word show, Mr. Reilly."

"Fine," Reilly snapped. He turned away from the lectern. Cal Emmons made an over-exaggerated, throat-clearing noise. Reilly went to him. He leaned in as Cal whispered something in his ear.

"What the heck is he doing?" Adam whispered to me.

"Beats me," I answered back. Emmons had handed his lawyer a note. Reilly crumpled it up but carried it back to the lectern.

"You said on direct that you had concerns about Dylan Woodhouse right from the beginning, didn't you?"

"I said he was an initial person of interest."

"And you said Woodhouse couldn't account for his whereabouts for over an hour the night Haley Chambers went missing, isn't that right?"

"I said there was a gap in his alibi from roughly eleven p.m. to midnight on the morning of April 3rd," Lance answered.

"So it's true that you have no idea where Dylan Woodhouse was during that critical time frame?"

"He didn't have a solid alibi during that time frame, no."

"And he doesn't really have a solid alibi for about a half an hour right around the time Haley went missing, right?"

"I don't know what you mean."

"Well, I mean, if the Woodhouse kid said he left Haley at 5:45 and didn't show up to dinner until 6:30, that's a pretty big gap of time, isn't it?"

"His cell phone hits the tower closest to his home at 6:05 p.m. His parents both saw him and spoke to him when he came home. So, no, your premise isn't supported by the evidence."

"His parents," Reilly said. "Sure. But wouldn't you agree that an hour is plenty of time to commit a murder?"

"What?"

"I mean, you could easily kill someone if you had a whole hour to do it, couldn't you?"

"Theoretically," Lance answered.

"You could shoot them. You could stab them to death. You could run them over with your car ..."

"Objection," I said, getting tired of this. "Defense counsel is giving speeches, assuming facts not in evidence."

"Mr. Reilly," Judge Saul said. "I'll let you finish your question, but get to it."

"Sure," Reilly said. "Will you answer, Detective?"

"Answer what?" Lance and I spoke in unison.

"Defense counsel doesn't have a question before the witness," I said. "He's got a speech."

Reilly slammed his fist against the side of the lectern. "Detective Lance, would you agree that it's entirely possible to carry out a murder in any number of ways within an hour's time?"

"Yes," Lance answered.

"Dylan Woodhouse could have strangled Haley Chambers between the hours of eleven and midnight the night she went missing, couldn't he?"

"Objection," I said. "Once again counsel is assuming facts not in evidence."

"Sustained, move on, Mr. Reilly."

"Your Honor, I have the right to cross-examine this witness. My question is within the scope of direct examination."

"You're right," Judge Saul said. "And he answered it. I'm telling you to move on."

"Detective," Reilly snapped. "So I'm clear, when you first went to Cal Emmons's property, you didn't have a warrant of any kind, did you?"

"I wasn't acting under a warrant, no," he said. "I was there to follow up on concerns raised by one of the members of the search party for Haley Chambers."

"Detective, do you know how many people Mr. Emmons employed at the garage you visited?"

"I didn't the day I went out there. I believe he may have or had one or two part-time porters working at that garage."

"Did you question any of Mr. Emmons's employees in connection with this case?"

"No other employees were on the premises the first time I went out there."

"But you haven't questioned any of them since either, have you?"

"I spoke to one employee, Lincoln Maguire, on the phone. Mr. Maguire worked for the defendant as an assistant. I spoke to another former employee, Rodney Fowler, a porter. He left the defendant's employ about six months before Haley Chambers disappeared though."

"I see," Reilly said, scribbling some notes

"Did you ask Mr. Fowler and Mr. Maguire about the blue Mercury Sable?"

"I did. Mr. Fowler indicated the vehicle belonged to Mr. Emmons, which was consistent with the registration. Mr. Maguire concurred."

"Did you ask Mr. Fowler or Mr. Maguire whether they'd ever been out in the barn on the Emmons's property?"

"I did," Lance answered. "They said they hadn't."

"So I'm clear, you indicated that Cal Emmons was on a volunteer search team with Tom Steele and Phil Majewski, correct?"

"That's correct."

"So Mr. Emmons wasn't searching for Haley Chambers alone, was he?"

"No," Lance said. "None of the search teams were permitted to search alone."

"I see," Reilly said.

"Detective, isn't it true that you yourself have taken a mower to the defendant's garage for repairs?"

"What?"

"Cal Emmons, he fixed a mower for you late last year, didn't he?"

"Yes," Lance said. "I had an issue with the starter. I took it to Emmons Garage."

"How long was your mower in the shop?"

"I have no idea. Two days, I think?" Lance answered.

"And you, yourself, were on the premises, weren't you?" Reilly asked.

"Yes," he said. "I dropped off my John Deere. When it was ready, I drove back and got it. Like one does."

Reilly smiled, big and wide. It was downright creepy.

"Thank you," he said. "I have no more questions."

"Ms. Brent?" Judge Saul said.

I looked over my notes. Reilly had done nothing. He'd refuted none of the physical evidence. I couldn't for the life of me figure out what his strategy was with that cross-examination.

"Your Honor," I said. "I have no further questions for Detective Lance."

"You may step down, Detective," Saul said. "We'll adjourn until tomorrow morning. The jury is excused with the admonition that they are not to discuss this case or what happened in court today with anyone. My bailiff will give you further instructions. Thank you for your time and attention today. We'll get a bright and early start in the morning."

Saul banged her gavel and left the bench. I gathered my things and Adam followed me out. Brody Lance was a few steps ahead of us. We all walked over to my office together.

"What the hell was that?" Lance said once we were safely inside my conference room.

"I don't know," I said. "Reilly seemed flustered. Unprepared."

"What do you suppose that note was about?" Adam asked. "The one Emmons passed him in the middle of his cross?"

"Honestly? I think it was to do with you getting your mower worked on, Lance. I don't think it matters, but that's something you should have told me."

Lance shook his head. "You're kidding me. More than half the town has taken their tractors into Emmons. And this was last fall. Something like six months before Haley Chambers went missing. You think he's gearing up to claim I planted evidence? That's physically impossible, never mind insane."

"I know," I said. "It's a nothing burger. And it felt like Reilly didn't even want to ask it. If he's letting Emmons call that many of the shots ... I mean ... I can't believe he's letting him call that many of the shots."

"I was watching the jury," Adam said. "Obviously I can't read minds, but I really don't think that impressed any of them. We already know from voir dire that three of them have either taken things to Emmons for repair or had family or friends who have."

"I don't know," I said. "I just don't know."

Kenya walked in. She had her own spies in the courtroom and no doubt already knew everything that happened.

"You're off to a good start," she said.

"We got in most of the physical evidence," Lance agreed.

Caro walked in just after Kenya. She had a pink note in her hand and set it in front of me.

"Dylan Woodhouse," she said. "He seemed pretty upset."

"He wasn't even in the courtroom for Lance's testimony," Adam said.

"Word's out then," I said. "Reilly's going to try to convince the jury Dylan's the real killer."

"That poor boy's been through enough," Caro said.

"It won't stick," I said.

"Are you sure?" Caro said, her voice breaking. "Mara, I know Dylan's mother, Heidi. This thing is destroying their family."

"I'm sure," I said. I put a hand on Caro's arm. "Reilly's trying to suggest that Dylan did something to Haley between the hours of eleven and midnight the night she went missing. Tomorrow, I will call the medical examiner and we can put that argument to rest."

"How?" Caro said.

Lance and I exchanged a look. "Because the evidence strongly suggests that Haley was still alive then. She was in that barn being tortured by Cal Emmons."

Caro squeezed her eyes shut and said a prayer. I found myself mouthing the words with her.

20

We had a treasure tucked away in our little town. A true gem in Dr. Wayne Pham. The man had an affable demeanor and rock-star looks that juries responded to. He had a bright smile and eyes that twinkled, hiding a tragic past that he didn't like to talk about, yet everyone kept asking. More than fifty years ago, Wayne's father, also a physician, had worked as a translator for the U.S. Army. At two years old, Wayne had been on one of the last helicopters off the embassy rooftop during the Fall of Saigon. There's a picture somewhere of his crying mother throwing him at a U.S. service member. Wayne was lucky. His mother was not. He never saw her again.

But we discussed none of that during Dr. Pham's foundational testimony. Wayne educated the jury on his impressive credentials. Pre-med at the University of Michigan followed by Harvard Medical School. He'd been Maumee County's chief medical examiner for the last five years.

"Dr. Pham," I said. "Can you tell me the major findings from your autopsy of Haley Chambers?"

"Yes," Dr. Pham said. His written report had already been entered into evidence. "The victim's cause of death was drowning. I found fetid fluid in the trachea, main bronchi, paranasal sinuses, lungs. There was a high concentration of algae and other bacteria in it. Additionally, as you can see from exhibit 41, there were fine grains of sand and dirt underneath the victim's fingernails. I also found the presence of vegetation in her mouth. In layman's terms, it was consistent with a type of seaweed."

"Seaweed," I repeated.

"Yes," Dr. Pham.

"In your expert medical opinion, can you estimate how long Ms. Chambers would have to have been submerged?"

"That's hard to say specifically," Dr. Pham said. "Generally speaking, when deprived of oxygen, and submerged in water, someone will lose consciousness after about three minutes. The natural response when held underwater would be to hold one's breath. On average, a person can hold their breath for about thirty to sixty seconds. Certainly, there are people who can go longer. But after a certain time, biology takes over. You inhale, even though you'll take in nothing but water. The airways will close involuntarily. After about five minutes submerged, the brain's oxygen supply diminishes. Clinical death could take as long as twelve minutes."

"I see," I said. "Dr. Pham, what other injuries did you find upon examination?"

"If we could go back to exhibit 49 for a moment," he said. Adam was quick on the laptop and clicked back to the photograph Pham needed. It was a close-up of Haley's upper body. Her opaque, sightless eyes stared upward. At this resolution, you could clearly see fine grains of sand around her mouth. It stuck to her eyelashes. At the center of the frame was a blackened, ugly circle over Haley's sternum.

"Here," Dr. Pham started. He used a laser pointer to isolate the wound on her chest. "This was one of the most prominent physical injuries to the victim including the breaks to her thumbs, collarbone, and the bruising and lacerations. But this one on her chest, you notice right off the bat. It's a burn mark, likely made from a cigar. It's fairly deep, which would indicate the cigar was pressed into Haley's skin for at least a few seconds."

"Dr. Pham," I said. "Do you know whether this wound was made when Haley was still alive?"

"I believe it was," he said. "Here, at the edges, you can see it's beginning to blister. That indicates that the healing process had already begun. That's not something you see on a wound that would have been delivered post mortem. It's my opinion this burn was administered at least twelve hours before the victim died. There are significant signs of healing."

"What other injuries did you discover?" I asked.

Photograph by horrid photograph, Dr. Pham continued. "The bases of both Ms. Chambers's thumbs were crushed. The metacarpals are little more than powder on each hand. It's actually quite interesting that the skin itself wasn't more damaged beyond the bruising you see."

"Do you have any theory as to what could have caused that kind of injury?" I asked.

"Well, with the bruising you see around the base, I'd say a tool of some sort was used. My best guess, a hammer. Once again, you see significant swelling around the base of the thumb. That's one of the first signs of healing."

"What does that mean, Doctor?" I asked.

"It means Ms. Chambers was very much alive when her thumbs were pulverized."

Someone in the courtroom gasped. I didn't react, but from the source of the sound, I was fairly sure it was one of the jurors. Haley's family wasn't in the courtroom. I said a prayer of gratitude for that.

"I see," I said. "You're certain of that?"

"I am," Dr. Pham said. "To put it bluntly, dead tissue does not heal itself. All of the non-life-threatening injuries on Ms. Chambers's body showed preliminary signs of healing. The broken thumbs, burn marks to her chest, cuts to her forearms, labial tears, these all showed signs of healing."

"Doctor," I said. "Were you able to determine how old these wounds were?"

"All of the wounds I've described were fairly fresh. That is, I would estimate they had been inflicted within hours of her death."

"Hours, not days?" I asked.

"I would put it at no more than thirty-six hours from the time of infliction to when Ms. Chambers expired."

"Is there any doubt in your mind that Ms. Chambers was alive when these wounds were inflicted?" I asked. I had choreographed this question with Adam. The moment I asked it, he switched the overhead to a long shot of Haley's body on the exam table. Her torso was covered with a thin sheet so you couldn't see any of her privates, but the cuts, bruising, and broken bones were all visible.

"I have no doubt," Dr. Pham said. "Just as I have no doubt that Ms. Chambers was conscious when many of these wounds were inflicted."

"How do you know that?" I asked.

"If we can move back to exhibit 44," he said. Adam complied. Haley had deep lacerations on the top of her feet corresponding to the shackles we found in the barn.

"I found evidence of burn marks on the bottom of the victim's feet." Pham pointed out where on the photographs. "These weren't cigar marks like what was found on her chest. These were electrical burns, likely made with a prod of some sort. In any event, you'll see deep lacerations at the top of her feet. These are consistent with the victim trying to pull her feet against the shackles, away from the source of her pain."

"Thank you," I said. I needed a moment. The jury needed a moment. As experienced as he was, Wayne Pham also needed a moment.

"Dr. Pham," I asked. "Can you tell me whether you found any evidence of sexual assault on the victim?"

He had. He described it. He reiterated that the wounds related to the probable assault also showed signs of healing. Haley had been alive. When he finished, I took another breath.

"Thank you, Doctor," I said. "I have no further questions."

Peter Reilly took a moment himself. Cal Emmons had his ear. Red-faced, the defendant jabbed a finger into Reilly's arm.

"Mr. Reilly," Judge Saul said. "Do you have any questions for this witness? If so, are you ready to ask them?"

"Yes, Your Honor," Reilly said. He almost looked relieved for the reprieve from his client's lecture.

"Dr. Pham," he said. "You've given very detailed testimony about the extent of the injuries you claim you found on the victim. Answer something for me, if you will. Isn't it true you found no foreign DNA on Haley Chambers's body?"

"That's correct," he said.

"So you claim you found evidence of sexual assault, but that didn't include any semen, did it?"

"We didn't find the presence of any semen on the victim, no. But I found evidence of injury to the victim's genitalia consistent with forceful penetration and sexual assault."

"You didn't find any other foreign DNA on the victim though, did you? No hair. No skin under the nails, no blood that didn't belong to the victim?"

"That's correct," Pham said. "Though I didn't find it odd that we found no skin under her nails. There was evidence that the victim's hands were bound. Both by shackles and there was also tape residue. She was duct taped around the hands and mouth. Additionally, the body had chemical burns around the genitalia consistent with bleach being poured on her. Those burns also showed signs of healing. She was alive for it."

"Dr. Pham, you're familiar with the practice of bondage in sexual play, aren't you?"

"Objection," I said. "Foundation."

"Sustained, Mr. Reilly," the judge said.

"Hmm. Well, you're aware, aren't you, of the practice of bondage in sexual play? I mean, you've heard of it?"

"Of course," Dr. Pham said.

"Isn't it true you've even handled cases where the victim died from injuries related to bondage play?"

"I have," Pham said.

"And you've ruled those deaths were accidental, didn't you?"

"In some cases, yes," Pham said.

"Shackles can be used in that sort of thing, can't they?"

"I would assume so," Pham said.

"Electrical stimulators might also be used in that sort of activity, mightn't they?"

"Objection," I said. "Lack of foundation again. This witness is a medical expert. He has no expertise in the activities Mr. Reilly wishes to describe."

"The witness has already admitted he's handled forensic examinations in accidental deaths caused by exactly these activities," Reilly said.

"Overruled," Judge Saul said. "But you've made your point; move on, Mr. Reilly."

"Ms. Chambers didn't die from any of the injuries you described, isn't that right? She didn't die from burning. She didn't die from broken bones. She didn't die from cuts or bruises, correct?"

"Correct. Those were not fatal injuries, in my opinion."

"You said she died of drowning," Reilly said.

"Correct."

"But you have no evidence whatsoever that Ms. Chambers was held down, do you?"

"Excuse me?"

"Well, you don't really know how she came to drown. You don't know if she went into the water willingly. You don't know if she fell in. You don't have any evidence that anyone else was with her at all when she allegedly drowned, do you?"

"Well," Dr. Pham said. "She wasn't found floating in water, Mr. Reilly. She was found buried upside down in a Christmas tree field a mile away from where she died. She didn't rise from that pond like a zombie and walk herself over to Gunderson's farm."

Reilly pounded his fist against the lectern. "Yes or no, Dr. Pham; you don't know if Ms. Chambers went into that water alone, do you? You didn't find a single bit of the defendant's DNA on the victim's body, did you?"

"That's two questions," Pham said, utterly unflappable. "To the first, her body was moved. The soil and water samples in and on the victim's body were from a pond a mile away from where she was buried. To the second, no. I didn't find any

DNA evidence on or in her body that matched the defendant's."

"Thank you," Reilly said. "That's all I have."

It was as good a cross as Reilly could do. He'd left himself one small hole. It was ludicrous. But I'd seen juries do strange things. I just prayed they would keep their heads. My next witness should blow Peter Reilly's defense strategy to bits.

21

You can lose a jury on science. Throw statistics and vectors and probabilities at them long enough and many become numb to it. We saw that play out in real time in the nineties with perhaps the most famous DNA-based murder trial of all time. There isn't a prosecutor in the country who doesn't think about the O.J. trial when presenting blood evidence. For me, Dr. Janice Greer was my ace in the hole. A solid, serious witness, she always came to court wearing the same navy-blue pantsuit with a pink and blue paisley scarf tied loosely around her neck. She had a pretty, round, apple of a face with deep dimples and a calm presentation.

We'd gotten through all the foundational questions. All the scientific basis for the conclusions she was about to draw in devastating clarity. I looked over at the jury. They were taking notes. Good.

"Dr. Greer," I said. "What can you tell me about the blood samples you found in the area marked A?"

Above me, Adam had thrown a large image of the corner of the wooden table in the center of the Emmons barn. It had a yellow marker with the letter 'A' on its label.

"That sample contained a fairly large concentration of human blood, type O positive. I was able to extract a usable DNA sample from it. We had an exclusion percentage of 99.999. Meaning there was only a .001 percent chance that the DNA in Cal Emmons's barn belonged to anyone other than Haley Chambers. That's about as statistically conclusory as it gets."

"What about sample B?" I asked. The image changed to show another large bloodstain on the floor of the barn; you could easily see a drip pattern from the table.

"This was a match to the other DNA samples extracted from the barn. It came from the same person," Janice answered.

We went through the rest of the barn. For the first time, I'd been given the go-ahead for 3D modeling of the crime scene. Adam hit play.

I put Janice Greer and the jury in the barn. With the click of the touchpad, Janice took them through each bloodstain inside of it.

"You see a large concentration near the top corner of this table. Based on the positioning of other samples we took, sweat, hair, vaginal fluid, it's my opinion, within a reasonable degree of scientific certainty, that the victim was positioned supine, with her head at the top here, her hands and feet shackled, spread-eagled."

Later, in closing, I would juxtapose this imaging with one of Haley's autopsy photos. The jury would be able to see the cuts on her body.

Janice catalogued each of the samples of body fluid. Every single one came back as a positive match for Haley Chambers's DNA. She was everywhere. She was speaking.

"Thank you, Dr. Greer," I said. "Your witness, Mr. Reilly."

Cal Emmons was still whispering in Reilly's ear. This had become their pattern at the conclusion of all my witnesses. Most of the time, Reilly had to break away from Emmons so he could get up and begin his cross.

"Dr. Greer," Reilly started. "In all of your sampling, isn't it true you found no DNA matching any other person?"

"Well, there were other DNA samples taken. It's true that my analysis of those samples were inconclusive."

"So you didn't find a match for the defendant's DNA in that barn?"

"I said my analysis on the other samples was inconclusive. The samples were degraded. The place had been sprayed down with a chemical substance. Bleach. The samples might have belonged to the defendant."

"But they might have belonged to someone else; you simply can't draw that conclusion sitting here today, can you?"

"That's correct," she said.

He went on and on, detailing a dozen other degraded samples, recommitting Janice to her inability to positively identify the presence of Cal Emmons's DNA.

"This is bad," Adam wrote me a note.

I wrote back. "It's Cal's barn. I've proven Haley was in it and that she was there. That's all that matters right now. Relax."

Reilly took a theatrical pause. He even scratched his head. Then, he stepped back behind the lectern.

"Dr. Greer, if Haley Chambers was in that barn, she was alive, wasn't she?"

"Well, I know she was actively bleeding, sweating, leaving her DNA markers, yes."

"You can't offer any opinion on how she died, can you?"

"That wasn't the scope of my analysis, no."

"You have no idea if she walked into that barn of her own volition or walked out of it the same way."

"That's correct," she answered.

"And you cannot say whether anyone else was in the barn with her or who they were."

"I can't, no."

"Thank you, that's all for me."

"Dr. Greer?" I said, rising. "Can you remind me how long you've been a forensic DNA analyst?"

"I've been at this for twenty years," she said.

"Can you estimate how many crime scenes you've processed?"

"Oh, it's in the thousands," she said.

"Can you give me an idea how this particular crime scene compares to those thousands in terms of the amount of DNA evidence present?"

She took a beat. "Ms. Brent, the victim's DNA was everywhere in that barn. The table. The floor, splattered on the far wall. She bled. She sweat. This victim was held in that position, on that table, for a very long time to have left all of that evidence behind. As I testified, we found large concentrations of bleach everywhere in that barn too. But there was quite simply too much to clean up ... I mean, for there to be that much left behind even after all the efforts to wash it away. In all my career, that was one of the most horrific things I've ever seen."

Her words echoed through the courtroom. Through me. And I hoped, through the jury. This time, Cindy Chambers was present. Silent through all of it. Until that moment, when a deep, mournful sob escaped from her.

"Thank you," I said. "I have no further questions."

22

Braden Hughey bit his nails to the quick as he testified. The mother in me made subtle gestures to try and get him to stop.

"Braden," I said. "How did you know Haley Chambers?"

"We're shirttail cousins. Her mom and my mom are second cousins, I think that is how it goes.."

"Did you know her well?"

Braden shrugged. "Not really. She was two years ahead of me in school. I'd see her at family reunions and stuff. But we moved to Tecumseh for my dad's job two years ago."

"I see," I said. "Braden, tell me how you heard about what happened to Haley?"

"My mom got a call from another one of her cousins. Aunt Cindy ... that's what I call Haley's mom. Anyway, her sister is Aunt Annie. She called my mom and told her Haley was missing. That was, I think, the afternoon afterward. April 3rd."

"What did you do?"

"I was on spring break from school. My mom was pretty upset. She wanted to go down there. In case Aunt Cindy needed anything. She asked me to come with her. I have to admit, I was pretty freaked out too. I said I didn't know Haley very well. That doesn't mean I didn't care about her. Aunt Cindy used to babysit for me when I was a kid. I like her a lot. So we came down here to Waynetown. Stayed with Aunt Annie."

"Did you at some point have involvement with the search for Haley?" I asked.

"Yeah. Um ... yes. By the morning of Sunday the 4th, they were starting to organize search teams to cover the fields around Waynetown. I still have some buddies here. I called two of them. Nate Overmeyer and Henry Gunderson."

"What did you do?"

"We all were supposed to report to Waynetown High School in the gym. They split us up into groups of three and handed us a map with grid marks. We were team 17. Deputy Smythe was who we were supposed to report to if we found anything or had any problems. He gave us his card. We were supposed to walk the four-mile grid between Forsythe Road and the railroad tracks that go behind the school."

He pointed out the area on a map.

"Do you remember what time this all happened?"

"We did two miles over the course of the day going north to south. We went back out on the 5th and picked up where we left off. There was heavy rain on the morning of the 5th so we got a later start. I think we went out around three in the afternoon. From there we went south. Our grid took us to that wooded area behind Forsythe."

"Were the three of you always together?"

"Yes," he said. "That was one of the rules they gave us. Don't split up. We walked in a straight line. Me on the right, Nate in the middle, Henry on the far left."

"Braden, do you know Dylan Woodhouse?"

"Yeah. I knew he was dating Haley. He'd been over at Aunt Cindy's house and I knew she was really mad at him. She was upset he hadn't stayed with Haley the night she went missing."

"Did you know where he lived?"

"Yeah," he said. "I knew he was on Forsythe Road."

"So you knew your search area would take you near Dylan's house?"

"Oh yeah," he said. "There's a big woods that runs behind that neighborhood. They don't own that. But I knew we were close to his house."

"Do you recall what time you searched near Dylan's house?"

"It was the last stretch we did. Like I said, we knew Dylan lived there. I just had kind of a feeling it was important. If Dylan had anything to do with what happened to Haley, I wanted to make sure we'd done our job and looked really good."

"I appreciate that, but what time was it?"

"Oh. We walked along that fence from four thirty to five thirty."

"How can you be so specific about the time?"

"We walked it back and forth. Nate was getting irritated because it was getting late. He had to go to work. I wanted to walk it one more time. I knew it was going to take us like twenty minutes to walk back to Nate's car once we finished. I promised him we'd be done by six. I got a call from my mom at five forty-five just when we'd reached the end of the woods. That's when we broke off and went home."

"Okay, did you find anything that day?"

"No," he said. "Nothing."

I pointed to the area behind the Woodhouse home. "You're certain there was nothing there? No clothing, no footprints, nothing?"

"I'm sure. There was nothing but woods. And I remember that rotted-out tree stump about fifty yards behind Dylan's house. It was covered with mushrooms. You can't miss it."

"Braden, did you ever become aware of reports of an article of clothing being found in that spot near the tree stump?"

"Yes," he said. "A day or two after, they found Haley's body out at Gunderson's. That's Henry's grandpa's place. I heard they brought Dylan in for questioning. Deputy Smythe called me, Nate, and Henry in and asked us that same question. Had we seen any clothing near that stump? We hadn't. Then I found out on the news that they found Haley's shirt wadded up at the bottom of that stump about an hour after we went out there. That didn't make sense. We would have seen it. I'm telling you. It just wasn't there at five forty-five on April 5th."

"Thank you," I said. "I have nothing further."

"Braden," Reilly started. "You liked Haley, didn't you?"

"What? Of course."

"I can't imagine how difficult this whole thing has been for your family. I imagine there's been a lot of pressure on you regarding what you know."

"I don't think it's pressure. I think everyone in my family is just still so sad and angry about what happened to Haley. And this ... this trial is really tough on everybody, especially my mom and my aunts."

"Of course," Reilly said. "And your family wants someone to pay for what happened to Haley, don't they?"

"Objection," I said.

"Sustained, Mr. Reilly."

"I'll rephrase," he said. "Braden, you're hoping someone gets convicted of killing Haley, don't you?"

"Well, sure. Of course. Haley didn't deserve that. Nobody would."

"Thank you, that's all I have."

I waived redirect. Shaky though he was, Braden had been a model witness for me.

"Ms. Brent?" Judge Saul said.

"The prosecution calls Phil Majewski to the stand," I said.

Majewski walked with a pronounced hitch in his left hip. He grunted as he climbed into the witness box. He stared straight at Cal Emmons as I began to question him.

Phil Majewski had lived in Waynetown his whole life. His daughter went to school with Haley Chambers. Like my son Will, his son had been one of Valerie Emmons's students.

"How did you come to be on a search team with the defendant?" I asked.

"It was kind of random," he said. "I showed up with Tom Steele. They were doing groups of three and Deputy Laurie Gavin put us all together. We were team 13. We were searching in the woods behind the ball fields at Waynetown High on April 5th."

"So you were nowhere near Forsythe Road?"

"It wasn't our area, no. Not initially."

"Why don't you tell me what happened?" I asked.

"We started out around two, two thirty that day. It took us a good three hours to finish those woods. There was another team doing the western part. We met up in the middle right around five o'clock or a little after. Well, we could have gone home, but all three of us had some energy left in us. I just couldn't help thinking how I'd feel if it were my kid out there. Anyway, Cal said, well, let's head on over to the woods on the other side of the tracks."

"Me and Tom said okay, but I said we should call Deputy Gavin. Well, Cal said we can call her when we get over to the tracks. Tell her what we were doing. Cal had the card with the deputy's number. He drove us in his truck and parked at the entrance to Summit Acres."

"Summit Acres," I said, pointing to it on the map. "That's the subdivision that abuts the woods off Forsythe Road?"

"Yes, ma'am," he said. "Well, I'd say that was just after six by the time we got out there. We agreed we were gonna go to the railroad tracks. But Cal started walking that big fence on the other side of Summit Acres. It doesn't go all the way around. It ends and then you've got all these houses with the woods behind them. I said we gotta stick with the plan. And we gotta tell the deputy where we were now. You know, so there wasn't overlap. I didn't want to cover old ground. There was a system."

"What did Cal say?"

"He got kinda angry. He said the deputies weren't gonna turn down more help. He was walking really fast too. Like almost running. Well, I need a hip replacement. This was a much thicker area of woods than where we were before. I was having trouble keeping up. Tom kind of hung back with me because he saw me struggling. Well, I'd say Cal got about fifty yards ahead of us. After a few minutes, we saw him kinda change direction real quick. He circled back and waited for us. Well, about that time, Cal started acting funny. He started waving his arms and yelling like crazy. He's pointing to this tree stump. Tom was closest to it so he got there and just kind of froze. I was just a couple of steps behind him. That's when we saw what Cal had been pointing to."

"What was that?"

"There was a hot-pink shirt wadded up on the ground near that petrified tree stump."

"Was it easy to see?"

"Sure was. You couldn't miss it. It was all green around there and some brown from the branches. That shirt is what I'd call neon. Bright pink. And it was that athletic material, you know. With a logo that'll reflect against headlights in the dark."

"What did you do then?"

"Well, I told Cal we gotta call the sheriff right away. We had a picture of that girl. We all did, all the teams. The description we got said she'd last been seen wearing this bright-pink shirt. And the one we saw on the ground, there was a dark, brownish stain on it. It looked like blood."

"Then what happened?" I asked.

"We waited. About fifteen minutes later, the deputies showed up and took over. They asked us to tell them what happened. Cal did most of the talking. Like he cut me and Tom off a few times."

"Then what did you do?"

"They told us we could go home but kept our phone numbers. I got another card from Detective Lance. He told me if there was anything else I remembered, to give him a call. Day or night."

"Did you?"

"Yeah," he said. "I called Deputy Gavin. I don't know. I just had a bad feeling about the way Cal was acting. He told the deputies we all saw that shirt together. Well, we didn't. And we weren't where we were supposed to be."

"Did you think he was lying?"

"No, it wasn't that. Not then. I don't know. It was just a feeling. Then, I don't know. Once the dust all settled, I guess Deputy Gavin must have told the detective that our group was searching where we weren't supposed to be. So the detective called me to ask me about it and I told him everything I just told you. I found out they found that poor girl the morning after. Just awful."

Phil Majewski began to cry. Great heaving, silent sobs.

"You think she might have still been alive? When we started searching? If we'd searched sooner?" he asked.

"I don't think so, Mr. Majewski," I said. "Thank you. I have nothing further."

Reilly asked a few questions. All he could do was get Majewski to admit he hadn't actually seen Cal Emmons plant Haley's shirt against that tree stump. But I didn't think it would matter.

Braden Hughey had no reason to lie. Tom Steele and Phil Majewski had no reason to lie. I hoped the jury was smart enough to see that.

As Majewski left the stand, Judge Saul adjourned us for the weekend. Two days for me to make the biggest decision of my case.

23

Saturday evening, the bottom fell out. I'd spent the day going over admitted exhibits and reviewing points from every witness I'd called.

"It's here," Adam said. Kenya and Hojo had just left. Adam stood with his coat on. He'd made like he was going to leave four different times while I sat at the end of the conference room table staring up at my whiteboard.

"You have it," he said. "You've put Haley in the barn. It's clear to everyone what happened to her there. You've got her in his car with the carpet fibers. You've got his tire treads leading to and away from the kill site on his pond. And to and away from the burial site out at Gunderson's. Hughey and Majewski were good yesterday. I think the jury is going to believe them that Emmons planted that shirt out by Dylan Woodhouse's place. I mean, other than a confession, what else could you give them?"

"I could give them Dominique Bright," I said. "She could put a face and actual words to the horror Emmons put her through. And put Haley through."

"So why don't you?" Adam asked.

"Emmons was never charged with Dominique's assault. Grace County is hedging their bets, waiting to see how this trial shakes out before they go after him for her."

"I don't get it," Adam said. "They can prove Dominique was in his car. She provides his M.O. Other than the torture barn and the actual murder, everything that happened to Haley happened to Dominique. Why aren't they moving on it?"

"Because of Dominique," I said, hating it. "She's shaky. She's had a complicated relationship with law enforcement. I'm worried she won't hold up on cross. Heck, I'm worried she won't even make it through direct. So, the question is, is putting Dominique on the stand worth the risk?"

I'd weighed this question a thousand times. Five minutes later, a text came through that tipped the scales once more.

"Mara, it's Sam. I'm downstairs. Can you let me in?"

I stared at the phone screen. "Dammit," I whispered. I couldn't think of a single, case-related good thing Sam would be here for at this hour on a Saturday.

"I'll be right back," I said, not cluing Adam in just yet.

I met Sam at the service door into the building. His grim expression did nothing to sway me from my initial instincts.

"What's going on?" I asked as we made our way back into the conference room. Sam paused, surprised to see Adam still sitting there. An odd moment seemed to pass between them, as if Sam didn't want to talk in front of him.

"If this is about the Chambers trial," I said, "Adam needs to hear it too."

"Right," Sam said. "Listen, I just got off the phone with Detective Amanda Berry down in Allen County."

My heart dropped. "Dominique," I said. "Sam, what happened? Is she okay?"

"More or less," he said. "Detective Berry wanted me to hear this before it got picked up by the local news. She's a friend. We worked another murder case about ten years ago. It wouldn't even be news at all if it weren't for the connection to the Chambers case."

"Sam, what?" I said, my patience wearing thin.

Sam sighed. "They're about to charge her with filing a false police report."

"What?" Adam and I said it together.

"She and the current boyfriend, Vinny Meyer, got into it again. She filed a report that he'd stolen her car. Meyer produced some texts between them where she very clearly gave him permission to use it last week."

I felt hot. I couldn't sit still. "She promised me she wouldn't have any contact with him. The Silver Angels were working on getting her into an apartment just outside of Waynetown. Where did this all happen?"

"Meyer's place outside of Lima," Sam said. "Dominique moved back in a few weeks ago after they started talking."

"Reilly probably already knows," I said.

"He most definitely does," Sam said. "Berry said she's gotten a call from him. She hasn't returned it. She wanted to talk to me and Brody Lance first."

I covered my face with my hand. "Dominique never mentioned any of this to me. Not a word. Nicole Silvers had her in counseling. There was a restraining order in place. She wasn't supposed to have any contact with Vinny. Oh, lord."

"She's spiraling," Adam said. "You think it's to do with the trial? She's falling back into old patterns?"

"More than likely," Sam said.

"This isn't just a potential problem for Haley's case. If I were the prosecutor in Grace County, I don't know if I'd be able to bring charges against Emmons."

"Yes, you would," Sam said. "You'd do it anyway. I know you. You'd rather risk losing than protecting your stats or turning your back on a victim like that."

"Thanks," I said. Though Sam's praise meant a lot to me, it wouldn't solve my Dominique problem.

"I need to talk to her," I said. "Have they booked her yet?"

"About an hour ago," Sam said.

"Dammit! Your Detective Berry should have called me. I would have liked to be there for it, or at least sent Hojo down. Ugh. This is the absolute last thing Dominique needs."

"I'm sorry," Sam said. "This girl has been through hell. I wish there was something I could do for her. I'm going to try talking to Detective Berry again. See if I can lean on her to let this one go."

"I'll talk to the prosecutor down there too. Though she's already in the system on it. This is another probation violation. Sam, I'm worried she won't make bail on this."

"One thing at a time," Sam said. I smiled. It was the advice I always gave to witnesses and victims.

Sam's phone went off. He frowned as he looked at it. "Mara," he said. "You better get down there. Things aren't going so well at the jail with Dominique. Come on, I'll drive you."

24

She'd lost weight. Dominique Bright wasn't that big to begin with. Her hair had lost its luster and hung in strings around her face. She'd been crying. I wanted to tell her everything would be okay. The trouble was, this woman knew that would always be a lie.

"You'll have a bail hearing in the morning," I said. "Your probation officer is going to recommend it be set at something reasonable. I don't expect any problems with that ..."

"Mara," she said, her voice barely audible. "I'm sorry."

"Sorry? Dominique, you don't owe me anything. Not even an apology."

"I know you told me not to talk to Vinny anymore. I know he just tells me lies. He's been cheating on me for years. He throws it in my face. I know these girls. They're all the same. They don't know him like I do. They don't take care of him like I do. I've done everything for him. I've proven it over and over."

"Dominique," I said, my tone firm. "This isn't about Vinny. This is about you. You just have to worry about working on you."

"Is this going to mess up your case?" she asked.

"It has nothing to do with my case," I said, though I wished that were true. It only affected my case if I chose to put Dominique on the stand. If the Grace County prosecutor wouldn't go forward with charging Cal for Dominique's abduction and rape, her testimony in Haley's case might be the only chance she had to tell her story.

Dominique got quiet. She leaned over, resting her head on her arm over the table. For a moment, I thought she'd actually fallen asleep. Then, she took in a great breath and let it out with four honest words.

"I can't do it."

"Can't do what?" I asked.

"I can't testify for you. I can't face that man. I can't relive all the horrible things he did to me. It'll break me. I'm already broken. He wins."

"No," I said. "He doesn't win. Not as long as you draw breath. You win. Do you hear me? You do."

"He'll do it again," she said. "Someday. Somewhere. He'll just do it again."

"We have a strong case against him."

"I get what I deserve," she whispered. Her eyes went glassy. She went to a dark place for a moment and I wondered if she could still feel Cal Emmons's hands around her throat, pushing her down into the water. "They always get what they deserve."

"You didn't deserve what happened to you. But you're not what happened to you, Dominique. You're not responsible for it. Do you hear me?"

She raised her head and leveled a cold stare at me. "That's what they all say."

I saw movement in the window over Dominique's shoulder. Nicole Silvers and Dominique's caseworker, Diane from the Silver Angels had arrived. They would stay with her tonight. They would be here at her bail hearing Monday morning. It was past four in the morning on Sunday. She had a long day ahead of her. But so did I.

"Do whatever you have to do," Dominique said. "Help Haley. I'm a bit of a lost cause."

"I don't believe that," I said, my heart breaking for her. But I had to leave her to the professionals. This girl needed help I couldn't give right now. It tore at me to leave her, but I had no choice. There was one other victim who needed my voice.

"I'll check in tomorrow," I said. "I need you to stay strong. There are good people out there on your side. Listen to them."

Dominique nodded, but her eyes stayed hollow. I left the room as the caseworker walked in. I met Nicole in the hallway.

"She's in rough shape," I said. "She feels guilty about whatever impact she could have made for Haley. But I just don't think that should be a priority for her right now."

Nicole gave me a sad smile. "You sure do have your work cut out for you. I don't envy you."

"Thanks," I said. "It'll help me to know you guys are going to be with her today. She needs to know people will fight for her. I don't think she's had much of that in her life."

"No," Nicole agreed. "She hasn't. And we're not going anywhere. You do what you have to do."

"I will."

"Mara? I know this isn't what you want to hear, but I just don't think Dominique is in a place where she can face Emmons yet."

"I know."

"This hold Vinny Meyer has over her is strong. I thought we were making some headway. But she's been in communication with him all along. She lied to us about breaking it off with him. He's not good for her."

"She thinks she deserves the way he treats her. I think she thinks she deserves what Cal did to her."

Nicole shook her head. "That sounds like Vinny talking. On Emmons though, can you nail that bastard without her?"

I didn't answer. It was bad luck to make predictions about how a jury would rule. There was still a lot of trial left to go. Peter Reilly had gotten off to a rough start, but I wasn't cocky enough to think he couldn't do damage during his case in chief. "I'll do my best." I smiled. Nicole knew me well enough to understand my fears. She shared them.

Sam waited for me at the end of the hall. "She's going to be okay," he said. "She's in good hands."

"I hope you're right," I said. "Because right now I just feel like Cal Emmons is re-victimizing her and there isn't much else I can do."

Sam put a supportive hand on my back as we walked out of the police station together.

Nineteen hours later, I stood at the lectern in front of Judge Saul. Dominique's sad eyes still wavered in my vision. So did Haley's. I went over everything I'd done again and again. Every witness. Every scrap of evidence. It was enough. Even without Dominique, it had to be enough. When Judge Saul questioned me, I squared my shoulders and faced her.

"Your Honor," I said. "At this time, the prosecution rests."

25

"We call Valerie Emmons to the stand, Your Honor," Reilly said, calling his first witness for the defense.

Valerie wore a floral print blouse and blue skirt. The pretty woman I'd always known with too much makeup had taken some style advice. Today, she wore none. Her skin was remarkably pale, her lips almost invisible. In fact, the only color on her face were the dark-gray circles beneath her eyes.

"Mrs. Emmons," Reilly started. "Can you explain to the jury how you're related to the defendant?"

"He's my husband," Valerie said. Reilly then had to remind her to speak up so the jury could hear.

"How long have you been married?"

"Since right after college," she said. "I went to the University of Toledo. Cal worked as a mechanic at one of the Ford dealerships in Toledo. I think it was my sophomore year, I had to take my car in to fix something with the transmission. That's when we met. He was so good-looking. And he knew how to do things, you know? Like he could fix anything. He could just ... handle stuff. Men like that are hard to find anymore."

"Sure," Reilly said. "What do you do for a living now?"

"Well, I got a psychology degree. But I didn't pursue that. Cal and I got married just as soon as I graduated. I didn't have the greatest home life. We'd already moved in together and that caused a lot of problems for me with my parents. Anyway, Cal was making good money. He told me I could do anything I wanted. He was always a little old-fashioned. A throwback. He was fine if I stayed home while he went to work. He gave me space to figure out what I wanted."

"Where do you live now?"

"Oh, it's been fifteen years now. But Cal's grandfather passed away and left the family farmhouse to Cal and me. It was a shock. By that point, Cal wasn't working for the Ford dealership anymore. His grandpa, Ralph Emmons, he'd taken Cal into the family business. Small engine repair. By the time Grandpa Ralph passed on, Cal was pretty much running it."

"Where is that business located?"

"It's out on Kidman Road. We live in the house, and Cal's garage is on the property. Emmons Garage. He's got a lot on the other side of the barn."

"How close are the garage and barn to the house where you live?"

"It's a thirty-acre plot of land. We don't farm it anymore. We've got some woods in the back and a pond. A yard right behind the house. The business property sits about a hundred yards away from the main house. But I can see it from the kitchen."

"To be clear, you're saying the barn is in sight of the main house?"

"It sure is. The garage too. The house sits up by the road. The barn's behind us. The garage is on the other side of the barn but set back a little ways. But you can see it from the windows on the west side of the house. The paved parking lot Cal uses for the business is between the barn and the business garage."

Reilly entered photographs showing the layout of the Emmons's property.

"Mrs. Emmons," Peter said. "Do you work outside the home?"

"Part time," she said. "Or rather, I did before all of this happened. Now, people just won't leave me alone. I got a job at Grantham Elementary about eight years ago. I work as a Title I reading specialist. I take the first and second graders who are struggling a little bit with reading and give them some one-on-one attention."

"Okay, what hours do you typically work?"

"Part time," she answered. "Like I said. I go in around seven a.m. during the school year Monday, Wednesday, and Friday. I work until two. So it's just about twenty hours a week with lunches in there."

"Were you working on April 2nd of this year?" Reilly asked.

"I was," she answered. "That fell on a Friday so I got home around two thirty. Cal and I have two small children. Bailey is seven. Carter is five now. They both go to school at Waverly

Elementary. They get off the bus at three thirty so I make sure to get home before they do."

"They're not at Grantham, where you work?"

"No, sir," she said. "Grantham is a private school. We can't afford that. Even with the tuition break I would get for teaching there."

"I see," Reilly said. "Can you tell me what you remember about the afternoon of April 2nd?"

"I've been asked that a lot," Valerie said. "It was just a regular day. Like I said, I worked then waited for the kids to get home. Cal was working too. He's practically never off. He works seven days a week out in the garage. In the summertime, I help out with bookkeeping when I can, though the kids keep me pretty busy with their camps and swimming lessons and play groups."

"Sure," Reilly said. "Why don't you tell me what you remember about that afternoon."

"It was a school day. I told you, Carter and Bailey get off the bus at three thirty. I made them their snacks. But we had to hurry cuz Carter had an eye doctor appointment. He needs glasses, it turns out. That appointment was at four fifteen with Dr. Milliken. So we had about ten minutes for snacks and off we went. Bailey came too cuz she's still too little to stay home by herself. Anyway, we went to the appointment. Just made it on time. We were home by five thirty."

"Then what happened, if you remember?"

"I do planned menus," she said. "Cal doesn't always like that. He says it gets boring, but with working and little kids who can be picky eaters it's a must. And see, I said Cal is kind of a throwback. There are good and bad parts to that. Sorry, honey, but it's true. Well, if I'm the one doing all of the cooking, then I will pick the menu. On Fridays it's pork chops, baked potatoes, and another vegetable. Salad, if I can't think of anything else or am running out of time. I was that night. I usually have dinner on the table by six. It was closer to six forty-five that night."

"Did Cal eat dinner with you?" Reilly asked. I sat with my hands folded, my face neutral, staring straight at Valerie Emmons. Her gaze kept drifting to me.

"Yes," she answered. "He takes a lunch hour and dinner."

"Was he in the house?"

"No," she said. "He was still working. He usually goes back after dinner and works until about eight every night. That's been a bone of contention. I'd rather he quit by six and not go back after dinner. You know, so he can spend some evening hours with the kids during the week. But that garage is always busy. Or it was. I'm so thankful for that. Our community has always been very good about keeping their business local. You ask anyone. They trust Cal. They know he's going to do good work and not rip them off. It's not easy to find an honest mechanic. Well, my Cal ..."

"Objection," I said. "This is improper character evidence."

"Mrs. Emmons," Judge Saul said. "Stick to the questions asked. Mr. Reilly merely asked you whether your husband was in the house at dinner time."

Val trembled. Tears filled her eyes. "He was working," she said. "I called out to him when dinner was ready. He was still out in the garage. We have a little triangle on the back porch.

That thing is probably sixty years old. Cal's grandpa put it there so his grandma could call him into dinner the same way. The kids like to take turns ringing it to call their daddy in for dinner."

"What time was dinner on the table?" Reilly asked.

"By six forty-five," she said.

"And what time did your husband come in from the garage?"

"Within maybe a minute of when Bailey rang the dinner triangle. She gets a little overly enthusiastic with that thing. But it takes Cal at most three minutes to walk from the garage up to the house."

"How long did dinner take?" Reilly said.

"The kids have an eight thirty bedtime. They help clear their plates and load the dishwasher. Then they take baths and Cal reads them a story when he comes back to the house. He was there for all of that."

"He did all of that the night of April 2nd?" Reilly asked. "Dinner. Baths. All of that?"

"He did," she answered. "Cal's a wonderful father."

"Mrs. Emmons," Reilly said. "How do you know Cal was working in the garage when you left for the eye doctor appointment that afternoon?"

"Because I texted him when I was leaving. He texted me back saying he had to finish a transmission repair."

I had stipulated the entry of Cal and Valerie Emmons's phone records. Reilly moved to admit them. The transcripts verified what Valerie said and we already knew Cal's phone pinged the tower closest to his garage at 4:10 p.m. when the text was sent. That phone didn't move until the next morning. I knew Reilly would try to argue that Cal never left the house that evening. I hoped he would so I could hang him with the rope he left me.

"Is that the only way you knew where Cal was, because of that text?" Reilly asked.

"No," she said. "I could see Cal's truck parked in front of the garage. I have to drive by it to get back out on Kidman Road and head toward town. And his truck was there when I got back a little after five thirty so I could start dinner."

"Mrs. Emmons," he said. "Can you hear Cal when he's working in the garage?"

"Oh yes," she said. "It's noisy out there."

"Can you hear Cal when he's working in the barn?"

"Yes," she said. "In fact, we used to keep chickens out there. Had to get rid of them because they were so loud."

"How often do you go out to the barn?" he asked.

"Once a week at least," she said. "We keep all of the yard and gardening equipment out there. And that week I was doing some of my spring planting. We've got a John Deere tractor and I cut the lawn. Cal doesn't like that always. He likes to do it. But so do I."

"Mrs. Emmons," he said. "Have you ever been inside the back room of the barn?"

"I don't go in there, no," she said, her voice wavering.

"Do you know what's inside that back room?"

"Just extra supplies. Stuff Cal doesn't want the kids getting into. Pesticides. Equipment that could hurt them."

"Do you ever go in that back room?"

"Gosh. I can't remember the last time I was in there. It's been years. Cal keeps it locked. I don't even have a key. They're out in the garage, I think."

"So sitting here today, you can't tell me what was in that barn on April 2nd?"

"I can't," she said. "I was as shocked as anyone to see what they found. I don't have a good answer for any of that. I know what it sounds like. But I'm telling you the truth. We don't use that room."

"Mrs. Emmons," Reilly said. "Did you ever see Cal going in or out of the barn the weekend of April 2nd?"

"No."

"What time did you go to bed that night, if you recall?"

"I'm usually in bed by ten. Sometimes Cal watches TV downstairs. He comes to bed by midnight."

"He was in bed by midnight the night of April 2nd?"

"Yes."

"Did you both sleep through the night?"

"Objection," I said. "If the witness was asleep, she has no firsthand knowledge of what her husband was doing."

"Sustained," Judge Saul said.

"Mrs. Emmons, did you wake up at all during the night?" Reilly asked.

"I don't remember. I do usually wake up once around three in the morning to go to the bathroom."

"Was Cal sleeping beside you at three a.m.?"

"Yes."

I scribbled notes as she spoke.

"What do you remember about Saturday, April 3rd?" Reilly asked.

"We had a soccer tournament. Both kids play in a community league. I had to have them out at the field by ten in the morning. We were all up by six. The kids are early risers."

"Did you have breakfast together?"

"We did," she said. "Then Cal left to go work in the shop. He was going to meet me at the field by nine thirty. Cal coaches Carter's team."

"Did he make it?"

"Oh yes," she said.

"How long did the soccer game last?"

"I think we were home by two p.m.," she answered.

"Where was your husband, Mrs. Emmons?"

"He was with us, of course. Well, he drove separately, but he was with us."

"He didn't go back to work that day?"

"I don't think so," she said. "We had dinner with another family. Cal's assistant coach, Mike Sutter, and his wife Amy. Their two kids, Josh and Christy."

"You had dinner at your house?" he asked.

"No, sir. We went to Luigi's pizza place. Saturday is buffet night."

"Anything unusual happen at dinner?"

"Well, that's when we heard about that poor girl, Haley Chambers. The rumors were going around the restaurant. It's a small town. I knew the Chambers family. They had a TV on at Luigi's and they were calling for people to come out and help search. Mike and Cal both said they wanted to help."

"What time did you get home?"

"I think it was about seven. The kids were extra tired from all the activities. So was I. So they were in bed earlier, by eight. Cal and I stayed up for a little while. He was on the phone with Mike. They were making plans to go out to Waynetown High the next day and maybe help with the search for Haley. See, Cal was very upset. We all were. It happened just a couple of miles down the road from us. I ride bikes with the kids down Kidman Road all the time. Cal told me he didn't want me doing that and he was adamant. He said not until they catch whoever did this to Haley."

Reilly scratched his chin. He looked through his notes, then up at Mrs. Emmons. "Thank you," Reilly said. "I have no further questions at this time."

"Your witness, Ms. Brent," Judge Saul said.

I rose, choosing to ask my questions from where I stood rather than moving to the lectern.

"Mrs. Emmons," I said. "Just a few things while they're fresh in your mind. You just testified that on the evening of April 2nd, you went to bed at ten and your husband didn't come to bed until midnight. In what part of the house is your bedroom?"

"It's in the front of the house," she said.

"Facing the road," I answered. "Not the barn."

"Correct," she said.

"So if you were in your bedroom, you can't see the barn from your windows, right?"

"That's correct. You can see the road and the field across from us."

"So for at least two hours on the night of April 2nd, you admittedly couldn't see the barn, or your husband, for that matter. I mean, if he was downstairs watching television."

"I could hear the TV," she said.

"Not what I asked you. So when you said you didn't see anyone coming or going from the barn on April 2nd, for at least two hours from ten to midnight, you weren't in a position to even see the barn, correct?"

"Well, I ... no."

"And you slept until six. Meaning you were in your bedroom from ten p.m. to six a.m., correct?"

"Yes," she said quietly.

"Eight hours," I said. "You didn't have eyes on that barn for at least eight hours, right?"

"That's right."

"You said your kids went to bed by eight thirty the evening of the 2nd. You said you went to bed by ten. Where were you between the hours of eight thirty and ten then?"

She bit her lip, thinking. "I just did normal things. Tidying up. Laundry."

"Laundry," I said. "Where is your laundry room, Mrs. Emmons?"

"It's in the basement," she said.

"The basement," I repeated. "Are there windows in your basement?"

"Just a couple of those glass block ones."

"Can you see through those?"

"They let light in, but not really."

"Your washer and dryer are actually toward the front of the house in the basement, correct?"

"Yes."

"So if you were in the basement between eight thirty and ten p.m. on April 2nd, you couldn't see the barn, could you?"

"Um, no."

"And Cal wasn't with you?"

"No, ma'am."

"Because Cal's old-fashioned. Laundry is a wife's job, right?"

"Objection," Reilly said.

"Sustained, Ms. Brent. You know better," Judge Saul said.

"I'll rephrase," I said. "Isn't it true you did the laundry by yourself? Cal didn't help you."

"That's true," she said.

"So from the time period of eight thirty p.m. to ten p.m. when you say you went to bed, you don't know where your husband was, do you?"

"He was home," she snapped.

"Home," I repeated. "But he could have been in the garage. He could have been out in the yard. He could have been in the barn. You don't know, isn't that right?"

She squirmed a little. "I suppose so."

"The morning of April 3rd, you said you got up at six thirty as a family. What time did you leave for the ball field?"

"It was a little before nine. I had to pick up snacks for the team," she said.

"You did that alone," I said. "Just you and the children?"

"Yes," she said.

"You said Cal wanted to meet you at the field, correct?"

"Correct. He wanted to get some things done around the house. You know. Get a head start. There's a lot of meandering that goes on after the games. Socializing. He wanted to have his own car."

"Of course," I said. "What time did you finish breakfast?"

"Probably by seven," she said.

"What were you doing between seven and just before nine when you left then?" I asked.

"The usual. Running around getting the kids ready. Somebody's always missing a shoe. Or can't find their pants. There's just always a level of chaos with little ones on game day."

"Sure," I said. "Did your husband help you manage that chaos that morning?"

"What?"

"Did he help you find shoes, mitts, pants, whatever it was you had to pack to get out the door?"

"No ... he ..."

"He wasn't with you, was he?" I asked.

"He was ... I mean, he was around."

"Around," I said. "Was he in the garage?"

"I don't know."

"Was he in the basement?"

"I don't know."

"Was he in the barn?"

"I don't ..." She froze, understanding the implications of that answer.

"Objection," Reilly said. "Counsel is badgering the witness."

"Overruled," Judge Saul said. "But let's keep this moving, Ms. Brent."

"Understood, Your Honor," I said. "Mrs. Emmons, isn't it true your husband owns and drives a blue Mercury Sable wagon?"

"He owns one, yes," she said.

"He parks the Sable in the business parking lot, doesn't he?"

"I guess," she said. "I don't drive that car. Cal calls it his beater car. He's had it since it was new. Twenty-some years. He drives a brand-new Ford F-250."

"You claim you saw Cal's truck parked in the lot when you left around four on April 2nd. And you claim you saw it parked there when you came home around five thirty, correct?"

"That's correct," she said. "Cal was working in the garage the whole time."

"Really? Because you testified you saw his truck. You didn't actually see your husband, did you?"

"No."

"You didn't go in the garage, did you?"

"No."

"You texted him. You didn't walk those hundred yards and speak to him directly, did you?"

"No."

"He could have been in the garage. He could have been in the barn, he could have even been in the woods on the property, you don't know for sure, do you?"

"He said he was in the garage."

"He said," I repeated, then let it hang for a moment. "You didn't actually lay eyes on your husband until almost seven o'clock that Thursday night when you called him in for dinner, did you?"

"I saw him when he came in, yes."

"You were cooking dinner from approximately five thirty until six forty-five, isn't that right?"

"That's right. I was looking right out that kitchen window. I could see the barn and the garage the whole time."

"You saw the buildings," I said. "You didn't see people, did you?"

"I saw the buildings."

"And you can't see Cal's blue Sable from that window, can you?" I asked.

I pulled up the aerial photo we had of the Emmons's property. The Mercury Sable was clearly visible on the opposite side of the garage from where the house sat. Cal's truck was parked on the side closest to the house.

"I can't see through buildings, Ms. Brent. That's correct." She laughed at herself and looked toward the jury as if they might laugh with her. They didn't.

"Likewise, from the kitchen, you couldn't see whether any cars, including the Sable, entered or exited the garage parking lot. You could only see if a car coming after it rounded this curve and happened to park on the side closest to the house, where your husband's red F-250 is parked in this photo, isn't that true?"

She gritted her teeth. "Yes."

"You don't let your children play unattended in the barn, do you, Mrs. Emmons?"

"Of course not. I don't let them play outside unattended anywhere. We have a pond in those woods. I need my eyes on them all the time," she answered.

"And you certainly don't let them go out to the garage without you or your husband, do you?"

"No," she said. "And as a rule, they aren't allowed in the garage. It disrupts Cal when he's working. And it's dangerous. Someday, Cal will teach Carter the business, if he shows some interest."

"Just Carter?" I asked. I knew it was a cheap shot, but I was getting pretty tired of the picture she wanted to paint of Cal Emmons as a model father.

"Objection!" Reilly popped up.

I raised my hand. "Withdrawn."

"Did you go out to the barn on the evening of April 2nd?" I asked.

"I don't remember," she said.

"Did you go out to the barn on the morning of April 3rd?" I asked.

"I don't remember," she said. "I don't think so."

"Thank you," I said abruptly. "I have no further questions."

"Mr. Reilly?" Judge Saul asked.

"Mrs. Emmons," he said. "Just to reiterate. You said you can hear noises coming from the barn, can't you?"

"I sure can. I said that's why we had to get rid of the chickens."

"Thank you," Reilly said. He flipped through his notes. I expected him to say he had no further questions. Instead, Valerie Emmons exploded.

"I would have heard!" she practically screamed. "You think I would have just ignored something like that going on in our barn? What they say? What they think happened to that poor girl? Right under my nose? No way. No chance. Cal's no monster and neither am I. You think he tortured that girl, then went to coach his kids' soccer game? You're out of your mind!"

Judge Saul banged her gavel. I rose to object. Reilly stood there with his mouth hanging open. Cal Emmons reached out, as if trying to give his distraught wife an air hug.

"I don't know what happened to that girl or why everyone thinks she got hurt in my barn. Maybe her boyfriend took her there. I don't know. I don't know. I don't know!"

"Mrs. Emmons," the judge said. "I understand this is challenging for you. But if you indulge in another outburst like that, I'll have to hold you in contempt. You must answer questions as they are asked. That is all. Mr. Reilly?"

"Thank you," he said. "I have no more questions for Mrs. Emmons."

"Fine," Judge Saul said. "The jury should disregard everything this witness said after being asked about whether she heard noises in the barn. You may step down, Mrs. Emmons. Mr. Reilly, call your next witness."

Valerie brushed past my table in tears. There was no one here for her. The Railroader protest group had all but dwindled after the physical evidence came in.

"Your Honor," Reilly said. "The defense calls Calvin Emmons to the stand."

26

I heard the collective gasp of about a hundred courtroom spectators as Calvin Emmons rose from his seat and slowly walked toward the witness box. He didn't look like the same man in his mug shot, or the scruffy-bearded mechanic everyone in town knew. No. Today's Cal Emmons was clean-shaven, his brown hair cropped close. He wore a black suit with a yellow tie. Without all the scruff on his face, his chin seemed to disappear into his neck. His dark eyes darted from me to Peter Reilly as he took his place behind the lectern.

"Mr. Emmons," Reilly started, after a few standard background questions. "Can you tell me how long you've lived at 41345 Kidman Road?"

"The property has been in my family for sixty years," Emmons said. He had a deep, gravelly voice from years of smoking that he'd later say his wife made him quit.

"My grandpa bought it from the farmer who built the place. The house and the barn were built in 1910. Grandpa added on some. Expanded the porch. I've kept up with all of that.

Grandpa built the garage, the parking lot, along with getting all the variances so we could run the family business off the property. Emmons Garage opened fifty years ago. Until all of this, we'd never missed a business day."

"Thank you," Reilly said. I sat with a pen poised over a pad of paper. Never in a million years would I have thought Reilly would actually put Emmons on the stand. Instead of the pen, I needed duct tape. I felt ready to leap out of my chair, eager to cross-examine this bastard. Adam must have sensed it. He put a light hand on my upper arm. It was only then I realized I'd been tapping my pen against my notepad.

"I'd like to talk about the barn itself," Reilly said. He pulled up several photographs of the interior and exterior of the barn. After committing Cal to the layout, he settled on the hidden back room where Haley Chambers had been tortured.

"Mr. Emmons," Reilly said. "Has this room always been there?"

"As far back as I can remember," Emmons said. "When I was a kid, I was never allowed back there. Grandpa kept some of the more dangerous implements in there and the pesticides. He'd whip you something good if you didn't follow the rules."

"It was kept locked?"

"Yes, sir," Emmons said.

"What is it used for today?"

"Same thing," he said. "You can see those barrels in the back. Those are pesticides. We don't farm the land anymore so I can't even tell you the last time anybody's got into them. I'd been meaning to clear everything out of there. Just hadn't gotten around to it."

"Do you keep that room locked?"

"I do. I gotta be honest. I generally don't even go into that room."

"I see. Where is the key kept for that room?"

"I've got a rack of keys in the garage."

Reilly pulled up a photograph of the back wall of Emmons's garage. It showed a hook bar with roughly eight sets of keys hanging off it.

"Keys to the barn are the second from left in that photo," Emmons said.

"Can you describe for the record how many copies are there of the barn keys?"

"Well," Emmons said. "There are two sets of doors. The outer door. I keep one of those on my keyring. Valerie's got one on her keyring too. But the keys to the tool room ... sorry, that's what Grandpa Emmons called that inner room there. The tool room. Anyway, that hook, second from the right in that photo. You see four keys hanging from it. They all go to the tool room. They're duplicates."

"You don't keep a key to the tool room on your person?"

"No, sir," he said.

"Does anyone else have a set of keys to the outer barn door?"

"Yep. Um, yes. That hook on the far right, you see one key hanging. That's the outer barn door key. I keep a spare there too."

"In the garage? Your commercial garage?"

"Yes," Cal answered.

"So how many keys are there in total for the outer barn door?"

"Just the three, as far as I know. Those locks were all changed about ten years ago. We had some wood rot on the doors and I had all that fixed."

"All right," Reilly said. "I see four other hooks with various keys hanging off them. Can you tell me what these go to?"

"Far right is the keys to the commercial garage. You see two rings there. We got a front and back door. I keep a set of those on my person. Those are spare sets for the guys I have working for me. The next ring over to the right is where I keep the spare keys to Valerie's car. Next to that, there's a spare set of keys to my truck. And in the middle there, those are a set of keys to the Mercury Sable."

"Were you in the habit of keeping a set of keys to the Sable on your personal keyring?"

"No, sir," Emmons said. "I don't drive it all that much. My truck is my work car and my personal vehicle."

"Your Honor, at this point I'd like to introduce defense exhibit 12 into evidence."

Reilly held up a keyring in a bag.

"Ms. Brent?" Judge Saul asked. Reilly brought the bag over to me.

"The state objects," I said. "There's been no offer of proof that these keys are in the condition they were at the time of Haley Chambers's disappearance."

"You'll have your chance to cross-examine the witness on that point," Saul said. "I'll allow the admission."

"Mr. Emmons," Reilly said, handing the set of keys to him. "Tell me what these are."

"Those are my keys. I've got a house key. Key to the main barn door, business garage door, key to my truck. That's it."

"You maintain you never kept a key to the inner barn tool room on your person."

"No," he said. "Like I said. I rarely ever go in there."

Reilly paused. Beside me, Adam scratched a quick note. "I can't believe he's going to claim he didn't know about that torture room. That can't be his whole defense."

"Mr. Emmons," Reilly said. "I'd like to direct your attention to the photograph marked 31. Can you tell me what we're looking at?"

"That's the interior of the tool room," he said, barely audible.

"Mr. Emmons, I'm going to ask you point blank. Is that your picnic table in the center of the room?"

"Yeah," he said. "My grandpa built that too."

"And what's that at the four corners of the table?"

Emmons dropped his head. He buried his face in his hands for a moment before answering. "I bolted some chains, some shackles to the ends of it."

Adrenaline shot through me.

"When?" Reilly asked.

"I'd say five years ago," he answered.

"Why, Mr. Emmons?"

"My wife ... she was ... we were going through a bit of a rough patch. She was having a hard time losing weight after the kids were born. Now listen, it wasn't something that I noticed. You've seen Valerie. She's beautiful. Well, she just wasn't feeling so good about herself. We were having trouble. I thought maybe if we experimented a little. You know, spice things up when we were ... intimate ... I thought maybe that would help."

"You're saying you installed those shackles as a way to spice up your marriage?"

"That's what I'm saying. Only, I don't know. I chickened out. I was going to surprise her with it. It was our wedding anniversary. But the day I was going to show her, her mom passed away suddenly. She was in a car accident. Well, Valerie took that pretty hard. She was really depressed. She got over it. But for a few months, things were really, really rough. It just never felt like the right time to bring it up. So I never did. Then eventually, things just got better between us and I kind of forgot all about it."

"Mr. Emmons," Reilly said. "Who else knew about that room in the barn?"

"Obviously Valerie knew it was there. But to my knowledge, she never went in it. The keys to it have been hanging on the hook in the garage for years. Like I said, it's not unusual for me not to even go in that room for weeks, months at a time."

"How many employees do you have working for you at Emmons Garage?"

"There's me, one or two apprentice mechanics. Then I usually try to keep one or two porters or runners around. But it's hard to hire these days. Kids don't want to work. It's a physically demanding job. In the last year, I've only had one apprentice mechanic, that's Lincoln Maguire. He goes by Linc. Then I've run through about three different runners or porters in the last year."

"Who was working for you on April 2nd of this year?"

"Linc was. And I had a new kid. His name was Shep. That was his last name. Short for Shepherd. I'm not even sure what his first name was."

"Don't you have payroll records?"

"Valerie does the books," he said. "Linc's the only one who's a W-2 employee. The porters I usually pay under the table once a week."

"You pay them cash?"

"Yeah. Look, I know maybe that's not the smartest way to do it, but like I said, it's been real hard to keep these kids working."

"When did you hire this Shep?" Reilly asked.

"It was right after Christmas."

"What were his duties?"

"Well, Linc and I were ultimately trying to train him on small engine repair. The kid had a bit of a knack. But a lousy work ethic. He wouldn't always show up. Beyond that, he was kind of a johnny-on-the-spot kid. If I needed errands run. He'd do the shop clean-up."

"Cal, did Shep and Linc have access to all parts of the garage?"

"Yes."

"Including this rack of keys?"

"Well, sure."

"Did Shep or Linc ever go out to the barn?"

"Yeah. Both of them. There's parking space behind it and when we had overflow with the vehicles or engines we were working on, Shep or whatever runner I had working for me would park over there."

"Did he ever drive any other vehicle?"

"Yes, he drove my Sable on occasion."

"Shep drove the Sable?"

My pulse skipped. I stayed stone still. I didn't want the jury seeing me frantically flipping through Detective Lance's witness statements. At no point had any of Cal Emmons's other employees reported someone named Shep driving the Mercury Sable or any other vehicle on Emmons's behalf.

"He's lying," Adam whispered.

"Yeah," Emmons answered. "If I needed the kid to drive somewhere to pick up parts, I'd have him drive the Sable. That way I didn't have to pay him mileage or gas."

"Where did Shep get the keys to the Sable?"

"I showed him when I hired him. I told him what keys were what on the hook in the garage."

"Did he have to ask for permission to drive the Sable?"

"Every time? No. Shep, Linc, and any other of my guys knew where the keys were. I didn't have time to hold their hand with everything."

Reilly clasped his hands together and rested them on the lectern.

"Mr. Emmons, did you know Haley Chambers?"

"No, sir."

"To your knowledge, did Haley Chambers ever frequent your business?"

"Not that I know of," he said.

"Mr. Emmons, were you part of a search party relating to Haley Chambers's disappearance?"

The muscles in Cal Emmons's jaw twitched. "Yes," he said, biting the word.

"What can you tell me about that?"

"It was like my wife said. Mike Sutter and I saw that news story on the TV at Luigi's. I can't remember if it was him or me who said we wanted to volunteer to look for her. The next day or the day after, I went out to the high school to help look."

"What about Mike Sutter, did he go?"

"I don't know," Emmons said. "I didn't talk to Mike after that day at Luigi's. They put me with Tom Steele and Phil Majewski. We finished early on the afternoon of the 5th."

"You heard Mr. Majewski's testimony," Reilly said. "Would you agree with how he characterized events?"

"No, sir," Cal practically shouted. "We all agreed to keep on searching after we finished our assigned grid. But Phil was slowing us down. There was some friction there. I thought it was noble that he wanted to help, but he had no business walking out there. You've seen him. He was limping pretty badly. I thought he was gonna keel over. So did Tom. I didn't rush ahead of them. Phil just couldn't keep up."

"Mr. Emmons," Reilly said. "Did you know Dylan Woodhouse?"

"I knew the name," he said. "I'd seen the family on television. But I didn't know they lived in that neighborhood on Forsythe. And I'm not the one who found that pink shirt. Tom Steele did. I didn't plant it. That's a flat-out lie."

"Mr. Emmons, did you take Haley Chambers into the barn on your property?"

Emmons flinched. As if a switch was flipped, tears flowed down his cheeks.

"No. God. No. I didn't know Haley. I didn't hurt that girl. If she was on my property, if she was in that barn, I didn't take her there. I didn't know. I swear to God, I didn't know. I didn't kill her. You gotta believe me. I have no answer for what they found out there. It wasn't me. I didn't hurt her. I didn't do those things to her. I'm a father. I've got a daughter myself. How could anyone think ... No. I am innocent of this. I never hurt Haley Chambers. I never hurt any woman. Not ever. Please. I'm as horrified with what happened to that poor kid as anyone. But it wasn't me. I swear to you. On my life. It wasn't me."

"Thank you, Mr. Emmons, I have no further questions."

My whole body went rigid, waiting for Judge Saul's next words. In some ways, I knew what I did afterward could define my career.

"Ms. Brent," the judge said. "Your witness."

27

"It wasn't you." I repeated the final words of Cal Emmons's direct examination.

"No, ma'am," he said.

"You admit you were the one who installed those shackles on that picnic table in your barn, correct?"

"Yes, ma'am," he said.

"Yet your wife, who took the stand this morning, never mentioned a word about that, did she?"

"No."

"So did she just forget to mention it, or is it your claim she's never seen them?"

"She's never seen them," he said.

"In five years, she's never seen them, that's your answer?"

"That's my answer."

"The barn is in plain sight of your kitchen window, isn't it?"

"You can see the barn from the kitchen window, yes. If you're standing in the right spot."

"The right spot?" I repeated. "It's a large structure, 48 x 64 is it not?"

"That sounds right."

"So isn't it true that if you're standing near a window, any window, in the back of your house, you pretty much can't miss the barn, right?"

"Objection," Reilly said. "Calls for speculation. Plus this question has been asked and answered."

"Your Honor," I said. "There's no speculation here. There's simple common sense."

"I'll allow it," Judge Saul said.

"Mr. Emmons?" I said.

"What are you asking me?"

"I'm asking you, isn't it true that the barn behind your house is actually larger than the house itself in terms of square footage?"

"That's not what you asked me. But that's accurate," he said. Something changed about Cal Emmons. When his own lawyer questioned him, he'd remained cool, calm, with almost a bumpkin demeanor. Now, Cal leaned forward into the microphone, his lips curled into a snarl.

"And because that barn is actually bigger than the house, if you're standing near a window facing it, you can see it, isn't that right?"

"If you choose to look, I suppose," Emmons answered.

"You pretty much can't miss it."

"Is that a question?" he said.

I paused. Ice filled my veins as I stared Cal Emmons down. He crossed his legs and picked a piece of lint off his pants. My eyes went to his hands. They were large and wide through the palms. He had long fingers. They would have easily wrapped around Haley Chambers's neck as he held her down in that pond. She had been tiny. Just five feet tall and one hundred and two pounds. He outweighed her by eighty pounds, stood a foot taller.

"Mr. Emmons," I said. "You never bothered to mention an employee by the name of Shepherd to the police, did you?"

"I wasn't willing to speak to the police without a lawyer present," he said. "That's my right, isn't it?"

"But even when your lawyer was present, you never offered the name of Shepherd to any of the investigators, did you?"

"I don't know everything my lawyer told the police."

"But you told Mr. Reilly about Shep, didn't you?"

"Objection," Reilly said. "Communications between my client and myself are protected by attorney-client privilege."

"Sustained, Ms. Brent," Judge Saul said.

"We've seen your tax returns," I said. "There's no mention of a Shepherd listed as a W-2 employee," I said. "Isn't that right?"

"That's correct."

"Likewise, you never listed this Shep as a 1099 contractor either, did you?"

"That's correct. I said when my lawyer was questioning me, I paid Shep and my other porters under the table. I paid them in cash."

"So you never reported the payments to Shep to the IRS, did you? As far as they know, he doesn't even exist, does he?"

"Objection." Reilly jumped up.

"On what grounds?" I turned to him.

"Mr. Reilly?" the judge said.

"Counsel is badgering the witness. She's not letting him answer before she bombards him with another question."

"Fine," I said. "I'll speak more slowly."

"Ms. Brent." Judge Saul gave me a pointed stare over her glasses.

"Mr. Emmons," I said. "You've never reported this Shep's existence to the IRS for tax purposes, have you?"

"I never claimed him as a contractor, no. I didn't issue 1099s."

"Do you have an address for Shep?"

"Not off the top of my head, no."

"Mr. Emmons, you're aware you were required to submit your business documents to my office as part of pre-trial discovery."

"I know we sent some records. We sent everything you asked for. I have nothing to hide."

"Except the shackles in your special room in the barn, right?" I said.

"Your Honor!" Reilly snapped.

"It's a fair question," Judge Saul said, surprising me. "The witness may answer."

Emmons squirmed. "I didn't hide anything in the barn. My wife had access to the keys just like anyone who worked for me out in the garage."

"I see," I said. "Back to this mysterious Shep. There's no mention of him in your employee records, is there?"

"He wasn't an employee," Emmons answered. "I think we covered that already."

"Enlighten me, Mr. Emmons. What exactly were Shep's duties when he worked for you?"

"I think I already answered that. His official job description was as a porter."

"Now he's official?" I asked.

"I mean that as just an expression. I called him a porter. My assistant mechanic, Linc, called him a porter. He did that. Cleaned the tractors we worked on. Moved them from place to place. He went and picked up parts for me from other shops when I needed them. He was there to just pretty much do whatever I needed on a given day. It wasn't always the same."

"I see," I said.

"Mr. Emmons, you claim Shep often drove the Sable. However, isn't it true you never reported that to your automobile insurance company?"

"I wasn't aware that was something that was required," he said.

"Is that a no?"

"That's a no."

"And the Sable is registered in your name, not the company's, right?"

"I guess so."

"You have a corporate structure though, correct? Emmons Garage is a domestic corporation in the state of Ohio, isn't it?"

"Yes," he said.

"Your story is that this Shep was allowed to drive your personal vehicle, the Sable, when he drove to pick up parts, is that true?"

"That's true."

"What suppliers would those be?"

Emmons let out a sigh. "I get parts from all over."

"Name your top three."

"Excuse me?"

"Give me three supplier's names that Shep drove to with your 2000 Mercury Sable."

"I mean, we get parts from all over the state and sometimes up in Michigan. It depends on what I'm working on. And we get parts from dealers too."

"Great," I said. "So tell me three of the most common places Shep would have driven in your vehicle at your direction?"

"I don't always keep a record of who picks up what from whom. But I suppose he would have gone out to Toledo, Lima, Liberty Center, really all over."

"When would he have done that?"

"I told you, I don't keep detailed records on that stuff. He would have gone when I needed him to go."

"Did he go to Lima on April 2nd?" I asked.

"Might have," Emmons answered.

"Did Shep go to Liberty Center on April 2nd?" I asked.

"I don't recall. It's possible. Heck, sometimes, I'd just have him run errands for me of a more personal nature."

"Did you have him run errands for you on April 2nd?"

"I don't remember specifically. But there were also some times that Shep's car would break down. I know we worked on it here at the shop. I let him drive the Sable so he could get to and from work."

"But you can't say one way or the other if that happened on April 2nd because you don't remember?"

"It was just a typical day," he said. "If I'd known I was later going to be asked all these questions, I would maybe have kept a diary or something."

"Mr. Emmons," I said. "You've done work for Dylan Woodhouse's parents, haven't you? You fixed a mower for Stephen Woodhouse, Dylan's father, didn't you?"

"Yes."

"That was in March of this year, wasn't it?"

"Sounds about right. You said you have the records, so you'd know."

"About those records, they listed Stephen Woodhouse's address on them, didn't they?"

"Well, sure," he said. "I would have needed his billing address."

"Haley Chambers's disappearance was all over the news, wasn't it? I mean, that's how you knew there was a search party forming, right? That was your testimony?"

"I saw it on the news, yes."

"And it was Stephen Woodhouse on the news asking for help, wasn't it?"

At that point, I replayed a clip from the six o'clock news on April 3rd. Dylan's father stood next to Haley's stepfather and did the talking. "We're looking for help," Stephen said, his eyes red from crying. "Our families are torn up. We need strong bodies out to meet out behind Waynetown High tomorrow morning. If you're out there, Haley. Don't lose hope. We haven't."

I turned off the tape.

"Yeah," Emmons admitted. "I saw that. I already told you that."

I left it there. It would be easy to argue Emmons found Stephen Woodhouse's address from his own business records. I resisted the urge to give him another chance to explain his actions during the search party. Braden Hughey and Phil Majewski had been credible witnesses in my case in chief.

"Mr. Emmons, I've got a few more questions about this mysterious Shep."

"Objection," Reilly said. "Counsel's characterization of Shep as mysterious amounts to badgering. She can save it for her closing argument."

"Sustained. Let's be precise, Ms. Brent."

"Fine," I said. "Mr. Emmons, you claim you kept your more dangerous equipment in that locked anteroom in the barn. You and your wife both testified you had pesticides out there. You never had Shep or any other porters doing farm work for you, isn't that right?"

"We don't farm the land," he said.

I paused. I could have pressed him further, but I had enough for my closing on this point. That's always the trap. Don't give the defendant room to explain something away.

"Your wife never saw Shep or anyone else besides you going in and out of that barn, did she, Mr. Emmons?"

"I don't know. She would have said if she did."

"She didn't see Shep near the barn, did she?"

"Objection," Reilly said. "Mrs. Emmons has already testified. This witness can only testify to what he observed."

"All right," I said. "You never saw Shep going in or out of that barn, did you, Mr. Emmons?"

"I don't recall that. But I wasn't watching the barn all the time. Shep knew where the keys to it were."

"You never saw Shep going in or out of that barn because there is no Shep, is there?"

"That's not true."

"You never saw Shep going in or out of that barn because you were the only one going in or out of it on April 2nd, isn't that true?"

"That's not true."

"You struck Haley Chambers with your car on Kidman Road, didn't you?"

"I didn't," he said. He lifted his chin and stared straight at me. I held my ground.

"You threw Haley Chambers's unconscious body into the back of your blue Mercury Sable with the gray carpet and took her to that barn, didn't you?"

"No."

"You shackled her to that picnic table in your barn. You tortured her for at least twelve hours, didn't you?"

"No. That's not true."

"When you were done torturing Haley, you put her back in the trunk of your car. You drove her to the pond behind your barn and you held her under water until she drowned, isn't that true?"

"No. That's absolutely not true."

"You took Haley Chambers's body, stuffed her in the back of your car and drove her out to Gunderson's tree farm, didn't you?"

"No!"

"You buried her in a hole head first. You left her for the animals to find, didn't you?" I shouted the last of it, letting my words echo through the courtroom.

Cal Emmons shook. He gripped the sides of the witness box. He broke his stare, then looked at the jury.

"I did not kill that poor girl. I never knew her. I never touched her. The only thing I'm guilty of is trusting the wrong people. I gave people I didn't know enough about too much access to my property. So yes. I'm guilty of that. I will regret that until the day I die. I'm sorry for that. But no. I didn't kill her. I didn't hurt her. I've never hurt anyone. I've never killed anyone. Not ever. I swear."

When he finished his diatribe, the courtroom fell silent. Had I done enough? The jury looked back at Cal. I couldn't read them. They seemed stunned. Shell shocked. Behind me, I heard the soft whimper of Cindy Chambers as she cried into her son's shoulder.

"I have no more questions for this witness," I said.

When Peter Reilly deferred the redirect, Judge Saul removed her reading glasses and quietly folded them. "Then we are adjourned until tomorrow morning."

Cal Emmons rose. Two deputies waited to take him back to his cell for the night. He walked with slow deliberation as he passed me at the lectern. He got so close I could feel his breath on me. I held my ground as he paused for the briefest of moments, then made his way out of the courtroom.

⁂ 28 ⁂

"We got him!" Adam pumped his fists as we walked into the conference room where Kenya and Hojo waited. "We got that motherfu—"

"Stop," I said. "Don't say another word."

My blood roared in my ears. I had to remind myself to breathe.

"She was brilliant!" Adam said. "Nailed his butt to the frigging wall!"

"Adam, sit down," Kenya said. "I want to hear what Mara has to say."

"I can't believe Reilly put him on the stand," I said. Sinking into the chair at the far corner of the room, I gave Hojo and Kenya the highlights of Emmons's testimony. By the time I finished, Detective Lance came in, followed by Sam.

"He admits to installing the shackles in the barn," Kenya said. "He's got no real alibi for the time frame when Haley went missing. He offers no explanation for how her DNA got all over that barn."

I looked straight at Lance. I'd kept my temper mostly in check. Even with Cal Emmons, only a few brief spurts of rage had seeped out while I cross-examined him. Now, I felt a crack in the dam.

"You never questioned this Shep," I said through a clenched jaw. "For the love of God, tell me something good, Lance."

He'd been in the courtroom. So had Sam.

"He's not in your witness statements. Where is he, Lance?"

"He doesn't exist," Lance said. "Mara, you all but got Emmons to admit that. There is no Shep. He's lying. It's a convenient excuse, nothing more. The jury is going to see through it."

"Are you sure about that?" I couldn't sit anymore. I started wearing a path through the carpet. "Reilly spent a lot of time on direct talking about this mystery man. Of course I've seen his name on his witness list along with about a hundred others that nobody's ever talked to. Nobody's ever been able to find a Shep."

"It's going nowhere," Lance said.

"No," I said, shaking my head so hard my brain rattled. "No. No way. Reilly's made some questionable choices during this trial. He's not an idiot. He doesn't bring this Shep up without being able to produce him. If he can find him, why couldn't you?"

"If he exists at all, he's some fly-by-night drifter. Emmons can't even put him at the scene during the time frame of

Haley's kidnapping and murder. It's a red herring. It's just a game. The jury will be smarter than that."

"You should have found him!" I shouted. "Lord. Am I the only one capable of seeing what's going on here? Reilly's got him. There's nothing stopping him from dragging this guy into court tomorrow."

"It's a bluff," Hojo said. "I think Lance is right."

"Yeah? I'd bet my right arm it's no bluff. I should have had more discovery on this guy."

"Linc Maguire didn't even talk about him," Lance said. "The wife didn't talk about him. Emmons made him up. I'm telling you. Or he made up all the other stuff. It's nothing more than a self-serving statement. He's got to say something."

"No," I said. "He doesn't have to say anything at all."

"So what?" Lance said. "Worst-case scenario, Reilly shows up in court tomorrow with this Shep character. You think the guy would come willingly? You think he's going to corroborate Emmons's story? It makes no sense. If he testifies at all, he'll be doing it to save his own skin. You think he's going to get up there and say, oh yeah, that's right, I just happened to be driving that car around with Haley's DNA in it. Maybe my psycho ex-boss was right."

I plopped back down in my seat.

"I think that's enough for the day," Kenya said. "Mara, you did great. I get why you're worried, but I think Adam and Detective Lance are right. Emmons did nothing but hurt himself on the stand today. Why don't you head home? Get some rest. Come at this fresh in the morning."

I shook my head. "I don't have that luxury. This is 24/7 for me until the jury gets it. I have to prepare a cross for a witness who may not even exist. Except I know he does. I can feel it. Adam? I'll need a brief on all the evidentiary objections I can raise to this Shep taking the stand."

"On what grounds?" he asked.

"I don't know. Just figure out what you can."

I didn't like the looks passing between Kenya, Adam, and Hojo. I didn't like any of this.

"Well, you should work from home then," Kenya said. "Get something to eat. Want me to order something?"

I shook my head and waved her off. She took her cue. Kenya shooed Hojo and Adam out, taking Lance with her. I'd have to put him back on the stand to clean this up on rebuttal. But that was a project for another day. Reilly likely had at least one or two more days of witnesses until I got the case again.

When everyone left, I buried my face in my hands and kicked off my heels. The conference room door quietly closed, but I wasn't alone. Wordlessly, Sam slid into the chair beside me and waited until I was ready to talk. When I showed no signs of that, he dug in.

"You're going to win," he said.

"You're going to jinx me."

"No. Mara, this is as solid a case as I've ever seen. Never mind putting him on the stand, the biggest mistake Reilly has made is not begging you for a plea deal. That jury is never going to let Emmons see the light of day again. His explanation was absurd. They will see through it."

"Emmons has a lot of supporters ..."

"Had," Sam interrupted. "Those so-called Railroaders have pretty much dwindled to just his friends and family. We've kept much of this out of the public, but they know. The physical evidence is overwhelming. He's getting the needle for this."

"Lance has been sloppy," I said. "If this were your case, or Ritter's, you'd have dragged this Shep guy in by the short hairs. You'd have cleared him as a suspect the right way. Now I'm going to have to do it on the fly while he's in the witness box."

"If," Sam said. "If he even exists."

I met Sam's eyes and raised a brow. "And you know as well as I do, he does. Reilly's got him. Some way. Somehow."

"Well, the idiot would have to come in willingly then. Reilly's served no subpoenas as far as anyone's aware. Unless Valerie Emmons has the guy shackled in that barn ..."

"Don't joke," I said. "Not about that."

"Sorry," Sam said. "That was in poor taste. I was going for some gallows humor."

"I know. I don't mean to jump down your throat. It's just been a really long day."

His face darkened. I had that feeling there was something he wasn't telling me. "You've got more, don't you?" I asked.

Sam shrugged. "No. Nothing that you need to worry about."

"Sam."

He pursed his lips, then made a decision to let me in on what had been ruining *his* day. "I'm sitting in on a tri-county task force. We're working on trying to match any other cold case, missing person, sexual assaults, or murders to Emmons's profile."

I sat back hard. "How many, Sam?"

"Mara, just—"

"How many?" I said, more firmly.

"About a dozen," he said. "So far. But that doesn't mean they'll all end up going anywhere. Dominique's case is at the top of the list, of course."

My head hurt. "Any other cases with survivors like her?"

"No," Sam said bluntly. "There are four or five where we've got missing girls but no bodies ever found. One of the girls went missing around the time Haley did. But we've got none of her DNA in that barn. Two cold case murders in Southern Ohio and one in Indiana that look promising in terms of some of the injuries found on the bodies. But nothing definite. No positive DNA. In two of them, we just know Emmons was potentially in the area when the girls disappeared."

"She was so lucky," I whispered. "Dominique. I think that's part of what is causing her so much grief. Survivor's guilt."

"Makes sense. Poor thing." Then Sam gave me a smile. "Come on. Let's get out of here. Kenya's got the right idea. You need a good meal. If you won't leave, let me run out and grab some takeout. We can brainstorm."

I laughed, maybe harder than was appropriate.

"What?" Sam asked.

"Nothing. It's just you sound like Jason. When he ... before we ... well, he used to be in charge of my care and feeding when I was in the middle of a trial. That's what he used to call it. I do tend to forget to eat."

I hadn't meant to make things awkward, but the mention of Jason and so intimate a memory suddenly felt unsettling.

"Well," Sam said. "I'm glad to hear the man has some redeeming qualities. But I'm not Jason."

There was weight to his words. Almost a promise. Had it been any other time, I might have said something else. But that evening, there were too many other things I knew needed my attention.

In any event, the door flung open and Adam poked his head in. "I'm about to grab some Thai takeout," he said. "What can I get for you?"

Adam fixed an oddly intense stare on Sam. My spine tingled a bit and I had a sneaking suspicion that Adam had been eavesdropping this whole time. His timing was just too perfect.

"I'm good," I said. "I think I'm just going to head home. I'll see you in the morning, Adam."

He lingered for a moment, still focusing on Sam. Sam leaned back, making himself comfortable. When Adam saw Sam made no move to leave, he finally cleared his throat and excused himself. When the door closed, Sam turned back to me.

"I'm not sure I care much for him," he said.

"He's been invaluable during this trial," I said. "First time I had an intern I didn't feel the need to babysit. Though I'll admit his bedside manner is a little off-putting. He's taken a lot of the load off me, so I'm grateful."

"He's done at the end of the term then?" Sam asked, apparently not hearing anything I just said.

"He is."

Sam nodded, but offered no further comment.

"You know," I said, changing the subject. "Why did you have to go ahead and accept that promotion? I could have used you on this one, Cruz."

He smiled. "You've got me. Anytime, anything you need. And you also know I don't have to tell you that. What I will tell you is this. Stop second guessing yourself. The creepy intern was right. You nailed Emmons to the wall today. This ... what you're doing? Doubting? It's what you do. It's what every good prosecutor does and you happen to be one of the best. Cocky means careless and you're never that. Just stay on target. Whatever Reilly throws at you, you'll handle. Yeah. Lance has a different style than I do. But he handed you a solid piece of police work. It's going to hold up. We can't save Haley, but that monster is never going to hurt another girl."

"Thanks," I said, slowly rising.

"If I know you, your wheels are already turning with how you're going to obliterate anything else Reilly does on rebuttal."

This finally got a real smile out of me.

"Yeah," he said, rising to join me. "I knew it. You wanna bounce anything off me?"

"Not yet," I said, though my nerve endings started to thrum with a new strategy. My riskiest one yet. But Emmons himself had opened the door without even realizing it.

"Give me a day," I said to Sam, feeling a thousand times better. "Then I may need your help after all."

29

"Ms. Brent?"

A light hand on my shoulder jarred me awake. For a moment, I couldn't remember where I was. Then, a shooting pain through my right shoulder clued me in that I'd actually fallen asleep at my desk. After dinner with Sam, I'd done the opposite of what he told me and come back to the office.

Jackie, one of the building maintenance crew members, smiled down at me. "Were you here all night?"

I wiped a spot of drool from the corner of my mouth. "Shoot. Yes. Lord! What time is it?"

Adrenaline jolted me. Had I missed court?

"It's okay," she said. "It's just about six a.m. You've got a couple hours to get in gear and uh, grab a shower."

"Thanks. Sorry. I'm embarrassed."

"Don't be. Nobody should ever feel bad about putting in a hard day's work. How long do you think it'll be before this case is over?"

Jackie took a seat at one of my desk chairs. She'd been here longer than I had. I think even longer than Caro had. She had a daughter I'd counseled through part of law school. She made it through half her second year before deciding on social work instead. "By the end of the week," I said. "I think Emmons's lawyer is going to call one, maybe two more witnesses. Then it's up to me to put on rebuttal."

"Well, I'm sure you'll be amazing at it." Jackie rose and gave me a wink. Lights went on in the hallway behind her.

"Is someone else here?"

Jackie looked back. "I think it's the intern. He's been coming in early for the last month or so. Combing through all those files you've got on this case. Probably has them all memorized."

She was right. Adam walked back, looking fresh-faced and wearing a sharp, gray suit. More importantly, he had a cup of coffee in each hand. The good kind, from the shop down the street.

"I'll leave you to it," Jackie said, excusing herself. She brushed past Adam, looking him up and down with an expression I wouldn't call kind.

"Is one of those for me?" I asked.

"Both of them are," Adam said.

"Well, that's genius," I said as he put both tall cups of coffee in front of me.

"One's a latte. Figured the sugar would put you in a good mood. The other is black, just for business."

"Thanks," I said, carefully sipping the latte.

"Sit," I said. "You've got a look. And you're buttering me up. What's going on?"

"I finished your brief," he said. He had a file folder tucked beneath his arm. Two of them, actually. He put the first one down.

"You'll argue undue surprise, of course," Adam said. "But I don't think it's going to go anywhere. I found some precedent when there's been a lengthy witness list filed. Most of those are in civil cases though. Judge will probably figure it's better for her on appeal if she just lets the guy testify."

"What else?" I said. He still had that second file folder under his arm.

"Late last night, Peter Reilly filed a new subpoena."

The floor dropped out beneath me. "I knew it," I said. "He's been planning this crap all along."

"I argued that in the brief too," Adam said as he handed me the second file. Bracing myself, I opened it. At eleven thirty last night, Reilly had served a subpoena on one Dalton Shepherd in Taylor, Michigan.

"He's been sitting on this," I said.

"Heck of a risky move," Adam said. "What if Saul really won't allow Shep to testify?"

"She will," I said. "Your instincts are right. She'll want some CYA if Reilly later has to file an appeal. She's not going to want to be the judge that left a door open for a monster like Cal Emmons if the jury convicts. She might adjourn trial for a day or two, but I doubt even that. I pretty much want to murder Brody Lance myself. If Reilly could find this guy, Lance should have. So now, I'm going to pretty much have to cross-examine him from the seat of my pants."

"You think he's going to get on the stand and admit he was driving Emmons's car the day Haley Chambers just happened to be abducted in it? No way. Won't happen. All Reilly can do, I mean, at best, is prove Shep exists. Everything else is too far a stretch."

"I appreciate your vote of confidence," I said.

"Plus," he said, rising from his chair. "I'd put money on you getting Saul to disallow his testimony. My briefs are that good."

I got up from my chair and flipped through the brief Adam wrote. He leaned over, pointing to a particular case he wanted me to review.

"This is good," I said. "It might even work if I tried it."

"Aren't you?" Adam asked. He was right next to me. Close enough I worried he could smell my coffee-laced morning breath.

"It's what Reilly expects me to do. You're right that I can handle this Shep character on cross. So maybe I roll the dice and force Reilly to put him on when he's not ready."

Adam smiled. "And I get a front row seat to watch all that. God, I love watching you in action."

It happened quickly. Adam took a step closer then hooked a finger under my chin. I let out a gasp and tried to step back, but his arm was already around my back.

He kissed me.

I went numb for a second. It took that long for my brain to process the physical sensation of it. As I did, I managed to step back, pushing against him. Adam's eyes stayed closed, his lips parted.

"Stop," I said.

"Mara," he said.

"Mara?"

Jason's voice spiked through me. I turned. My ex-husband stood in my office doorway, his face red with fury.

30

"Congressman Brent?" Adam said, straightening.

"I'm going to need you to step away from my wife," Jason said, emphasizing the last word.

"Adam," I said. "Please go down to your office. We need to have a conversation but I have a trial to prepare for."

Adam looked awkwardly between me and Jason. "Congressman, I just wanted to let you know I've been a huge admirer of your work. Your ideas on housing and ..."

"You're done here," Jason said.

Adam's jaw dropped. He looked to me for an answer I couldn't give just yet. My own rage poured through me only I didn't know who I was more angry with. Finally, Adam took the hint and walked out of my office. Not before Jason moved sideways and jammed him with his shoulder.

"What are you doing here?" I said after Jason shut the door.

"What are you doing?" he said, charging toward me in three long strides. "What the hell was that, Mara?"

"I'm not doing this scene with you," I said. "Why are you here? Where's Will? Is he okay? He's supposed to be in D.C. with you."

"Will's fine," he said. "Thank God he *is* in D.C. right now."

I crossed my arms in front of me. "Are you seriously judging me right now?"

"Are you sleeping with him?" Jason asked.

"No," I spat. "Not that it would be any of your business if I were. That was ... I don't know what that was. A misunderstanding."

Jason's shoulders dropped with relief. Then his eyes flashed with new anger. "Did he put his hands on you? I'll handle it if ..."

"You won't do a thing," I said. I wanted to kill him. I wanted to kill both of them. Unfortunately, I didn't have time for either. I was due in court in an hour and still looked every bit like someone who'd slept in their clothes. It occurred to me then, that to Jason, it had to look like something else.

"What are you doing here?" I asked once more.

"I have a meeting with some local labor leaders downstairs later this morning. I drove by the house and you weren't there. I figured you had to be here. I wanted to see how you were doing. I know how you get when you're in the middle of a trial. Whether you like it or not, I still care about stuff like that."

I didn't want to fight. I had no energy to spare for it.

"I'm great," I said. "But I don't have room for any side drama. Where is Will?"

"He and Kat are hanging out in Georgetown. They were going to see a movie. Everything's under control on my end. You, however ..."

"Jason, let's not. You are the last person to give me any grief for seeing someone, which I'm not."

"Then you need to tell that guy. Because he isn't getting the message. I saw how he was looking at you. It was predatory. Trust me."

"Really? I guess you'd know." I picked up the files Adam left me and stuffed them into my briefcase.

"I'll take care of it," he said. "He'll be out of your hair within the hour."

"Stay out of it. If I find out you said or did anything, I'm the one who's going to need a defense lawyer!"

"I'm trying to help you. Why do you have to be so stubborn?"

"Mara?" A soft knock on the door and Kenya poked her head in. By the expression on her face, I knew somebody had already clued her in that Jason would be in here. "Do you need any help with anything?"

"Jason," I said. "I'll talk to you later. Go to your meeting. I've got a murder case to win."

"I was hoping you wouldn't mind if I sat in on that for a bit after I get done with my business," he said.

"It's a public building," I said. "Though you're supposed to be spending quality time with our son. That's really the very best way you can help me."

An awkward moment passed, then Jason finally got the hint. He exchanged quick pleasantries with Kenya, then left my office.

She whistled low when we knew he was out of earshot.

"Don't ask me if I'm okay," I said. "I think I might scream."

"I can see that," Kenya said. "How about if I ask you if you need a fresh suit to wear? I've got one in my office that'll probably fit you. You won't have time to go home."

I shook my head and thanked her. She wrinkled her nose. "And Caro keeps a pack of travel toothbrushes in her drawer."

This got a laugh from me. But my humor was short-lived. Adam waited at the elevator. I had two messages from Judge Saul's clerk. She was ready for us. My life would have to wait.

31

"The defense calls Lincoln Maguire to the stand," Reilly said.

I'd interviewed Linc. So had Brody Lance. He was a quiet, thoughtful man who didn't particularly trust the police. He'd had run-ins with them in his younger days. He freely admitted to gang involvement before he turned his life around and got steady work as a mechanic.

Reilly did what I would do. He got Maguire's more colorful history out of the way. His answers were short, to the point, but read earnest.

"I'm not proud of the choices I made in my past," Linc said. "I didn't have a lot of positive role models growing up. But as soon as someone gave me a chance, I got straight."

"Who was it that gave you that chance, Linc?" Reilly asked.

"I started working for Cal Emmons," he said. "I was twenty-five. My probation officer recommended me to him. Said Mr.

Emmons wouldn't judge me for things I'd done wrong as long as I worked hard for him. As long as I was willing to learn."

"I see," Reilly said. "How long have you worked for Cal Emmons?"

"Three years," he said. "Almost four."

I made a note. Those dates would matter.

"Linc, do you know a man named Dalton Shepherd?"

"I knew a Shep," he said. "Cal hired him as a porter about a year ago."

"What do you remember about him?"

Maguire shrugged. "Kept to himself. Wasn't much of a talker. That's fine by me. When I'm working, I'm working."

"That's fair. What did Shep do around the shop?"

"Odds and ends. He didn't show much promise as a mechanic. He was more of a gopher. You know. Go for stuff. He'd clean up the shop at the end of the day. He was pretty good at general maintenance. That sort of thing."

"How many hours a week did Shep work?"

"Maybe thirty. He'd come in around eight in the morning. Open things up. Then he'd work until three or so. But I can't say for sure every day. I did my thing. I wasn't in charge of his hours."

"You say he opened up the shop. Alone?"

"Cal usually got there before anybody else," Linc explained.

"Was that every single day? You're saying Cal was always there before any other employee?"

"Most days," Linc answered.

"Most days. But there were days you got there before he did?"

"On occasion," Linc answered.

"Were there days Shep got there before you or Cal?"

Linc got quiet, considering the question. "I don't know about that."

"You don't know? But it's a possibility?"

"I don't know."

"Never. In all the months Shep worked there, you're saying he may or may not have gotten there before Cal?"

"Objection," I said. "Mr. Reilly got his answer. Mr. Maguire said he doesn't know."

"Sustained," Judge Saul said. "Move on, counselor."

"Okay," Reilly said. "Linc, I want to be clear here. Did you have a set of keys to the shop?"

"I did."

"So you could have opened the garage when Cal wasn't there?"

"I could have. I don't remember doing that though. Cal lives on the property. He was there before me, from what I remember."

Reilly pulled a photo of Emmons's blue Mercury Sable. "All right. Linc. What can you tell me about this car?"

"It belonged to Mr. Emmons. He called it his beater car."

"What was it used for?"

"Not much," Linc answered. "He drove it sometimes. Couldn't tell you when or how often."

"Do you know where he kept the keys?"

"Not really."

"Not really?" Reilly pulled up the photo of the hook board on the wall of the garage with the sets of keys dangling from it. Linc identified the ones to the front and back doors of the shop.

"What about this set?" Reilly asked, pointing to the keys to the Sable.

"Those are car keys," he answered.

"To what car?"

"Not sure," he answered.

This went on for a few minutes. I let it go. Lincoln Maguire was doing my work for me. After Reilly's seventh attempt to get Linc to identify the car keys, I objected.

"Asked and answered, Your Honor," I said.

"You took the words from me, counselor," she said. "Move on, Mr. Reilly."

Over at the defense table, Cal grew increasingly agitated. He kept mouthing something I couldn't make out, as if he were trying to get Reilly's attention, but his back was turned. The jury started to notice.

"Fine," Reilly said. "Did Shep have the same access you did to these keys here on the board?"

"Well, they were on the back wall of the garage. Anybody walking by would have access. But nobody got to that part of the garage. That is, nobody had any business in that part of the garage except employees."

"Okay. And on April 2nd of this year, who were the employees working at Emmons Garage?"

"Me and Shep. Though I don't know if he was legally an employee. And I hadn't seen him for a few days before that. Honestly, I was getting ready to ask Cal if Shep had maybe moved on. Of course, Cal was there too. And Mrs. Emmons would come in sometimes but I never saw her in the employee area."

"Thank you. To your knowledge, did anyone other than Cal Emmons ever drive the Sable?"

Reilly practically shouted the question. Across the way, Emmons gritted his teeth. Linc looked at him. He looked at the jury.

"Once or twice," he answered.

"Once or twice what?"

"Once or twice maybe somebody other than Cal drove that car."

"Who else drove it, Linc? Was it you?"

"No, sir. I never drove that car," Linc said, his voice breaking.

"But someone else did; who was it?"

"I know Shep drove it a couple of times."

"You mean Dalton Shepherd?"

"Yes."

"So you're telling me, Mr. Emmons routinely allowed Dalton Shepherd to drive the Sable?"

"Objection," I said. "Counsel is putting words in the witness's mouth."

"Sustained. Rephrase, Mr. Reilly."

"Did Cal Emmons routinely allow Shep to drive the Sable?" Reilly asked.

"He let him drive it. I didn't ask beyond that. It wasn't my business."

Reilly's shoulders sagged. "Thank you. You've been very helpful, Linc. I have no further questions."

"Ms. Brent?" Judge Saul said.

I waited for a beat. Without looking at the jury, I thumbed through a few pages of notes. Lincoln Maguire sat with his hands folded, waiting as I approached the lectern. "Mr. Maguire," I said. "This isn't easy for you, is it?"

He blinked, considering my question. "No, ma'am."

"Do you remember how many times you were interviewed by the police in connection with this case?"

"Twice, I think. Maybe three times."

"Do you remember being asked about the blue Mercury Sable?"

"Yes, ma'am."

"What did you tell the police in April of this year about that car?"

"I told them it belonged to Mr. Emmons. I told them he used it as a beater car."

"Do you remember being asked by the police about Dalton Shepherd?"

"They asked me who else worked in the garage. I told them Shep and me."

"When was that? If you recall. When were you questioned by the police?"

"It was after they found that poor girl's body. They came out with a warrant and that's when everything just blew up."

"Did they question Shep at the shop that day?"

"No, ma'am. Not that I'm aware."

"Why not?"

"He wasn't there. It was just me and Cal."

"Where was Shep?"

"I don't know. I hadn't seen him that day."

"In fact, you hadn't seen him in several days, had you?"

"No. I hadn't seen him that whole week."

"Was he still working for Cal at that time?"

"I don't know. I hadn't seen him for a while. Gophers like Shep tend to come and go. We weren't close."

"Mr. Maguire," I said. "You never told the police you saw Shep driving Emmons's car did you?

He looked down. "I don't think I did. They didn't ask me though. If I'd known that girl was in that car, I might have thought to say something. I don't know. I answered wat they asked me. I swear."

"Did you ever have occasion to go into the barn on the Emmons's property?"

"No, ma'am," he answered.

"Why not?"

"That was Cal's private property. I didn't go in there."

"Did you ever discuss the barn with the defendant?"

"Discuss it. Not really. I mean, you could see it from the garage. Cal was pretty clear what my boundaries were."

"How so?" I asked. This topic had been well covered during Linc's police interviews. So far, he was answering almost word for word what he'd told Brody Lance.

"That was Cal's private property. When he hired me on, he told me where the garage property ended and his private residence started. He said not to go over there. He said that's where his family lived and if I wanted to keep working for him, I needed to keep to my place."

"Keep to your place? Those were his words?"

Linc shrugged. "It was something like that. He said I needed to know my place. I was an employee of the garage. He said the barn was off limits."

"Do you know whether Cal had that same conversation with Shep?"

"I don't know about Shep in particular. But it was Cal's habit to say that to all the workers on their first day. We had a lot of gophers like Shep come and go over the years. Cal always said, business is business. His private property is private. He said his residence was off limits."

"And you understood that to include the barn?" I asked.

"Yes, ma'am. More than understood it. He said it. He said the house, the barn, the yard, and the woods behind it was off limits. So that was that."

"Thank you," I said. "Mr. Maguire, you said you could see the barn from the garage where you worked."

"Yes, ma'am," he said.

"Did you ever see anyone besides Cal going to or from that barn?"

"No, ma'am," he said.

"Did you ever see Dalton Shepherd in or around that barn?"

He shook his head. "No, ma'am." He dropped his shoulders and started to shake.

"Are you all right, Mr. Maguire?" I asked.

"No," he said, his voice breaking. "I could see that barn. Every day. Every single day."

"Mr. Maguire, surely you don't blame yourself for what happened?" I said.

"If I'd known she was in there. I worked there. Five days a week. I helped search for that girl too. If I'd known she was in there ..."

"Your Honor," Reilly said, though his tone was gentle. "The witness is unresponsive."

"Sustained. Ms. Brent, if you have a specific question, please ask it."

"No, Your Honor," I said. "I have no more questions for this witness."

"Mr. Reilly?"

"Just one," Reilly said. "Linc, I know this is tough for you. But you didn't work at Emmons Garage twenty-four hours a day, did you?"

"No," he answered. "Of course not."

"So your knowledge of that barn would have likewise only encompassed your working day, right?"

"I saw it when I worked. That's true," he answered.

"Nothing more from me, then," Reilly said. Judge Saul instructed Lincoln Maguire to step down.

He'd come into the courtroom with his head high. When Lincoln left, his head hung low and the tears he'd kept back started to flow.

"Your Honor," Reilly said. "The defense calls Dalton Shepherd to the stand."

"Your Honor!" I shouted as the courtroom doors opened and a pale, skinny kid came through.

Judge Saul leaned toward her microphone. "I'm calling a ten-minute recess. Both of you, in my chambers. Now."

32

"I've had no opportunity to interview this witness," I yelled. Vivian Saul had hung her robe on the back of her chair. She wore an eggplant-colored pantsuit and impressively high heels. She stood bracing herself on the back of her desk chair.

"This witness has been on my list since the beginning," Reilly said. "The cops have known about him. Lincoln Maguire just testified to having answered Detective Lance's questions about him."

"You've been hiding him," I said.

"Why in the world would I do that? I'm fighting for my client's life out there. You think I'd actually hide an exculpatory witness? If anything, you've been hiding him."

"This is ridiculous," I said.

"Mara," Judge Saul said. "I have no idea why this witness was never questioned by the police. He's been known. Reilly's right. Vague though it was, he's been on his witness list. This is a capital murder case. I am not going to deny defense counsel the right to call a witness. You'll have your chance to cross-examine. Mr. Reilly, this isn't the end of this. If I find out you've known about Mr. Shepherd's whereabouts before this, I'll have your license. That'll also be the least of your problems. Mara's office will be able to make a credible case for obstruction of justice. Are we clear?"

"We're clear," Reilly said. "And I swear on my law license ... hell, I'll swear it on my life; until yesterday, I didn't know where Dalton Shepherd was. I got a tip from my private investigator. That tipster wishes to remain anonymous. But I swear I will cooperate with law enforcement within the confines of attorney-client privilege, if it comes to that."

"Oh, it's going to come to that," I said.

"Fine," Judge Saul said. "Let's get on with this." She grabbed her robe off the chair and swirled it around her shoulders.

Sweat poured down my back. As I stormed out of Judge Saul's chambers, Adam waited for me.

"Not now," I said as I brushed past him.

Five minutes later, I was back at the table as Dalton Shepherd was sworn in. He looked about twelve years old and he was so thin. He wore a dingy yellow tee shirt and jeans. He kept rubbing his hands on his thighs, wiping off the sweat.

"Will you state your name for the record?" Reilly asked.

"Dalton Thomas Shepherd," Shepherd answered. He trembled so badly the witness chair squeaked.

"Mr. Shepherd," Reilly said. "Have you ever met me before today?"

"No," Shepherd said.

"How is it you came to be in court today?"

"I got a subpoena yesterday," he said. "A couple of deputies drove me here."

"Are those deputies in the courtroom today?"

"Yeah. They're sitting at the back of the courtroom."

"Thank you," Reilly said. "Mr. Shepherd, do you know the defendant, Calvin Emmons?"

Shep rubbed his brow. He wouldn't look up.

"Mr. Shepherd, have you worked for the defendant, Calvin Emmons?"

With shaking fingers, Shep pulled out a wrinkled piece of paper and read from it. Each word was like a nail right through my heart.

"I exercise my right not to incriminate myself under the fifth amendment," he said.

"Mr. Shepherd, I'm merely asking you if you worked for the defendant," Reilly said. "Can you not answer with a simple yes or no?"

"I exercise my right not to incriminate myself under the fifth amendment," he said again.

"Did you work for Cal Emmons in April of last year?" Reilly asked.

"I plead the fifth."

To his credit, Reilly at least appeared surprised. Beside him, Cal Emmons gave a quick fist pump.

"Did you ever have occasion to drive a blue Mercury Sable wagon owned by Calvin Emmons?" Reilly asked, his words a staccato beat.

"I plead the fifth."

"Did you know Haley Chambers?"

At this, Dalton Shepherd looked up from his paper. Tears filled his eyes. "I plead the fifth."

I couldn't believe it. Adam swore under his breath. I shot him a withering look.

"Did you abduct Haley Chambers on April 2nd of this year, Mr. Shepherd?"

"I plead the fifth," Shepherd said. I felt a tap on my shoulder. Sam sat behind me and passed me a note. I read it quickly.

"Lance just got a call from a defense lawyer in Taylor. He's sitting in back. Someone retained him for Shepherd."

Someone. I'd bet *my* license that someone would trace straight back to Peter Reilly.

"Mr. Shepherd, did you torture Haley Chambers?"

"I plead the fifth."

"Did you kill Haley Chambers?"

"I plead the fifth."

"Your Honor," I said. "I respectfully request this witness be asked if he intends to invoke his fifth amendment right against all further questioning."

"Agreed," Judge Saul said. "Let's not waste anymore of the jury's time. Mr. Shepherd, is it your intention to invoke your fifth amendment right to all further questions?"

"Um ... I think so," Dalton Shepherd said.

"Fine," Judge Saul said.

"Then I have no further questions," Reilly said. I could tell he was fighting not to sound smug.

"Ms. Brent?" Judge Saul said.

"Your Honor," I said. "I have one question, if I may."

"Ask it," she said.

"Mr. Shepherd, were you working for Calvin Emmons four years ago?"

Shepherd blinked. "I plead the fifth."

"All right," Judge Saul said. "The witness may step down."

Shepherd practically ran out of the courtroom. Reilly stood at the lectern. When the doors slammed shut, Judge Saul looked at him.

"Call your next witness, Mr. Reilly."

Reilly took a breath and exhaled his words with grandeur. "Your Honor, at this time, the defense rests."

33

Late in the day, I had the blessing of Judge Saul's overcrowded calendar. She adjourned us until morning. I needed a few minutes of solitude but didn't get it. I got a call from Jason. I'd almost forgotten he'd planned to sit in on court today.

"Mara," he said abruptly. "Are you still at the office?"

"I am," I said. "And I'm tired. It's been a day."

"So I heard," he said. His heavy breathing on the other end of the line told me this was more than just a check-in phone call.

"Are you okay?" he asked, his voice filled with concern. Not so long ago, he was the one I leaned on after days like this. And he'd been there with a shoulder rub and a glass of chilled wine. He knew me. Just a look. Just the tone of my voice. He would comfort me.

"I'm fine," I said, my tone sharp. I had no time for nostalgia. It had taken me years to build up boundaries where Jason was concerned.

"Listen," he said. "I'm about to get on a plane. But you need to fire Adam Skinner."

Had I even told Jason Adam's last name?

"Jason ..."

"No. Listen. He's no good. I did some checking. I'm not even sure how he cleared the background check to get a county ID badge, Mara. It looks like he's never been able to end a romantic relationship without a court order."

"What? How do you know that? I *saw* his background check. There was nothing ..."

"His last girlfriend was getting ready to file a petition to get a restraining order against him. Said he was stalking her. Threatening her. It wouldn't have shown up on the sheriff's department check because she never went through with the thing. She withdrew it."

Jason would have had to call in a powerful favor to get information like that this quickly. "Jason, that's not even part of a public record then. How did you even ..."

I let the question die, realizing I didn't want to know. But another question sprang up in my mind with darker consequences. It meant Jason likely had a private investigator on retainer. An expensive one. Why?

"Just get rid of him," Jason said. "I don't like him around you. And I better never find out he came to the house."

"Thanks for the tip," I said. My head started to pound. "I've got to get back to work and you have a plane to catch."

Jason tried to move the conversation to something more pleasant, but I was done. I said a polite goodbye. Not two minutes later, I was disrupted again.

"Mara," Adam said. He didn't knock. He didn't just poke his head in or ask to come in. He came right up to me as I sat at the end of the table.

"We need to talk about what happened," he said. Had he been eavesdropping on my call? Jason was on a power trip, but I prayed there was nothing to what he said. More drama with Adam was the last thing I needed.

"We don't," I said. "I need to figure out how I'm going to undo the mess Dalton Shepherd just made of my case, Adam. That's what you should also be focusing on."

He grabbed a chair and pulled it in close. "You've got this," he said. "I know you. I've watched you. I've watched the jury watching you."

I had to suppress the urge to explode. "You don't know me," I said. "You work for me. You're right, we do need to have a conversation about this morning. Now isn't the time. Can you just ... I don't know."

A soft rap on the door cut off my train of thought and gave me respite. Brody Lance walked in.

"Mara, I'm sorry. I don't know how Reilly found that kid. But trust me, we're looking into it."

"It doesn't matter," I said. "You realize what's happened though."

Behind Brody, Kenya and Hojo walked in. Their funereal expressions did nothing to lighten my own mood.

"How bad is it?" Kenya said.

"As bad as it gets," I answered, throwing my pen on the desk.

"He said nothing," Brody offered. "Dalton Shepherd didn't answer a single question. He admitted to nothing. Reilly can't even establish where Shepherd was the night Haley Chambers disappeared."

"Can you?" I snapped.

"He's not talking," Brody answered. "Not in the witness box and not in any kind of formal interview. His lawyer has already contacted me. We're meeting later this afternoon. It's going to come to nothing. I promise."

"The damage is already done," I said. "For every question Shep evaded, he set Reilly's closing up. He'll argue Shep's invocation of the fifth amendment means he's got something to hide."

"It's just a smoke screen," Lance shouted. "Dalton Shepherd didn't kill that girl. He didn't torture her in that barn for a day. He didn't plant evidence to frame Dylan Woodhouse. Cal Emmons did all that. Shep is just convenient."

"Mara," Kenya said. "Brody's right. You can clean all that up in your own closing."

I shook my head. "I can't clean it all up. Not with what I've presented so far. If we go to the jury tomorrow morning, we don't have a unanimous verdict. No way. There will be at least one holdout. At best, we get a mistrial. Then at least we can sort out the Shep problem. If he'll talk. But if he doesn't have a solid alibi, I can't fix this."

"You can!" Kenya said. "You have a mountain of physical evidence. You have witnesses who saw Emmons planting that girl's shirt."

"This is capital murder," I said. "We're asking those twelve people to render a verdict that could end Cal Emmons's miserable life. I've been at this long enough, so have you, to know we're in trouble, Kenya. Big trouble. Unless ..."

I threaded my fingers and placed my hands on top of my head.

"Unless what?" Adam asked. I had my eyes locked with Kenya's. She knew what I was thinking. She'd spent enough years at the prosecution table to know we had no other choice.

"Do it," she said.

"Do what?" Lance asked.

"I'll get in touch with Nicole Silvers," Kenya said. "We'll have an army of Angels in that courtroom. She won't be alone."

"Good," I said. "I'll need them. And she needs to understand what Reilly's going to be able to do to her on cross. I can't protect her from all of that."

"Dominique Bright?" Lance asked. "You can't put her on, Mara. Reilly's not the greatest defense lawyer I've ever seen, but even a mediocre one will know how to rip through that girl's credibility. She's facing charges for filing a false police report right now."

"So we just have to pray that won't matter in light of everything else she's got to say. Dominique's my best weapon against Reilly's closing argument. I have no other choice."

The grim looks from the room did nothing to assuage my own doubts. Putting Dominique on the stand could break her. It could sink my case for good. Or it could save us all.

34

The next morning, Dominique barely made it out of the car. Nicole Silvers coaxed her out and got her as far as the first-floor bathroom before Dominique lost her breakfast. Nicole told me all of this later. Had I known, I might have stalled for more time. To her credit, Nicole knew I didn't have any.

So, at nine a.m. on the tenth day of trial, Dominique Bright slowly climbed into the witness box. She stumbled over her words as the bailiff had her take her oath.

"Hello, Dominique," I said, positioning myself in the center of the lawyer's area, in Dominique's direct line of sight. Cal Emmons could see her, but she could only see me. "Will you tell me your name, age, and where you live, just for the record?"

"I'm Dominique Anne Bright. I live in ... I've been staying in town. Do I have to say where exactly? Oh, I'm twenty-four years old."

She was being honest, even though it twisted my heart. She was still with Vinny Meyer. "Okay," I said. "I'd like to talk about what you were doing four years ago. Summertime. Do you remember?"

"I was taking classes at Grace County Community College. I thought I was going to be a dental hygienist."

"Did you finish school?"

"No," she said. "I didn't."

"Let's go back a little further than that. Dominique, can you tell me where your family is from?"

She looked down and picked at her nail. "No. I don't really have family. My mom died when I was five. I never knew my dad. That's when I went into foster care."

"Can you tell me what that was like?"

She sat sideways on the chair, tilting her body away from the jury, away from Cal Emmons. Twice, I had to gently instruct her to speak into the microphone.

"It wasn't the happiest life. I was unlucky with the homes I was placed in. There was a lot of chaos. A lot of moving around. I spent some time in a few bad homes. It was ... abusive. It wasn't a good time in my life."

"Dominique, have you ever been in trouble with the law?"

I knew I had to get Dominique's issues out in the open quickly. The more the jury could understand what she'd overcome, the more they might be willing to overlook some of the more problematic things about her.

"I didn't make the best choices," she said. "I didn't have a lot of attention from adults growing up. Not the good kind anyway. I have a record. It started out with what I thought were little, minor things. Shoplifting. It wasn't frivolous stuff though. I stole food. I stole money from one of my foster parents. I spent some time in juvenile detention. The first time, I found that better than the group home I was living in. When they let me out, the next home was way worse. So I started doing things hoping I would get caught. Jail was better than being homeless. Which I was. I ran away a lot before I finally turned eighteen."

"What happened when you turned eighteen?" I asked.

"By then, I had some trouble with drugs. One of the guys I'd dated got me into them. And ... other things."

This was just the first of the more heartbreaking things that had happened to this girl. In clear, steady words, Dominique explained how she'd turned tricks for a few months to support both her drug habit and the first loser boyfriend she couldn't break free from.

"Okay," I said. "So how did you end up in college?"

"My probation officer, Maggie Conroy, suggested it. After I'd done rehab and it felt like it was working, she helped me get my G.E.D. and into a job retraining program. I was doing really well. I liked school for the first time. It was a fresh start. I was able to remove myself from people who weren't such a good influence on me."

"Did you finish school, Dominique?" I asked.

She closed her eyes. "No."

"Why not?"

She took a breath. Kept her eyes squeezed shut. Then, she let the air out and locked her eyes with mine.

"Something happened to me," she said.

"What, Dominique?"

"I didn't have a ride to school. My roommate's car broke down. A friend was supposed to pick me up but we got our wires crossed and she wasn't there on time. I only lived two miles from campus. I'd driven that way a thousand times. It was in the middle of the day. I always carried pepper spray with me. But ... as I was walking along Jefferson Highway in Grace Park, someone grabbed me."

"Grabbed you," I said. "Can you tell me exactly what happened?"

"Objection," Reilly said. His voice split the air. Judge Saul called us over for the sidebar I knew was coming. As I passed my table, Adam handed me the brief he'd written. I knew I wouldn't need it.

"Look," Reilly started, his voice low so the jury couldn't hear. Judge Saul covered her microphone with her hand. "I feel for this girl. I'm sympathetic to whatever she's gone through. But this is irrelevant and highly prejudicial. My client was never charged with any crime in conjunction with Dominique Bright's attack. This has zero relevance to this case. If the Grace County sheriff's office thinks they have something, they can bring charges in a separate matter. Not here."

"Ms. Brent?"

"This is proper rebuttal," I said. "Cal Emmons got on the stand the other day and swore up and down that he's never hurt another woman both on direct and cross. This witness can give credible testimony that's not true. The defense opened the door on this one. That's how rebuttal works."

"Your Honor ..." Reilly started.

"I've heard enough," Judge Saul said. "Ms. Brent's argument is well founded. She's right. Your client opened the door. Whether you like it or not, the state is allowed to parade as many witnesses as they'd like in here if they have credible testimony that he lied about that. Though I'm warning you, Ms. Brent, don't overstep."

"This is the only witness I am planning to call on this particular point," I said. "She's the only one I'll need." The last bit, I fired straight at Peter Reilly.

"You may proceed," Judge Saul said.

Reilly stormed back to Cal Emmons's side. I ignored their furious whispering and placed myself in a protective position, once again blocking Dominique's sight of Emmons.

"Dominique, you said you were attacked. Can you tell me exactly what you remember?"

Something happened to her then. I'd explained to Dominique that Emmons's lawyer would try to stop her from testifying. She knew that objection was coming. With that one question, she knew his objection had failed. She would get to tell her story. In court. On the record. Right in front of the man we both knew hurt her.

A light came into her eyes then. One I'd never seen. It was as if she knew at that moment, she'd been granted power.

"What happened to you, Dominique?"

"I remember it was hot," she said. "Hotter than I realized. I hadn't brought water with me like I normally do. I regretted that. Two miles didn't seem like such a big deal but as I was walking, it was hard. The road was uneven. I was just wearing flip flops. One of them kept breaking. You know, the little plastic disk thing kept popping out of the hole in the sandal part. I should have called a cab. I should have called ... anyone. But I didn't.

"I was going uphill. It was steeper than I thought, you know, from the times I'd driven that route. There were cornfields on either side of me and bugs were everywhere. Getting in my mouth.

"I was so thirsty. I heard a car coming from behind me. It was going really fast. It started to slow down. I turned. At first, I thought maybe they were going to offer me a ride. I don't know, but then I got terrified. I was all alone out there. There was nothing but fields. I was just about to turn around, when I got hit."

"Hit by what?" I asked.

"The car. It was going slow. I saw just the silver bumper. The car was blue. I don't know the make or the model, but it was blue. The car hit me and pushed me into the ditch. I remember falling. I remember pain in my knee. Then nothing. I just went to sleep. I was knocked out."

I paused, letting both the jury and Dominique catch their breaths.

"Dominique," I said. "Do you remember anything else about the car?"

"Not from when it hit me. Other than what I said. It was blue. But later, when I woke up, I was in it. In the back of it, lying down. That's when I knew it was some kind of station wagon. The whole thing smelled like cigars. Cheap ones. One of my foster fathers smoked those things. For a minute, while I was still disoriented, I thought that's where I was. Back at that house."

"You came to inside the car?" I asked.

"Yes," she said. "My hands were tied together in front of me with something plastic and there was more tape around my body. And there was thick tape covering my mouth going all around my head. Tape over my eyes. I was sweating. There was so much pain. It felt like my whole body at first. When I tried to move though, I knew it was my hands. I couldn't move my thumbs. For a minute, I thought he'd maybe chopped them off. I couldn't feel them. Couldn't move them. They were broken. After a little while, the edge of the tape around my eyes started to lift. I could just see under it. Not much. But enough that I could make out I was in the back of that car. I remember the carpet. It was gray. Really dirty. But gray."

"What happened next?" I asked.

"We stopped. I tried to kick my way out, but my head hurt so bad and my hands were just aching. I was dizzy. He pulled me out."

"He," I said. "Did you see who attacked you?"

"No," she said. "I never saw his face. I only … I saw his hands. He had big hands. Hairy hands."

Every member of the jury looked over at Cal Emmons. He sat with his hands folded. As Dominique spoke, he spread them flat, almost daring them to take a closer look. His hands were large, rough, and covered with dark hair at the wrist and dusting over the back.

"What happened next, Dominique?" I asked.

"He took me into this room. I could just see a little bit under the tape. I saw the lights from a gas station. I could read Sunoco. That was on one corner. The other was a McDonald's. And I saw a broken traffic light with the yellow light busted out."

"Where did your captor take you, Dominique?" I asked.

"The police told me later it was this dingy hotel room. It smelled like sweat and worse things. It had stained brown carpet. He ... he put me on the bed. Then he left. He was gone for a really long time. For a while, I thought maybe something happened to him. That he wasn't coming back. But then he did. That's when it all started."

"What started, Dominique?"

"He hurt me."

"How did he hurt you?"

She looked down at the floor. A tremor went through her. Then, Dominique Bright found the strength to call out her monster.

"He beat me. He had a belt. He beat me on my feet, my legs, my shoulders. I tried to scream but the tape muffled my voice. I remember thinking at least it took the pain away from my broken thumbs. This went on for a very, very long time. It got dark. Then it started to get light again."

"What else?"

"He raped me," she said. "Just ... the once. But I thought I would die from it. He choked me. Tried to smother me. When that was over, he dragged me out of the room. It was still early. Like the sun hadn't come fully out. He threw me over his shoulder and then back in that car. We drove for a while. I blacked out again. When I woke up, I couldn't breathe. I heard this cutting sound. He had a knife. He tore off the tape with it, cut my hair off. But I couldn't fight back. I didn't have any strength. It was cold and dark and wet. I didn't know where I was."

"Did you see his face?" I asked.

"No," she said. "I didn't. I couldn't. He held me face first. I was in mud. A swamp. He had his knee in my back. After he cut the tape off, he pulled me up, bent me backward. He was right in my ear. I could smell his sweat. God. He smelled so awful. And that cigar smoke. He had one in his mouth. I could feel it against my ear. He whispered. He said you always get what you deserve. Always. But he never even told me to do anything. I would have done what he wanted. Anything to keep him from hurting me like that. He bent me backward at the waist, you know, with his hand under my chin. He reached around and then ... he took that cigar out and while he held me like that, he put it out on my chest. He ground it in between my breasts."

"Dominique, what happened next?" I asked.

"He put me under," she said. "He pushed my face into the water of that swampy lake. I choked on it. He was trying to drown me. He'd push me in until I almost passed out. Then he'd pull me up just when I thought I was going to die. He did that over and over. It seemed like hours. My lungs burned so bad. Then, I don't know. There was a noise. Voices. He froze.

He took his knee off me and got up. I was just lying there, gasping. I felt so weak. I just waited for him to grab me again and push me under. But he didn't. The next thing I knew, I heard this lady screaming. I found out later I was at a campground. This couple had parked their truck and were about to set up their tent. The police think their headlights scared him and he ran off. If that couple hadn't come when they did, I'd be dead. I know it. I almost wished I was. It took me a really long time not to wish for that. It would have been so much easier than this. So many things would have turned out differently. People would have been better off."

She was crying. I was trying not to. "Dominique," I said. "Do you still have a scar from that cigar burn?"

"Yes," she said.

"Will you show it to me?"

She did. Reilly objected. He was overruled. I described the mark so the court reporter could get it all down for the record. Dominique opened the top two buttons on her blouse. She opened it so the jury could see her sternum. They no doubt noted how her left thumb was still bent oddly at the knuckle from that long-ago break. But there, directly between her breasts, was a deep, ugly, circular scar. Its shape and placement was identical to what they'd seen on Haley Chambers's autopsy photos. I knew it would sear into their memories like Emmons had seared it into Haley and Dominique's skin. A perfect match except for one thing. Through time and the grace of God, Dominique Bright's had healed.

35

"Good afternoon, Ms. Bright," Reilly said. He stalled, looking through his notes. He pursed his lips, relaxing them, then pursed them again.

"He doesn't know what to do with her," Hojo whispered to me. I'd made a change at the prosecution's table. Though Kenya didn't yet know the scope of my issues with Adam, I couldn't have him next to me right now. That fire would have to wait to be put out until the jury had this case.

"Ms. Bright," Reilly said. "I cannot imagine how difficult it has been for you to rehash all of this today. Are you nervous?"

"What?"

"Are you nervous? Is it causing you undue distress to answer my questions?"

"You haven't really asked me any yet," she said.

"Well, I want to be clear about something. If at any time you need a break, or if you need anything, just say so. Can we make that deal?"

"If I need something, I'll ask," she said.

"Fair enough," he said. "Okay, you've been very forthright in answering Ms. Brent's questions about things you've done in your past. Things you're maybe not proud of. I just have a few follow-up questions on that. Isn't it true that at the age of sixteen you were arrested for shoplifting and disorderly conduct?"

"Yes," she said.

"You slapped a police officer in the face, isn't that right?"

"They dismissed that charge," she said.

"Does that mean you didn't slap that police officer?"

"I wasn't charged with that, no," she said.

"I didn't ask you what you were charged with. I asked you if you did it."

"I don't remember exactly," she said. "I tried to run when the cops tried to question me. I think it was some clothing I tried to steal. It wasn't for me. It was for this little boy who was staying with me at the foster home at that time."

"You ran when the police tried to question you?" Reilly asked.

"I ran. It got physical. I didn't intend to hurt anyone."

"I see," he said. "How many times have you been arrested, Ms. Bright?"

"I don't know for sure," she said.

"More than five?"

"Yes."

"More than ten?"

"Not more than ten."

"It's eight times, isn't it, Ms. Bright?"

"If you say so," she said.

"In fact, you were arrested two years ago for assault. You went after a woman you told the police your boyfriend, Vincent Meyer, was cheating on you with, isn't that right? You threw a hammer at her."

"Those charges were dropped," she said. "The police said we were mutual combatants. She came at me first. I was only defending myself. Vinny will back me up."

"You were arrested this year, weren't you?" he asked.

"Yes," she said.

"You hit your boyfriend, Vincent Meyer, isn't that right?"

"It got all crazy," she said. "I was in a situation that wasn't good for me."

"You were charged with filing a false police report five months ago, isn't that true?"

"I was charged, yes. But they said they're going to drop it. Vinny and I worked it out. That's all behind me," she said.

"Two years ago, you were charged with obstruction of justice, weren't you?" he asked.

Dominique looked over at me. Though it killed me not to rise up and protect her, she knew this was a bed of hot coals she'd have to walk. Her past was her past. The only thing that mattered was how she held up today.

"I was ... Vinny was going through some things," she said. "He's clean now. I thought I was helping. I know now what I did was wrong."

"You flushed drugs down the toilet when the police were executing a valid search warrant in your home," Reilly said. "Those were the circumstances, weren't they?"

"Yes," she said.

"Okay, so you've routinely lied to the police and concealed evidence over the years, isn't that true?"

"Objection," I said. "That's a mischaracterization of both this witness's testimony and the record Mr. Reilly has right in front of him. He can argue as he likes later."

"Overruled, Ms. Brent," Judge Saul said. "I don't think we've veered outside the bounds of proper cross. The witness may answer."

"I don't trust the police," Dominique said.

"Is that a yes? You routinely lie to the police?" Reilly asked.

"No. I'm not a liar. I said I don't trust the police. That's not the same thing."

"Filing a false police report, concealing evidence: you don't consider that to be a form of lying?" Reilly asked.

"Your Honor," I said. "Counsel has asked, the witness has answered to the best of her abilities."

"Sustained. Let's move on, Mr. Reilly," the judge said.

"Fine," Reilly said. "Ms. Bright, of these eight arrests, two of them were for prostitution, isn't that correct?"

"Yes," she said.

"In fact, your most serious charge, the one that landed you in jail for a month, that was a prostitution charge, wasn't it?"

"Yes," she said. "I've told you. I don't always make the best choices when it comes to men. My last boyfriend before Vinny had an even more serious drug problem. There were times when he ... when I did things to try to help him. I thought I was helping him."

"Like you thought you were helping Vinny when you concealed evidence. Like you thought you were helping Vinny when you went after another woman with what might be considered a deadly weapon. And you turned tricks so this other boyfriend could buy drugs, is that what you're saying?" Reilly asked.

"Yes," she said.

"I'm sorry that happened to you, Ms. Bright. I truly am."

"I don't need your sympathy," Dominique said. Fire lit her eyes.

"I don't wish to belabor this point. I don't wish to expose you to more pain with my questions. But I need to clarify. You say you were attacked four years ago on Jefferson Highway in Grace Park, Grace County, Ohio. Is that true?"

"Yes," she said. "It's true I said it. It's true it happened."

"Isn't it also true you were arrested for prostitution six months prior to that alleged attack?"

"Yes," she said. "But those two things had nothing to do with each other."

"Got it," Reilly said, but I knew what he'd try to argue in closing. It was far too thin an argument, in my opinion. But I wasn't the one he'd need to convince.

"Okay," Reilly said. "So let's talk about that attack. Again, Ms. Bright. I'm so sorry that happened to you. Whatever happens with this trial, I'd like you to know how brave I think you are for coming forward today."

"Do you have a question?" Dominique asked. When she looked at me, I couldn't help but smile.

"I do," Reilly said. "You gave a detailed description of the events leading up to your attack. You claim you were blindfolded?"

"I said the man put tape over my eyes," she said.

"So you never saw his face?"

"No."

"You couldn't provide the police with a description of your captor, could you?"

"No," she said. "I only briefly saw his hands. He had tape over my eyes. When he cut it off, he was holding me down on my stomach."

"You never saw him," Reilly said.

"No, I never saw him."

"So sitting here, you're maybe twenty feet away from the defendant. You can't tell me or this jury that Cal Emmons was the one who attacked you, can you?"

"I know what the police found," she said. "I know what happened to me and what happened to that other girl, Haley Chambers."

"You've never seen Cal Emmons before the events of this trial though, have you?"

"No," she said. "I'd never seen him before."

"Thank you," Reilly said. "I have no further questions."

"No redirect from me, Your Honor," I said.

I tried to transmit a look of solidarity with Dominique as she quietly rose. She had one last hard thing to do. She had to walk within two feet of Cal Emmons as she made her way out of the courtroom. He didn't look at her when she did. But she looked at him. It was just a moment. A brief pause as she went by his table. But Dominique looked right at Cal Emmons and never blinked.

36

I called Detective Darma Shultz of the Grace County sheriff's department to the stand. The physical evidence she introduced, in my mind, put to rest any lingering doubt the jury might have about Dominique's testimony.

"You were assigned as lead detective into the abduction and rape of Dominique Bright?" I asked.

"I was," Detective Shultz said.

One by one, we introduced the photographs taken of Dominique after the two campers got her to the hospital. She looked so much like Haley Chambers. Pale. Thin. Her hair chopped off in jagged clumps. Then, there was the circular wound on her chest, raw and angry.

It was the same. It was all the same.

"Detective," I said. "What other physical evidence were you able to collect from the victim, Dominique Bright?"

"A standard rape kit was administered to Ms. Bright at the hospital. She had a number of strange gray, synthetic fibers embedded in her hair, on her skin, and under her fingernails."

"Were you able to identify those fibers?"

"We were," she said. "They were consistent with carpet fibers used in a particular make and model of automobile. That was also consistent with Ms. Bright's account that she'd been transported in the back of a car."

"What make and model automobile did you identify?"

"Those carpet fibers, dyed gray, were used in the 2000 Mercury Sable wagon. They were embedded with dirt and sand we were more recently able to match to the property surrounding the defendant's home. Additionally, we identified a set of tire tracks leading away from the pond area where the campers, Joly and Roger Kinsey, found Ms. Bright."

"What was significant about those tire treads?" I asked.

"They were mismatched. The treads on the front driver's side and back tires were consistent with a Bridgestone 16-inch all-season tire. The passenger side front tire was consistent with a 16-inch Goodyear ultra-grip winter tire. It was a snow tire. There was also a unique imperfection in that tread. The same imperfection was found in the tire on Mr. Emmons's vehicle," she said.

"Detective, did you have occasion to cross-check your physical evidence from Ms. Bright's rape kit with any other similar crimes?"

"Yes," she said.

"And what was the result of that analysis?"

"I was contacted by the Maumee County sheriff's department. Those fibers are in a national database. Much like we check DNA. The fibers were a match for those found on Haley Chambers's body."

"Thank you," I said. "I have nothing further."

Reilly popped up. "Detective, you've never charged anyone in Dominique Bright's case, isn't that true?"

"That's true as of now, yes," she said. "It's still an open investigation."

"In fact, you found the victim, Ms. Bright, to be a problematic witness, didn't you?"

"I don't know what you mean?"

"I mean, isn't it true you wrote in your report that you had concerns Dominique Bright would not make for a credible witness?"

"I found her evasive in some of her answers. She wasn't very trusting of the police," she said.

"Detective, you found no physical evidence tying any other suspect to Ms. Bright's attack, did you?"

"Other than what I've described, no."

"No DNA evidence?"

"No DNA evidence that held up to the rigors of our analysis. It was inconclusive," she answered.

"No foreign blood. No foreign hair. In fact, no evidence other than Dominique Bright's word for it that she was raped at all, isn't that right?"

"Son," Detective Schultz said. "This girl was brutally attacked and raped. She was beaten within an inch of her life. There is no doubt in my mind that if not for Joly and Roger Kinsey happening by when they did, Dominique Bright wouldn't be alive today."

"And yet even now, you still haven't charged anyone for that crime," Reilly snapped.

"Is that a question?" Schultz asked.

"No," Reilly said. "But here's one. You haven't got a shred of proof on who might have been driving the car you think Dominique was transported in, do you?"

"I've got a positive match on tire treads and carpet fibers to the one owned by the defendant and used in the commission of a murder against Haley Chambers," she answered.

"But you cannot say who was driving that car on the day Dominique was allegedly attacked, can you?"

"No," Detective Schultz said, sighing. "I can't say that."

"Thank you," Reilly said. "I have no further questions."

"Ms. Brent?" Judge Saul said.

"None from me," I said.

"Detective, you may step down."

Darma Schultz rose, straightened her tie, and left the witness box. As she did, I remained standing. The jury watched Schultz go. I knew their minds lingered on the one legitimate question Reilly raised. Detective Schultz had not yet charged Cal Emmons with a crime. It would be my job to refocus them on why that didn't matter.

"Ms. Brent?" Judge Saul said. "Are you ready to call your next witness?"

"Your Honor," I said. "The prosecution is prepared to rest."

My words echoed with finality. Judge Saul nodded. It meant as soon as this evening, the jury would get to decide Cal Emmons's fate.

37

At two p.m., October 28th, I walked to the lectern, leaving my notes behind. I wouldn't need them. For more than six months, I had lived, eaten, and breathed this case. I could no longer see any other path to justice except for the conviction of Calvin Emmons. As I took one last breath before I started, I just hoped that wouldn't be my downfall.

"Members of the jury," I said. "You know what happened out there on Kidman Road. You don't have to guess. There is no mystery here. There is only the horror that man left behind."

I pointed at Emmons. He glared back at me and kept his hands folded in front of him.

"You're looking at a predator," I said. "A man who has honed his skills and an appetite for killing over years. In a few minutes, his lawyer is going to stand up here and try to get you to doubt what you see, what you know. Don't let him.

"On April 2nd of this year, Haley Chambers was a smart, happy, ambitious young lady. She wanted nothing more than to dedicate her life to putting people like Cal Emmons away.

To keep them from hurting people just like her. Fate stepped in. What we may never know is whether Cal stalked Haley in advance, or whether she just happened to be in the wrong place at the wrong time. But make no mistake, Cal Emmons had planned this killing for years.

"He admitted to you how he set up a torture chamber in his barn. A secret room that he took great care to keep his wife and children out of. He wants you to believe he meant it as some ill-advised attempt to spice up his marriage. Really? Interesting then that his wife knew nothing about it. Logic tells us it's because he didn't want her to. Just like he didn't want any employees of Emmons Garage to go near that barn. Linc Maguire told you that. He was told right off the bat that Cal's private property was off limits.

"On that fateful evening, Cal drove up to Haley and struck her with his car. You saw the injuries. You heard Dr. Pham describe how the wounds to her legs, her broken collarbone were consistent with a low impact collision. Cal hit her just hard enough to knock her down and incapacitate her. Just like he did to Dominique Bright.

"Then, Cal restrained her with duct tape and threw her in the trunk of his car. We know that because Haley's hair was found in that trunk. And the carpet fibers from that trunk were found on Haley's body. They found her DNA in there too in the form of her sweat, her blood. He tried to clean up after himself, but failed. Haley couldn't be silenced in the end.

"We know, without a shred of doubt, that Cal Emmons took Haley to his barn. He shackled her to that table. And for hours. Hours. He systematically tortured and raped her until he had his fill."

At this point, I pulled the autopsy photos up on the screen. One by one, I reminded the jury of every injury.

"She was still alive, ladies and gentlemen," I said. "She was alive. Until Cal was through with her. Then, he took her to the pond at the back of his property and held her under water until she drowned.

"Haley can't tell us what happened. But we can see through Haley's eyes in the words of Dominique Bright. We are dealing with a monster. He has a killing routine. One he practiced on Dominique. Her abduction represents the Rosetta Stone by which we can imagine what Haley's last hours on earth were like. Like Haley, Cal Emmons took Dominique Bright to a body of water, just one mile away from the motel where he'd been torturing her. Just like Haley. Perhaps Haley woke up face down in the water like Dominique did, her hair cut from her head. A knee in her back. If it weren't for the Kinseys, God bless them, Dominique wouldn't be alive today. She wouldn't be able to take back her power and help give Haley a voice. We know Cal Emmons is a liar. He lied to you when he tried to imply anyone else committed these crimes. You don't have to guess.

"Dalton Shepherd is another victim of Cal Emmons. It doesn't matter if he drove that Mercury Sable. You know why? Because Dominique Bright's attack took place over four years ago. Dalton Shepherd didn't even live in Waynetown four years ago. He didn't know Cal Emmons. He didn't work for him. He had absolutely nothing to do with what happened to Dominique Bright and he had nothing to do with Haley Chambers. The defendant thinks you can be manipulated. That you're gullible. That he's in control. He isn't. You know the truth. There is no doubt.

"When Cal Emmons was done torturing Haley Chambers, just like Dominique Bright before her, he tied her back up and threw her in that car. He took Haley two miles away to a grave he may have dug in advance. That's one thing we don't know. But we know he must have scouted that location well before burying Haley's body there. Detective Lance told you they found two other identical holes dug near where Haley was found. He would have killed again. He was waiting. Stalking.

"Cal Emmons has tried to frame at least two other people for this heinous crime. In that, Haley wasn't his only victim. After he saw Haley's boyfriend on the news, he planted evidence outside his house, hoping to throw the police off his trail. And we already know he's tried to frame Dalton Shepherd. He's lying to you. You see the evidence, you know the truth.

"Listen to Haley, she's told you all you need to know. So has Dominique. With their bodies, their blood, their voices, they have told you what happened to them. They have pointed the finger at the monster who hurt them. That monster is Calvin Emmons. There is no doubt. I trust you'll do the right thing. Thank you."

When I turned to leave the lectern, I nearly walked right into Peter Reilly. He stood behind me, waiting like some gargoyle. I found it odd. It dawned on me later he may have done it to get away from the furious whispers of his client.

"You may proceed, Mr. Reilly," Judge Saul said, observing the whole bizarre exchange. As I took my seat at the table, Hojo gave me a quick thumbs-up. I looked behind me, searching the room for Dominique Bright. She was there, way in the back. Beside her sat Cindy Chambers, her face made of stone. I hoped I did right by them. I hoped I was enough.

"Members of the jury," Reilly started. "The only thing Cal Emmons is guilty of is trusting the wrong people. He's been naïve. But he's also been cocky and arrogant. It never occurred to him that anyone would believe he committed this awful crime. And you'll notice I said crime. Not crimes. I want to be clear on something. Cal Emmons has not been charged with anything in conjunction with Dominique Bright. The Grace County sheriffs have been privy to the same information you have. They know what's going on here today. If they thought Cal was guilty of attacking that girl, they would have charged him. They haven't. I'll put to you that it's because they know they have no case. So, don't let Ms. Brent fool you. She was eloquent today. She tells a wonderful story. But it's based on a foundation made of quicksand.

"The prosecution wants you to focus on what she claims you should know. She has twisted the facts and the science to support her theory of the case. The problem is, she has failed to answer one of the fundamental questions in this case.

"Where's the proof?

"She has proved Haley Chambers was injured. Was it torture? We don't know. We don't know if she consented to the sex play she engaged in. We know none of those injuries were fatal. We know she didn't die in Cal Emmons's barn. We know Cal Emmons's DNA was never found in that barn. No semen. No blood. No sweat. Not even any hair belonging to Cal was found on Haley's body.

"You know why? Because he rarely went in it. He told you that. The lack of physical evidence bears that out.

"What we do know? What Linc Maguire admitted. What the cops' own crime scene photos showed you ... the keys to that barn and the Mercury Sable were kept in a common area. Many people had access to it, including Dalton Shepherd.

"We know Shepherd was in that car. You sat here and watched what happened when he was questioned about all of it. Why haven't the cops more thoroughly questioned him? Why haven't they charged him? Because Detective Brody Lance has blinders on. That is criminal in and of itself. I can assure you, this isn't over. Not by a long shot.

"The law requires you to return a verdict of not guilty if you find reasonable doubt that the defendant committed the crime. There is a mountain of doubt in this case. There are fundamental, unanswered questions. Corners were cut. Assumptions were made. And now Cal Emmons's life hangs in the balance. It's in your hands. Think about what it would mean if you get this wrong. It's not just Cal Emmons's life that's at stake."

Reilly turned away from the lectern. He took a step, then turned back, grabbing the microphone.

"Think about that," he said, almost shouting it. "I know you'll do what's right. You'll render the only verdict you can based on the evidence presented and what the police and the prosecution have failed to answer. You must find Cal Emmons not guilty and give him back his life. Thank you."

I took my last moments of rebuttal to remind the jury of the science. But they were tired. Eager. And it was time to give them control of the case.

Judge Saul efficiently delivered the jury instructions. At five o'clock on the dot, the twelve members of the jury filed out of the courtroom. Now all I could do was wait.

38

By Tuesday afternoon, the third full day of deliberations, we still had no verdict. Lawyers exist in an anxiety-filled limbo during this time. You try not to read into the ticking minutes of the clock. Some say the longer a jury takes, the more likely they'll come back with a guilty verdict. In the hundreds of cases I've tried, that isn't true. As I finished packing up the last of my war room boxes, Kenya found me.

"Will comes back this weekend?" she asked. I jumped at her voice, not expecting her.

"Yeah," I said. "They're flying into Toledo Sunday morning. He's anxious to get back to school."

"That's good," Kenya said. "You holding up okay?"

"I'm trying. This case was ... I don't know. Some of them sink into you more than others. And there are more. You and I both know it."

She nodded. "That tri-county task force Sam's on has identified a dozen potential victims. Cold case murders and missing persons. They go back up to ten years."

I rubbed my forehead. It was hard to think about all of that now. "How many will be ours?"

"Maybe two victims will fall under the jurisdiction of Maumee County. But we can't get ahead of ourselves. The cops need to make probable cause. They're not there yet."

"I feel like I'll never get out from under Cal Emmons." I sighed.

"Well, for what it's worth, you were at the top of your game, Mara. I mean that. It'll be enough."

As she said it, Adam moved into the doorway beside her. Kenya pushed herself off the doorframe from the shoulder. I thought about asking her to stay. But she was already halfway down the hall as Adam stepped in. He started to close the door.

"Leave that," I said. I held a file in front of me. Adam seemed startled, but slowly took his hand off the doorknob.

"Kenya's right," he said. "It was a treasure to watch you in action. I'm going to miss my time here. I'll be finishing out the week, but then I need to focus on studying for exams."

"Good choice," I said. "And thank you for your help with this case. You're a good brief writer, Adam. That's hard to find."

He came further into the room. When I saw him getting ready to invade my personal space again, I lifted my file folder higher, as if it were a shield. The trial had occupied all my waking thoughts. I had yet to bring Jason's concerns to anyone else's attention. I wasn't even sure I ever would. Inappropriate as Adam's behavior was toward me, Jason's actions had been a clear invasion of this man's privacy.

"Mara," he said, reading my gesture. "I just told you. I'm leaving. I won't be your intern anymore. Look, I know it was wrong to act on this while we're still in the same office and all …"

"No," I said. "Adam, you're not seeing this clearly. There is no we. I'm not interested in you in that way. Not now. Not ever. To be honest, I don't even feel comfortable being alone in a room with you. I'm going to step out now."

Something changed in his face. Anger flashed in his eyes. He reached for me. I stepped out of his grasp.

"Stop it," I said. "Your actions have been inappropriate on every level."

"You pulled me off this case," he said. "Don't stand there and pretend you didn't want me to kiss you."

Alarm bells clanged in my head. This was way worse than I realized. I should have asked Kenya to stay. I should have documented everything days ago. Maybe I should have listened to Jason.

"I most certainly did not," I said. "You're completely out of line, Adam."

I turned for the door and he lunged for me, grabbing my arm. Adrenaline pumped through me.

"We're great together," he said. "There's no way you could have handled this case without me. I want to work with you again. I'm applying for a position here after I pass the bar."

"Let go of me," I said, keeping my voice cool. He did.

"Oh," Adam said. "I get it. Are you planning on making this difficult for me? If you stand in the way of my ambitions ..."

"Stop right there," I said. "I am not having another word with you without either Kenya or someone from HR present."

Adam smiled. "Sure," he said. "If that's what you need."

I didn't like the tone of his voice or the look he gave me. How in the world could this guy have misread the situation so badly? Or how had I?

Luckily, Kenya was heading back down the hallway. She wasn't alone. Sam Cruz and Brody Lance were with her. Sam must have read something in my face. He gave Adam a look that could melt glass.

"We thought you could use some dinner," Kenya said. "I found these two crawling out of their skin across the street. None of us are doing ourselves any good waiting around here."

"I'll get my coat," Adam said.

"Sorry," Sam said abruptly. "I think you better head on home."

He offered no further explanation. No diplomatic excuse for freezing Adam out. It was just pure instinct. Or perhaps Kenya said something. Either way, I was grateful for the respite and the company. I grabbed my own coat off the chair and fell into step behind Sam and the others, leaving Adam alone in the conference room.

39

Sam found a table for us in the back at the Blue Pony. Though I made it a point not to drink during the work week, I couldn't turn Lance down when he offered to pick up the first round. I asked for a white wine. While he and Sam headed to the bar, Kenya cornered me.

"How big of a problem is Adam Skinner?" she asked.

"Bigger than I thought," I answered honestly. "He made a pass at me a while ago."

"When?" she asked.

"Last week. In my office."

Kenya sat back hard. "Let me guess. The day Jason showed up. He saw?"

"He saw," I said, sipping my water.

"Son of a ... I should have guessed. I thought the testosterone levels in the office seemed a little high that day. So that's why you benched Adam from the trial?"

"I didn't bench him," I said. "I had him doing legal research and brought Hojo into the courtroom. I'm sorry. I've handled this badly. I just didn't want the distraction of it while I was still in trial. Now it's gotten a little out of hand. Adam seems to be having delusions about things. He also said he plans on putting in for a position here when he passes the bar."

"Not on my watch," she said. "Mara, I'm sorry. I should have read the situation better. I should have known Adam was too good to be true."

"Well, I think we need to get HR involved. Just before the three of you showed up, he made a bit of a veiled threat that he'd take it personally if I got in the way of that."

"Great," Kenya said. "Mara, are you okay? Did he hurt you? Your safety is the only thing I care about. Let that jackass bring whatever heat he thinks he can. I've got your back."

"Thanks," I said. Just then, Cruz and Lance arrived with our drinks. That glass of wine never looked better. I took a healthy sip as Lance slid in beside me and Cruz across from me.

"So," I said. "What's the word from the Grace County sheriff's department? Why aren't I getting cc'd on new charges in the Dominique Bright case?"

Sam ran a ring around his rocks glass. He'd gone with a gin and tonic. "They're hedging their bets. Waiting to see what happens with your jury."

"Any word on that?" Lance asked.

"Nothing. They haven't even asked to have any of the evidence brought back. No questions for the judge. I don't know what to make of it and am trying hard not to let my imagination run wild."

"It is what it is, at this point," Sam said. "You've done your job."

"A little optimism," Kenya said. "We can cry in our beer tonight, but tomorrow morning, it's full steam ahead prepping for the penalty phase. Because there *will* be a penalty phase."

I clinked glasses with her, then with Cruz and Lance. I didn't want to jinx anything, so I didn't verbally agree.

We changed the subject. Lance had another murder case come down. A drug deal gone wrong on the other side of town. Though there were eyewitnesses, Kenya still wanted to make sure he kept me in the loop as he secured an arrest warrant.

As the conversation veered to lighter topics, I heard a commotion at the bar. The four of us turned at the same time.

"Is that ..." Kenya started.

The woman's back was turned. She wore a halter top and denim shorts too light for the weather. She teetered on a pair of heels as her companion tried to grab her arm.

"I saw you!" she shouted, slurring her words.

"Crap," Kenya muttered. "That's Dominique."

"It's worse than that," I said. "That's Vinny Meyer she's with. Her abusive supposed-to-be ex."

"Mara," Sam said. "He's got a felony record. She's violating her probation just being around him."

"I don't suppose public intoxication will go over well either. I was afraid of this. She was rock solid on the stand, but dredging all that up could set her back. She was supposed to be staying put in the rental house Nicole Silvers got her. If Vinny followed her here ..."

"Crazy bitch!" Vinny shouted. The four of us rose together and descended on the scene.

"Dominique," I said. "Why don't you let me give you a ride?"

She wrenched her arm out of Vinny's grasp. "He thinks I don't know what he does. You can't treat me like that. I'm a human being!"

"You're a lunatic," Vinny shot back.

"What are you doing in town?" I said to Vinny. "You belong back in Ransom."

"She called me!" he said. "Begged me to come get her. Yeah. Please. Take her out of here. Take her far away from me. I'll get a restraining order next time. I'll call her probation officer. You guys think she's some put-upon saint. Big hero up there on the stand. She's a liar. She's crazy. She's trying to ruin my life."

"You're the liar!" Dominique shouted. "I've done everything for you. Everything!"

"Sure, baby." Vinny laughed. "You keep on telling yourself that."

He grabbed Dominique cruelly by the arm and brought her into him. "I know what *you* really are, you little psycho. Don't you ever forget that. You're mine to take, and you're mine to throw away!"

Sam jerked him back hard, separating Vinny from Dominique. He pushed him against the wall. "Time for you to get the hell out of here. I don't want to see you near this girl or anywhere in Maumee County ever again. You got me?"

Sam took his badge out and shoved it in Vinny's face hard enough to leave an impression on his forehead.

Sam glanced at me. He knew my mind and I knew his. He'd handle Vinny. I'd make sure Dominique made it out of here safely.

She staggered, but came willingly when I led her toward the door. Lance took a twenty out of his pocket and laid it on the bar to pay for Dominique's tab.

I got Dominique to my car and strapped her in. Once behind the wheel, I made a quick call to Nicole Silvers and explained the situation.

"Thank you," I said after Nicole agreed to meet me at the Silver Angel House. They'd been standing ready for Dominique all week.

"He lies to me," Dominique said as we drove away. "Cheats on me right in front of me and thinks I don't know. What's wrong with me, Mara? Why doesn't anyone love me?"

"They do," I said. "You have so many people in your life rooting for you. This has just been a stressful week for everyone. Is that why you called him?"

"Sometimes I think he's right. Nobody knows me like Vinny does. He's such a jerk. I know that. But he knows things. He's taken care of me."

"You deserve better, Dominique," I said.

She shook her head. "I deserve what happens to me."

She said that a lot. It broke my heart. "You deserve better," I repeated.

She listened. More importantly, I listened. She cried a bit. I let her. After a few minutes, I pulled into the Angels' parking lot and cut the engine. I didn't want her to be alone tonight. Nicole or one of the other volunteers could drive her home in the morning.

Dominique wiped her eyes. "Thanks," she said. "I know I'm going to regret all of this come morning. I know I shouldn't let Vinny get under my skin. I shouldn't be thinking of him at all. It's just ... I didn't want to be alone tonight."

"You won't be," I said. "There's a place here for you with Nicole and the others for as long as you need it. We want to help you. Accept it. I know it's hard."

Dominique looked at me. Her tears ripped me apart.

"They have to put him away, don't they?" she asked. "Emmons has to pay for what he did."

It gutted me not to be able to give her the answer she wanted. If that jury came back with an acquittal, I knew Dominique's case against him was so much weaker. And she'd have to get up there and go through this all over again.

She took my silence as an answer and slid out of the car. It heartened me a bit to see Dominique let Nicole embrace her. For now, she was safe and I'd done all I could.

I'd done all I could. I let that be my mantra as I slipped under the covers an hour later. Dominique's tears haunted my dreams though. I saw the sky wavering above me as hands held me beneath the water. Strong, hairy hands. My dream self tried to kick him away. Cal Emmons's hands, but he had Adam Skinner's eyes.

I startled awake, thinking I'd slept through my alarm. I hadn't. It was my phone ringing. Reaching for it, I knocked it to the floor. Swearing, I found it under the bed and brought it to my ear. The clock read just past eight a.m. Kenya was calling.

"Get up," she said. "Get dressed. We have a verdict."

40

I made it into the courtroom before anyone else. Even before Judge Saul's bailiff. It gave me an eerie moment of complete silence save for the constant hum of the courthouse ventilation system. I stared at the empty jury box. When I closed my eyes, I could see all twelve of them in their respective seats. We had a white-haired, seventy-year-old male sitting in the front. He took the most notes out of the bunch. Beside him sat a thin, African-American woman who always came to court in a solid-colored dress and the same set of large, two-strand pearls.

They listened. They absorbed. Of all the jurors I'd presented cases to, this one had stayed the most engaged. Would it matter? Had I done enough?

"They're coming," Kenya said as she entered the courtroom. Hojo was right behind her. She deferred to him, letting him take his seat at the table with me while she sat on the bench behind us.

Reilly walked in, his face flushed, but his gait confident. He'd made a ton of careless mistakes during this trial. Enough that I knew Emmons would argue ineffective assistance of counsel in his first appeal should the verdict go my way. But ultimately, Reilly had presented at least the basics of the defense I would have were I in his shoes. The lack of Emmons's DNA could be troubling to a layperson. And it was just the kind of thing a misguided jury could latch on to if they were looking for a reason to acquit.

Emmons came in next with his deputies at his side. They uncuffed him as he stood at the defense table. He caught my eye. The urge to avert my gaze from his pulled at me. I didn't. I stared him down. He smiled.

"Eyes on your own paper, Emmons," one of the deputies said when he saw what was going on.

Reilly was too busy shuffling through notes to pay much attention.

The rest of the spectators filed in. There was press. At least a dozen deputies, some on duty, some in plain clothes. Lance walked in last flanking Cindy and Rob Chambers along with her twin boys. They'd aged in the last week and a half. That certain wide-eyed look all fifteen-year-olds have hardened into grim wisdom, a haunted outlook that would stay with them until they went to their own graves. It would color the kind of fathers they might become. The kind of husbands. I hoped they would weather it. I hoped it wouldn't break them forever.

"All rise!" Judge Saul's bailiff came through her chamber door. She was right behind him, robe flying.

I didn't hear the preliminaries as the clerk and recorder took their seats. I barely heard the jury as they filed in. None of them looked at Cal. None of them looked at me.

I turned, searching for the other soul I hoped wouldn't break forever.

"Where's Dominique?" I whispered to Kenya. She looked behind her as well.

"Not sure," she said. "Nicole took her home early this morning. She said she wasn't sure Dominique wanted to come."

I didn't see Nicole either, but a handful of volunteers with the Silver Angels stayed with Cindy's family. I had no doubt they would text Nicole the second we knew anything. There was one other person missing. I caught Lance's eye and mouthed, "Where's Sam?"

He had enough time to give me a quick shrug before the judge began.

"Members of the jury," she said. "Have you reached your verdict?"

The white-haired juror in the front stood up. So they'd elected him foreman. "We have," he said.

The bailiff took a piece of paper from him and walked it over to Judge Saul. She opened it. Read it. She'd done this so many times, she knew how not to betray anything with her face. She handed the paper to her clerk.

A moment. An eternity. The court reporter poised her quick fingers over her keyboard as if she were a pianist about to begin a concerto. She just needed the conductor to raise his baton.

"The state of Ohio versus Calvin Louis Emmons. On count one of the complaint in the above-entitled matter, first degree murder ... we find the defendant, guilty."

Thunder clapped through me. Hojo put an arm around me. I felt so brittle, like he could crack my spine.

There were other charges. Four more in all. Kidnapping. Sexual assault. Abuse of a corpse. Obstruction of justice. All with aggravating circumstances. One by one, the verdict came down.

Guilty. Guilty. Guilty. Guilty.

Behind me, I heard the sobs of both Valerie Emmons and Cindy Chambers.

"It's over," Hojo whispered. "You did it."

But this didn't feel like a victory. It felt like a nightmare. A waste. It wouldn't bring Haley back. It wouldn't heal Dominique's wounds. But no other young girl would ever have to suffer under the hands of Cal Emmons again.

There were congratulations. Hugs. Slowly, as the jury's verdict finally sank in, I felt it.

Relief.

It took close to an hour before I could wind my way back to my office. I felt numb. Exhausted. I just wanted to curl up with a glass of wine and wait for Will to come home. When he did, we'd watch movies. He was trying to indoctrinate me into the Marvel Universe. Sunday night, Kat promised to cook us all dinner. She was bringing the woman she'd been seeing to the house to get to know Will. It was getting serious. Her name was Bree and I'd only met her once for a few minutes as she picked Kat up for a date.

I got a lot of pats on the back as I walked down the hall. Kenya was waiting in the conference room already. She'd given a brief statement to the assembled press. Justice was served. We were satisfied with the outcome. But there was still work to be done. The sentencing phase of this trial would begin in four weeks. We would now ask the jury to give Cal Emmons the death penalty.

"You were great, Mara," Brody Lance said. He had tears in his eyes. It touched me. I had no words. Instead, I drew Lance into a hug. He sank against me and I felt a little of the weight of this case lifting from him. I'd been so focused on my own job, I hadn't bothered to notice the toll it was taking on him.

"We did it," I said. "I couldn't have gotten this verdict without you."

"I want it to feel better," he said.

"Me too." I smiled.

I don't know how long we stood there. It felt late. Something happened. The room started to clear out. It was just me, Lance, Hojo, and Kenya. I looked up and Sam stood in the doorway.

No.

The word just thundered in my head. There was something wrong. His suit was a little rumpled. He had mud on his shoes.

"Dominique," I whispered, praying to God nothing had happened to her. But she'd gone radio silent since the verdict.

"No," he said. "But they found the remains of another girl last night. Another young girl. She went missing a few months ago, after Haley, but before we took Emmons into custody. She ... she fits the profile. Her injuries are consistent with his M.O. We think ..."

"No," I said, sinking into the nearest chair. "Not again."

41

"Her name was Talia Brewer," Sam said. Ahead of us, I could see the trucks set up. The yellow crime scene tape cordoning off a hiking trail entering the thickest part of the woods. We were on state hunting grounds, just beyond the borders of Waynetown's only Metropark.

"You're sure?" I asked.

"She's wearing jewelry that matches the description her mother reported to the police," he said. Sam parked the car at the edge of the crime scene. B.C.I. was still processing it. I recognized Wayne Pham's blue Lincoln parked alongside their van. They'd rolled an ambulance up on the north side of the park.

Wayne walked out into the clearing as Sam and I exited his vehicle. Wayne saw us approach and gave me a grim look. Detective Gus Ritter came out just behind him. I was glad to see him. I knew Lance was also on his way, but Ritter would take the lead on this one. Plenty of work to go around.

"What do we know, guys?" Sam asked.

"She's been dead for a while," Wayne said. "I've got a lot of work to do back at the morgue, but I'd say this girl's been dead for at least six months. When was she reported missing?"

"About that long," Gus answered. "She and her mother have been estranged for a while but she stopped showing up for work at a carry-out in Perrysburg. Last time anyone saw her was April 30th."

"Almost a full month after Haley went missing," I said.

"A couple of weeks after Emmons did," Sam said.

Fury heated my blood. "Dammit, Sam. This shouldn't have happened. I told Lance to keep eyes on that man."

"Mara," Gus said. "He wasn't under arrest then."

"But he knew he was under suspicion. We don't know where he was staying for weeks while he posted those ridiculous videos on the internet. God. He panicked. She was one last kill before the walls closed in."

"Maybe," Sam said. "Wayne, what can you tell us?"

Dr. Pham raised a brow. "She's pretty badly decomposed. Six months in a shallow grave and the weather's been mild after a pretty hot summer. There's an area on her chest that could be a burn."

"A cigar burn," I whispered.

"Maybe," Pham repeated. "I'll be honest, it's not likely I'm going to be able to give you anything conclusive on that. But ... there are a couple of injuries on visual inspection that *are* pretty conclusive. Her thumbs are broken. Smashed at the base, both of them. And her hair's been chopped off. Probably with a dull knife. She was found buried head first."

My legs trembled. Late October and only fifty degrees, but I was sweating. I unbuttoned my collar.

"It was Emmons," I said. "Those details never made it into the public domain. No one knows that besides the people involved in this case. Sam ..."

"I know," he said. "Dammit. I know. But let's not get ahead of ourselves. We're gonna do this step by step."

Just then, Pham's crew came out carrying a body bag. I walked toward them.

"Mara," Sam said.

"I want to see her," I whispered. "I need to."

There would be another mother to console. Another family shattered.

"No!" Sam said.

"I'll see her anyway," I said. "This will be my case just like Haley."

I walked over to the ambulance, waiting for the crew to join me. They did, gingerly lifting Talia Brewer's body into the back of it. Wayne Pham came to my side. He still wore his purple latex gloves. Slowly, he pulled back the zipper. He only showed me what was left of her face. Bones, mostly. The rest barely looked human. But she had thick, blonde hair. It curled at the root. As Wayne said, the ends were jagged and uneven where it had been cut off.

"That's enough," Sam said, putting a hand on my back. "It's time for you to go home."

"I have some phone calls to make," I said. "It's going to be a long night. Clancy's going to need to hold a press conference with Kenya in the morning. She'll want to be briefed."

"All that can wait," Sam said.

I smiled. "It can't. It's my job."

"Then at least let me drive you back to the office and buy you a cup of coffee."

"Better make it a pot," I said. As I slid into the passenger seat, my phone started to blow up. Steeling myself, I looked at the caller IDs.

"Son of a ..." I started.

"What?" Sam said as he climbed behind the wheel. I turned my phone screen toward him so he could see what I saw. My phone was still ringing and the caller's name showed up in all caps.

PETER REILLY.

42

"He just wants to talk," I said early the next week as we assembled in my office once again.

"No!" The chorus of three keyed-up male voices made the room shake. Sam, Gus Ritter, and Brody Lance crowded around my desk, none of them choosing to sit.

"I don't like it," Sam said. "Reilly's playing games. Emmons is playing Reilly."

"I agree with you," I said. "But we've got another dead girl out there with injuries fitting Emmons's M.O. She was his last, but we know she wasn't his first. And we also know the odds of there having been no other victims in the four-year span from Dominique to Haley are pretty slim. You said you've got at least a dozen cold cases that might fit Emmons's kill profile. Was Talia one of them?"

"Not until now," Sam answered.

"So it's thirteen girls," I said. "If Emmons is willing to talk now ..."

"This isn't just some crisis of conscience," Lance said. "That's the real reason I wanted to meet with you." Lance's glum expression wasn't helping my mood. He'd called me an hour ago and told me to clear my schedule. No small feat as I'd been doing that for six weeks in preparation for the Emmons trial. I had a pile of backlogged cases and phone calls to return.

"I got a call this morning from Valerie Emmons's lawyer," he said.

"What lawyer?" I asked.

Ritter and Lance kept looking at each other, their postures uneasy.

"What lawyer?" I asked again.

"She wants to change her statement," Lance said.

My head reeled. "To what?"

"The lawyer wasn't specific. Threw out a lot of hypotheticals. But I think she's going to say she lied about what she saw the night Haley disappeared. Though he didn't use the word lie. It was more like, upon further reflection and soul searching, she's remembering things with new clarity. Now that the trauma of the trial is over."

Lance couldn't hide the sarcasm in his voice.

"This can't be real," I said. "Let me guess, she saw Cal going in and out of the barn that night."

"Yeah," Lance answered. But there was a hesitancy in the way he said it that told me there was more to it. I felt a shot of ice through my veins.

"My God," I said. "She heard something. You're telling me she heard something?"

"The lawyer, she was cagey as hell," Gus offered.

"She's fishing," I said. "Val Emmons probably isn't going to say another word without an immunity deal."

Kenya came in. By the look on her face, I could tell she was already privy to these new developments. In the end, any further immunity deals would have to be her call.

"So Reilly was completely bullshitting me," I said. "Emmons probably already knows his wife's about to go south on him."

"She's scared," Sam offered. "Now that the dust has settled. I think she wants to make sure he never gets out of prison."

"Unbelievable," I said. "We could have protected her. I told her that when I interviewed her six months ago. So did you, Lance."

"Mara," Kenya said. "We know what kind of man Cal Emmons is now. You have to assume that Valerie Emmons did too. Maybe not the full scope of it. But she was afraid of him. If this thing hadn't gone how it did ... I'd be livid. But we got the conviction. Cal's not going anywhere. Like it or not, Valerie might know some things that could help in the Brewer case or ... others."

"Which is why I think you should tell Peter Reilly to go screw himself. No deals. Emmons doesn't get an audience with you," Sam said.

"It's not that easy," I said. "We don't know how credible Valerie will be. It's going to take a long time to unsnarl whatever new statement she's willing to give. Kenya, are you leaning towards an immunity deal for her?"

"Yeah," Kenya said. "I think we have to. If she has credible info regarding Haley, it'll only bolster your case during the sentencing phase. Saul and the jury won't be inclined to give him any leniency. This thing isn't quite over. And maybe she has something to say about Dominique's case too. If we could put that to rest without putting her through another trial. Not to mention Talia Brewer's family."

"It's the right call," I said, reluctantly. Though I wondered if we could have saved Haley's family and Dominique from the re-traumatization of trial if Valerie Emmons had come forward sooner. Reilly might have pushed harder for a plea deal.

"Good," Kenya said. "I'll talk to Valerie's lawyer and set it up."

"And I'll call Reilly and set up the interview with Emmons."

"No!" my male chorus chimed in again.

"If it can spare the Brewer family from going through what Cindy Chambers had to, it's worth it," I said.

"You'll agree to nothing," Kenya said. "Odds are Emmons is just trying to jerk all of us along. He had his people lean pretty hard into that railroader nonsense. He's still got online support. Those kooks tend to get louder when it gets closer to execution day."

"I know," I said. "I'll be careful. And I'll assume everything he tells me is a lie."

"He's gotta give us Talia Brewer and Dominique," Ritter said. "Period. Or no deals of any kind."

"We're clear," I said.

"And Gus is in the room," Sam said. I had to give Brody Lance credit. He was the first to agree.

"All right," I said. I picked up my desk phone and buzzed Caro. She was waiting for the call.

"Can you call Peter Reilly and tell him I'll meet with Cal Emmons?"

"Already on it," Caro said. "Just waiting for the go-ahead. I've arranged for you to see Emmons first thing in the morning."

I thanked her, hung up the phone, and prayed I wasn't making a huge mistake.

43

I've visited criminals in jail hundreds of times. I've even sat across from a few serial killers. But I'd never felt cold fear like I did when they brought Calvin Emmons into the room to sit across from me.

I couldn't shake the image of that room in Emmons's barn. The memory of the badly decomposed body of Talia Brewer floated before my eyes. And as always, there was the terror I still saw in Dominique's eyes. Terror that would never leave her. Terror that had broken her spirit and ruined so much of her life. She was making a fresh start for herself here in Waynetown. She was building a new support system.

Ritter, Cruz, and Lance sat behind the one-way glass, listening to our every word. A beefy deputy stood at the doorway, arms crossed, ready to tackle Emmons if he so much as blinked too fast. He sat in chains. His eyes and words were the only weapons he had against me.

Today, my weapons were far bigger.

"I want it on the record that my client is speaking to you freely and in part against my advice," Peter Reilly said. Just before I sat down, Emmons told him he'd do all the talking.

"We're not in court, Reilly," I said. "Your client isn't under oath. Yet."

"You're off the hook, Peter," Emmons said. He didn't break my gaze.

"I'm a busy woman, Cal," I said, taking control of the interview. "So I'm going to lay this out. Here's what I'm interested in. Give me the names of your other victims. And an admission. Tell me what happened with Dominique Bright."

"That's not in the scope of what I called your office about," Reilly said. "We're not here to talk about Dominique Bright."

"Then we're done," I said. I grabbed my briefcase and got up.

"Wait," Cal said. I turned back toward him.

"Cal!" Reilly shouted.

"Enough out of you," Cal said. "I said that before. You don't listen."

"Then I quit," Reilly said.

"No, you don't." Emmons and I spoke in unison.

"Sit down, Reilly," I said. "You're in this. I'm not talking to this man without his lawyer present. Whether you like it or not, that's still you. Now, you either tell me what happened with Dominique, or I'm walking out."

"You're so sure," Cal said, narrowing his eyes. "You think that girl is some tragic victim. Trust me. She's a world-class liar. Ask Vinny Meyer. She's made his life miserable."

"You made mistakes with her," I said, undeterred. "You like control. You wanted to spend more time with her. But it just happened, is that right? Your perfect victim that just fell out of the sky. Or walked alone down the road."

"She was built for it," Emmons hissed. "She asked me to pay her for it. Did she tell you that?"

"She was fighting for her life," I said.

"No," Cal said, shaking his head. His bitter expression cut through me. "No. Not that girl. She was a player. Smarter than you think she is. A thousand for the night, she wanted."

"Was that before or after you hit her with your car?" I asked. "Before or after you broke her thumbs, Cal?"

"After!" he shouted, lunging forward. I backed up and ran smack into the hulking deputy.

Cal laughed. I put a hand up, signaling to the deputy that I was okay. I looked at the glass and gave a slow nod, letting Sam and the others know too. Then, I sat back down across from Cal Emmons.

"So we're clear," I said. "Tell me how you met Dominique Bright."

"You're not that smart," Cal said. "She was smarter."

I pulled a two-page document out of my briefcase and set it on the table between us. I had a second copy and I handed that one to Reilly.

"Your wife turned on you, Cal," I said. "She remembers you running in and out of your barn on the night of April 2nd. She says she heard noises. She thought it was a barn cat. Screaming. And she says she saw you drive your Sable up to the barn that evening. She knows because she set a timer. So she could pull your dinner out of the oven. And she's not done talking. She's got some things to say about the summer of Dominique Bright's abduction."

No reaction. Cal didn't even look at the paper. Reilly did.

"I need a minute with my client," he said. "When did you get this?"

"Late last night," I answered. "Valerie's lawyer's name is written on the bottom. Feel free to reach out to her. For full immunity, Valerie has agreed to testify again at your sentencing."

"She can't do that," Cal said. "There's marital privilege."

"She's waived it as part of her deal," I said. "You know I'm recommending the death penalty. It might take years. Who knows, maybe you'll get some traction with your ineffective assistance of counsel argument. But eventually. They'll put a needle in your arm, Cal. You won't make it into the next decade."

"You gonna be the last sweet face I see, sweetheart?" he said.

"Yes!" I leaned forward, going almost nose to nose with him. "You can count on that."

He held my stare. Then, I saw it. That flicker of terror that I knew haunted him when he was alone in his cell.

"Tell me what you did to Dominique," I said. "And maybe you can live."

"She's not an angel," he said, spitting out the last word. It was a dig at the Silver Angels who had closed ranks around her. "None of them are. They all get what they deserve."

"No," I said. "She's not without sin. I want a full admission."

"That is not something I'm comfortable signing off on," Reilly said.

"Your client can only be lethally injected once, Reilly," I said.

"We want a reduced charge and sentence," Reilly said. "Second degree murder. What happened to Haley Chambers was an accident. You recommend the possibility of parole."

"Life without parole," I said. "First degree murder stays. You plead guilty in Dominique's case. I have an agreement from the Grace County prosecutor. No death penalty there either. But all of this is contingent on the names of any other victims and where they're buried."

Cal Emmons had found his smile again. "She drives a hard bargain. Look at you. Tough lawyer woman. Ivy league? Expensive shoes. Designer bag. No ring on her finger. Can't keep her man, is what I read."

"You think you're the first psychopath who's ever tried to get under my skin? You're nothing, Cal. Less than nothing. When I leave this room, I won't even remember what you look like."

"She lies," Cal said. "I know what you see when you close your eyes. Admit it. You're curious. What you saw in my barn stirred you up."

I pulled a blank legal pad out of my briefcase and a pen. I slid it across the table to Cal.

"Names," I said. "I want your other victims. All of them. If you don't remember their names or never knew them, then you tell me dates, descriptions. You tell me where. You give me the location of their bodies."

"They knew she was a liar too," Cal said. "They knew Dominique would fold on the stand. She lies more than she tells the truth."

"She didn't fold though, did she?" I asked. "She looked right at you and called you out for what you really are. She's going to sleep in her own bed tonight. Free. Alive. And knowing you'll never see a world without bars in front of them again."

A beat passed. Then another, as Cal got close enough to breathe on me.

"I've heard enough," I said. "I'm through with games. I'll see you both in court for your sentencing. You can try your act on Judge Saul or the jury again. Good luck though. You'll need it. Should I send your love to your wife, Cal?"

The only answer he gave was the flaring of his nostrils. I rose. I turned my back on him. As I took my steps toward the door, I heard him slide the legal pad across the table.

"Cal," Reilly said.

"No needle," Cal said. I lifted my chin and turned around.

"For Dominique," I said. "The whole story. An unequivocal admission. And all the other names and locations."

He started to write. I grabbed the handle of my briefcase. I heard a shuffling sound coming from the other room. I could only guess at the reaction from Sam, Gus, and Brody.

It took Cal nearly an hour to write what I asked. I took a chair away from the table and waited. Twice, he stopped to shake out the cramps in his fingers. He wrote in slanted, looping cursive.

When he finished, he turned the pad toward me. Reilly tried to grab it but Cal pushed his hand away.

"Cal," he said. "You need to let me review ..."

"No needle," Cal said, speaking only to me.

I reached for the pad. Cal moved with catlike quickness, grabbing my wrist. The deputy moved forward and the door behind him flew open. Sam burst in first.

I jerked my arm away and picked up the pad. I gestured to Sam to stand down. Cal Emmons would get no more answers from me until I saw what he'd written. I started to read. It was all there. He'd been in Grace County that summer picking up parts. He detailed how he spotted Dominique walking alone along Jefferson Highway, almost staggering from exhaustion and the heat. The crunching sound as he hit her with his front bumper and knocked her into a ditch.

He'd used a hammer to break her thumbs before she came to. So she couldn't wriggle out of her duct tape bindings. So she couldn't easily inflict any damage to his eyes or privates if he decided to take off the tape. The beating. The burning. All of it.

"No needle, Mara," he said. "That's our deal!"

I'd reached the final page on the pad. Three names. Three dates. Three locations.

Catherine Simpson, Swanton, Ohio. She's in a cornfield near a stream next to an industrial park.

He'd drawn a crude map.

Lindsay Goode. Her license said Gaylord, Michigan. Had her in the barn two years ago. Valerie knew. If she lies about it, promise me she goes to jail too. I put the girl in the ground at Gunderson's in the spruce field. Don't know why your dog didn't hit.

Eliza Mattis. Her license said Findlay, Ohio. Three years ago. Summertime. Buried her near the Maumee River behind the dump off Garfield Road.

This wasn't complete. There was no mention of Talia Brewer. I met his eyes again. He tried to read me. Could he? The corner of his mouth lifted in a smirk. He was playing me. He had to be playing me. I slid the pad of paper and pen back toward him.

"You went into hiding after we searched your barn," I said. "You knew you were going to be arrested. I want to know where you were. Write it down. Every single day between the day Haley disappeared and when you turned yourself in. Who did you stay with? Who did you talk to?"

He narrowed his eyes, confused. It was an act. It had to be. He knew I knew he was lying. He took the paper back and wrote something. He slid it back. He'd written an address in Sylvania, Ohio and the name of a cousin, Larry Emmons. We'd questioned him multiple times. This told me nothing new.

I rose. "This isn't complete. Emmons. Tell me about the last one or there's no deal."

A curious look came into Cal's face as my words sank in. Then, he gave me a wide smile and raised his shoulders in a shrug. Turning my back on him, I left him to the detectives and his lawyer.

44

Will had a rough night. It was my fault. I spent the last couple of days on edge after meeting with Cal Emmons. I hovered. Will's highly tuned sense of empathy had him feeding off my nerves. He woke up screaming from a nightmare at four a.m. He let me sit on the end of his bed for almost an hour, until he finally fell asleep.

It doesn't matter how old they are. When your child falls asleep, you can see the baby they used to be. Long lashes, lips in a pout. I missed the way he used to sink into me.

"I love you, buddy," I whispered. He was changing. He'd grown two inches in the last couple of months. His weight hadn't quite caught up and one lanky arm hung over the bed. I carefully lifted it and placed it under the covers. Though I hated leaving him, I knew my own night was over. There was work to be done.

Though I hadn't meant to wake her, Kat met me in the kitchen just as the coffee was ready to pour. I slid a cup to her.

"Did he calm down?" she asked.

"Yes," I said, sipping my coffee. I added a bit more cream to it to cool it down.

"Mara," she said. "There's something I've been meaning to talk to you about. Something I've noticed with him. The back and forth is stressing him out. He won't say it. And he loves D.C. He has a great time. It's just ..."

"It messes with his routine too much," I said. It was something I'd been worrying about too. "Have you mentioned that to Jason?"

She set her mug down. "I tried. My brother has a way of ..."

"Thinking he knows everything?" I finished for her.

Kat smiled. I made a point not to bad-mouth Jason in front of either Kat or Will. I hoped my comment hadn't crossed that line.

"Yeah," she said. "I think he's also aware. He just doesn't know what to do about it. It's easier pretending. And I think he'll adapt. I'm not saying that. But I think it's behind the issues he had at school earlier this year. Things Will could ignore or brush off, he's not as able to right now."

"Well, I appreciate you talking to me about it. I don't know the solution either. It's worth a conversation with his therapist. Jason and I swore we would always put Will's needs first. We'll find a way."

"I know," she said.

"Thank you for staying here this week," I said. "I'd hoped things would die down after the Emmons main trial. With this new victim and the sentencing hearing next week, things are just as crazy as they were before the verdict. In fact, if you don't mind, I'm going to head into the office as soon as I finish my coffee. Get a head start on the day so I can be home before Will gets out of school."

"He'd really like that," she said.

"I'll take you all out to eat. Is Bree free for dinner?"

Kat smiled. No, she blushed. I hid my own smile behind my mug.

"I'll ask her," she said.

"Will really likes her," I said. "He was talking up a blue streak the other day about what a big help she was with his latest Lego build. There was some issue he was having she helped him solve."

"Ugh," Kat said. "They were up there for hours the other day. At this rate, she's going to want to convert her spare bedroom into a Lego room. Will's created a monster."

I laughed. "Better Bree than me. So give her a call. How about we eat at Luigi's?"

"I'll make a reservation," Kat said. "Six work?"

"It's perfect," I said, sipping the last of my coffee. "So. Is she the one?"

Kat had adorable dimples when she smiled. Will and Jason had them too. Kat tried to hide them behind her own coffee mug. "Maybe. It's early. But yeah. I think so. I want you to get to know her better."

I slid off my chair and went to her, putting my arms around her. "I'd like that too. I'm really happy for you. We could use some joy around here. Things have been too dang dark."

"Bree'll be excited about tonight."

"Good," I said. "Me too." With the evening settled, I grabbed my briefcase and headed into town.

I didn't go straight to the office; instead, I stopped at the sheriff's department hoping to catch Gus and Brody. With the Talia Brewer murder still open, they'd been burning some midnight oil themselves.

I found them in the break room, an empty carafe of coffee between them.

"How are we doing?" I asked. Gus grumbled. But then, he always did.

"Pham just sent over his final autopsy report on her," Lance said. "It wasn't what we were hoping for."

"In what way?" I asked.

"A lot of his findings are inconclusive," Gus answered. "She's been in the ground for so long things aren't as clear-cut as they were on Haley and Dominique. Injuries to her thumbs are there. We've got tape residue and her hair cut off. There's a wound on what's left of her chest that could be a burn."

"He said it's most likely a burn," Lance offered. "And she had some sand and vegetation in her mouth. A case can be made that she died of drowning."

"They found her buried near a pond," I said.

"Look," Gus said. "The bottom line. If Emmons won't admit to killing her, we'll have a hard time even getting to probable cause."

"What did you get from her mother?" I asked.

"Layla Brewer hadn't seen her daughter in a couple of weeks," Brody said. "They weren't on great terms. The last time she saw her, she stopped over at Talia's apartment and they got into a fight. Talia was there with some new loser boyfriend. She gave a description. Dark hair. Brown eyes. Six one, six two, maybe. She said he came out of the bedroom bare-ass naked. She was able to describe a tattoo on his chest. Wings and a date. Twelve Eleven Sixty-Six. We're trying to track that down. Guy was drunk or high and Layla figured Talia was using again. That's the source of their estrangement."

"Nothing from her cell phone?" I asked.

"She was using one of those prepaids. None of the more recent calls on it lead us to anything concrete. It looks like she was hitting up a dealer a couple of times a week. We're trying to chase all of that down but it's slow going."

I heard footsteps behind me and turned. Sam walked in. "Good," he said. "You're all here. It'll save me the trouble of finding all of you. Any good news?"

"Not from where I sit," I said. "You don't have probable cause in the Talia Brewer case."

"Any more contact from Reilly or Emmons?" Sam asked.

"Nothing," I said. "Not since I told Reilly his deal is dead in the water."

"Well, I just heard from a detective in Swanton. They found female skeletal remains in a cornfield near their Fed Ex warehouse. We're waiting for dental records, but the girl was wearing a locket matching the description of one worn by Catherine Simpson. Then we've got what's left of Lindsay

Goode in Gunderson's field. Jan is devastated. He says he's never opening the farm again. He's looking to sell."

"Another one of Emmons's collateral victims," I said. "How awful."

"Needle's too good for him," Gus muttered.

"Emmons was telling the truth," I said. I couldn't feel relief. None of us could. Every one of the recovered victims had suffered the same set of injuries we now knew as Emmons's calling card. Broken thumbs. Hair cut off. Evidence of prolonged, brutal beatings. "Still nothing on Eliza Mattis?"

"Not yet," Sam said. "That one falls in Wood County's jurisdiction. But there was some significant flooding in the area Emmons described last year. Cops there think any remains buried near that area of Garfield Road might have been washed further into the valley. They'll expand their search."

"Let me know when you know," I said. "In the meantime, we're still proceeding as if this is a capital case against Emmons. We owe it to Haley's family. We owe it to Talia's too. He did this. He needs to admit it."

"Until he does," Gus said. "We don't have a solid case for the Brewer family. Coincidence alone won't be enough."

"I just don't get why he didn't confess to it," I said. "He doesn't want to die."

"He doesn't care," Sam said. "He just likes being the center of attention and that meeting with you was just that. More attention."

"He can't get attention after he's dead," I said. "He killed Talia Brewer. He had to have."

Gus got quiet. I knew that look.

"What," I said. "Gus ... what?"

"We can't rule out the possibility the Brewer girl was a copycat."

"There's nothing anybody could copy," I said. "The only people privy to the specifics of Dominique and Haley's injuries when Talia Brewer went missing were the cops in this building, me, and Cal Emmons. Period."

Gus was still quiet. So was Sam. I felt my skin crawl. "You think a cop on this case might have done this?" I said. Then, my own words played back in my head. My office. People in my office were privy to the specifics. My mind whirled trying to piece together a timeline.

"Whatever happened to that Skinner guy?" Gus finally came out and said it.

"He's gone," I said. "His internship is over."

"Have you heard from him since the trial ended?" Gus asked.

"No," I said, abruptly. "We didn't end on the greatest terms. He was ..."

"I never liked the guy," Sam said.

"Neither did Jason," I muttered. I hadn't told anyone about Jason's intel on Adam. As Gus and Sam stared at me, I began to wonder if Jason had already filled them in.

"If you hear from Skinner again," Gus said. "I want you to call me. We need to have a conversation with him at least."

It chilled me to think of it. But Adam Skinner knew the Chambers file inside and out. He'd memorized it.

"Is there anything else you need from us?" Sam asked, making a quick change of subject. "Before your sentencing hearing, I mean."

"I'll let you know," I said. "In the meantime, I'm heading over to Dominique's. I want her to hear about the other girls from me."

"I can drive you," Sam offered.

"No," said. "Dominique's seen enough cops lately. I think this will go over better if I'm on my own."

Sam and the others agreed. I left them with their promise to call me if they had any luck tracking down Talia Brewer's dealer or boyfriend. I had a sneaking suspicion they were one and the same. As much as it pained me, I knew I might need to call Jason and ask him for the file he started on Adam Skinner. Just in case.

45

Dominique's rental house in Waynetown was beautiful. Nicole and the Angels helped her get it a couple of weeks after we first met. It sat on the river with a nice big, wraparound porch. I found her there, waiting for me. She wore a pink-and-white striped top and a green polyester skirt. That, too, was courtesy of the Silver Angels. Dominique was working at Waynetown's most popular ice cream parlor. The hours were steady, the tips outstanding. It was a start. She wanted to go back to school and finish getting her certification as a dental hygienist.

"I think I might learn how to fish," she said. I felt a cold front coming in. A pair of kayakers rowed by and waved. It didn't seem wise to be out in the water this late in the year. Across the river, an older couple sat on their porch in a pair of matching rocking chairs. Dominique absently waved to them. Then they got up and went back inside.

I took a seat next to Dominique and watched the water with her. "Have you given any more thought about making a victim's impact statement at the sentencing next week?"

She didn't answer. She just reached down and untied her white sneakers. After that, she slipped off her apron. It clunked to the porch, heavy with coins.

"We were really busy today," she said. "Everyone's saying this is the last time we'll get in the mid-sixties. I asked Lisa, my boss. She said we stay just as busy in the wintertime. That'll be nice."

"Do you like it?" I asked. "I've never waitressed before."

"I like the money," she said. "Instant gratification. And I never realized how much people tip for ice cream. Some of them give us more than they pay for their food."

"That's great," I said.

A few minutes passed. I knew Dominique had a lot of questions about what to expect at the hearing. But there was something more important I needed her to understand right now.

"Dominique," I said. "You know that Emmons gave us information about other victims."

"You said you turned him down," she said. "That you weren't going to take the death penalty off the table. Did you change your mind?"

"How would you feel if I had?"

She looked down at her bare feet. "What he did ... Mara, there is no worse thing. It was ... bad."

"I don't believe he was being completely honest," I said. I had to be careful. We'd managed to keep the details of Talia Brewer's murder and the discovery of her remains for the most part out of the press. We didn't want to risk Peter Reilly or Emmons finding out what we knew. Not just yet.

"I need to tell you something," I said. "Emmons wasn't completely honest, but he did admit to some things. You know he admitted to what he did to you. He's going to plead guilty to that."

"I already know this," she said. "You told me. It should help. It's supposed to give me closure. I'm sorry, but it doesn't. It just makes me sad. I'm glad he said what he did. It just doesn't make it any better."

"I know," I said, then realized it was a stupid thing to say. I knew nothing. I hadn't lived through Dominique's nightmare.

"There were others," I said. "This hasn't been released to the press yet, but Emmons gave us the names and locations of three other women. As of yesterday, the police were able to find two of those women."

Dominique squeezed her eyes shut. When she opened them, she fixed them on me. "They're dead too?"

"Yes."

"He said he ... he hurt them? Raped them?"

"Yes."

"Did it happen after what he did to me?"

"Yes."

She dropped her head. "If they'd caught him. If I'd been able to remember more, would those girls still be alive?"

"That's not on you," I said. "Cal Emmons is the bad guy here. Not you."

"Everyone's bad, Mara. There are no good people."

I didn't know how to answer her. Dominique's eyes glazed over and I realized she wasn't asking for one.

It was only a matter of time before the rest of this story leaked to the press. Once again, it felt important that she hear it from me.

"Dominique, there's something else. There was another woman who went missing in Maumee County just after Haley was killed. Her body was found a couple of days ago. It will be hard to prove without Cal's admission, but her injuries fit his profile. We believe she was his last victim. I just want you to be prepared."

"What was her name?" she asked, her voice robotic.

I hesitated telling her but felt I could trust her. "Talia Brewer," I said. "We're still trying to piece it all together."

She got very still. She reminded me of a wax figure.

"You think Cal killed her too?"

"It looks that way, yes. Only he hasn't admitted to it. It's why I won't take the death penalty off the table. I need you to keep that detail to yourself. Cal has to make the admission on his own, without knowing what we know. Otherwise, he may try to manipulate things."

"Everyone's bad," she said. "They all deserve what they get."

She looked back out at the water. Time passed. Her faraway expression didn't change. I was about to say something, then Dominique's apron started to vibrate. She'd left her phone in the pocket. Reaching for it, she checked the caller ID then declined the call. The way she held the phone, shielding it from me, gave me an uneasy feeling. Whoever had called, she didn't want me to see.

"You don't have to say anything at the hearing if you don't want to," I said. "You aren't legally required to even be there."

"But you think it will help," she said.

"Yes. I think it will help if the jury fully understands the impact of what happened to you."

"Dead isn't enough?" she asked, tears starting to form. The shield she'd put up started to break.

"What?"

She turned to me. "Haley being dead isn't enough to make them understand how bad he is?"

"Sometimes it's hard for people to really know. Of course, they can never really know."

"You want me to speak for Haley. I can't. I never could. We aren't the same."

"No," I said. "You're not. And it isn't your responsibility to take this on if you don't want to. But it might be the last chance you have to confront Cal Emmons."

"Nicole says that's supposed to help give me closure. Like it's supposed to make me all better."

"Dominique, there's nothing wrong with you," I said. "You're not broken. You're not something that needs to be fixed. But maybe this could help you feel better."

Her expression darkened. She looked at me with what I can only describe as contempt. I knew she didn't hate me. Again,

I'd judged poorly. Who was I to tell this girl anything about how to feel better?

"I'm sorry," I said. "I should go. Just know that you can still call me anytime. I still want to know how you're doing. My door will always be open to you. I won't be prosecuting your case against Cal because it's not my county. But I'll be there. I promise."

Her phone rang again. She'd set it on the wooden arm of her chair. I stood at her shoulder. I glanced down.

A picture came up on her caller ID. It was then I understood what she hadn't wanted me to see. Vinny Meyer. I heard tires crunching on the gravel driveway.

"Dominique," I said. "You have a restraining order now. If that's Vinny, you can't ..."

The phone kept ringing. It sat on the chair arm between us. My eyes were drawn to it. I don't know what made me do it. I picked up Dominique's phone. She didn't stop me. There was a glare and I took a step away from her so I was better shielded under the porch. A text had come in from Vinny a few minutes before. As the phone rang, I read the banner across the top. It read simply, "About to pull in. Don't keep me waiting." Now he was calling.

In his caller I.D. picture, Vinny Meyer stood next to Dominique with his arm around her. She had on a bikini top. He was shirtless. I could just make out the tattoo on his chest.

Angel wings.

Beneath them. A date. Terror filled my heart. 12/11/66.

Talia Brewer's mother said Talia was seeing a man with that tattoo. My mind raced, trying to connect the pieces.

Vinny Meyer? A car door slammed on the other side of the house. A voice shouted.

"You don't answer your damn phone? I know you're there. I told you your ass better be ready for me. I'm done putting up with this crap!"

I kept staring. Unable to move. I saw a shadow cross in front of me. Then the base of my neck exploded in pain from the blow. I tried to stagger forward, but the ground gave way beneath me.

46

"You're bad. All you girls are bad. This is what you get. I told her. This is what you get!"

I didn't recognize the voice. Deep. Raspy. Unnatural.

The floor was hard under my cheek. My eyelids felt like they were made of cement. It would have been so much easier to just go back to sleep.

A ripping sound had me fully awake. I tried to sit up. My legs felt encased in sand. No. Not sand. And my eyelids weren't made of cement. I smelled the plastic, chemical scent of duct tape. It was over my mouth. My arms were wrenched behind me, bound at the wrists with more tape.

I tried to talk. My words were muffled behind the tape. Before I could get my bearings, I was dragged across the floor. Someone had me by the feet.

I screamed behind the tape, wriggling like a snake as pain ripped through my spine. I was being pulled down a set of stairs. Each one cut into me. Then, I hit the ground.

I could still smell the river. My body hit the grass. I tried to kick out. All I could manage was a twist to the side to keep my hands from scraping across the ground.

Sweat poured down my face. As I tried to clear my head and get my bearings. This was still Dominique's house. She'd been standing beside me. Behind me?

Someone let me go. My feet dropped to the ground. I tested the tape around my wrists. There was give.

I'd been dragged to the water's edge. Dominique had a rusted, steel sea wall along her property line.

I moved as quickly as I could, running the tape along the lip of the wall, sawing it back and forth. It gave a little more. I could hear arguing.

"I told you this would happen," a male voice said. "You never listen. What are you going to do this time? You keep making messes I have to clean up, Dom."

"Help me!" Dominique's voice. Cracked. Desperate.

Pulling for all I was worth, I got one hand free. Pain coursed through me. If I could get my legs free, I could roll into the river and let the current take me.

I ripped the tape off my face and mouth, tearing skin and what felt like most of my skin with it.

It was just me. I worked the tape around my ankles. Dominique's front porch and yard were empty. Where was she? Where was Vinny?

"It's for your own good!"

That deep, unnatural voice came from behind me. Hands grabbed at me, pulling my left hand up behind my head, pinning me back to the ground.

I looked up. It was as if my brain couldn't register what my eyes were seeing. The voice didn't match the face. Dominique straddled me. She pinned my right arm to the ground with her knees, and held my left arm out with one hand. In her other hand, she held a hammer.

"Be quick!" Vinny said. He was a blur, a mountain behind her. "She gets what she deserves, baby. It's your fault. You talk too damn much."

She swung it hard and quick, smashing my left thumb.

Pain shot through me as I heard the bones break. But she let go. She repositioned herself, ready to bring the hammer down again.

I kicked upward with both legs as hard as I could. Dominique lost her balance, toppling off me. My vision wavered with the pain shooting out from my broken thumb.

"Dominique!" I shouted. She looked at me, but through me. It was as if she weren't really there. With renewed horror, I knew she wasn't. She was somewhere else. She was inside a nightmare and planned to bring me with her. Behind her, Vinny's voice egged her on.

She rounded, drawing the hammer up over her head. One deadly swing, and she could smash my skull like a melon.

I crawled backward. I felt the air shift as the hammer came down. I rolled to the left as hard as I could. Dominique tripped. She came down on her knees and braced her fall with her hands.

I kicked out, making contact with her right hand. The hammer skittered away and fell over the wall into the river.

"Stop!" I shouted. "Dominique! Stop!"

She covered her face with her hands and curled into a fetal position.

"Stop," I said quieter. My legs were still partially bound with the tape. I couldn't feel pain anymore. Seizing the advantage, I pulled at the rest of the tape with my good hand.

She didn't stop me. She just rocked back and forth on the ground. But she wasn't alone. Vinny loomed over us.

"Worthless," he spat. "Gotta do everything by myself."

I screamed. This was a nightmare. I wanted that to be true. I wanted to believe some other monster had overpowered me today. But it hadn't. It had been Dominique. Vinny Meyer had triggered this broken girl and turned her into the thing she had feared the most.

He came closer, stooping down to pick up the hammer. He raised it. The water churned behind me. I was at the lip of the sea wall. There was only one thing left to do. As Vinny brought the hammer down, I rolled for all I was worth and let the current take me.

47

Later, I sat in the back of an ambulance. Dominique's yard lit up like Christmas, with all the emergency vehicles that descended. A neighbor had called them. He'd been sitting on his porch across the river and seen it all transpire.

Now, he stood next to a patrol car, saying the same thing over and over.

"That girl just picked up that sack of coins and hit the lady over the head. I started yelling. She couldn't hear me over the water. Then that man came running. I don't know why he didn't stop her. I saw them tape her up. Then that girl started dragging the lady to the water. That guy just stood there. Like he was telling her what to do. Had the wife call 911 and I started driving over here as fast as I could. The bridge was up. I'm so sorry, the bridge was up. You got lucky. If you hadn't gotten snagged on that fallen tree limb over there, who knows how far you'd have gone downriver."

"It's okay," I said for the dozenth time. "You did what you could."

He did everything. I found out later, the deputies were here less than two minutes after the 911 call was placed. A unit was on a call just one street over. Vinny and Dominique never made it out of the driveway.

Another car pulled up. Sam, Gus, and Brody poured out of it. Sam saw me first and ran toward me, white-faced.

"Mara," he gasped. The paramedics had wrapped my arm to my chest. My thumb throbbed with pain and had swollen to twice its size.

"I'm okay," I said, barely recognizing my own voice. Sam stayed with me while the detectives went to the responding officers and got the lowdown.

Just then, Dominique came out of the house, handcuffed and flanked by two female officers. That had been at my insistence. She still wasn't fully in her own head. I rose and walked over to the deputies. They'd already put Vinny Meyer in another patrol car, swearing his innocence up and down.

"Dominique," I said. "Can you hear me?"

"I didn't mean to hurt her," she sobbed. "I knew he was lying. I knew he was sleeping with that girl. I just got so mad."

I nodded. "She needs to be in the hospital, not lock-up."

Sam pulled me away, careful not to touch my injured thumb. "They'll take care of her," he said. "I'm more worried about you."

With my heart breaking, I watched the deputies put Dominique in a second ambulance. They followed behind in a squad car and disappeared up the hill.

"It was Vinny," I said. "The boyfriend Layla Brewer saw her daughter Talia with."

"What?" he asked.

"Yes. I saw a photo of him on Dominique's phone. He called her while I was here. Have him lift his shirt. You'll see the angel wing tattoo with the 12/11/66. It was him."

Sam shook his head. "I don't understand."

The pieces were still starting to take shape, but Dominique had already given her statement over Vinny's shouting protests.

"They killed Talia Brewer together," I said. "Dominique found out she was sleeping with Vinny. He tried to break up with her over it. Talia came here to confront her about it. Dominique snapped. She hit her over the head with a hammer. God. She'd done it once before with another one of Vinny's mistresses. Two years ago. There was a police report. Reilly questioned her on the stand about it. This time, it sounds like it was Vinny's idea to stage the body to look like one of Cal's victims to cover it all up. Dominique was the only one who knew how to do that. She told Vinny what Cal did to her. They took her body to those woods by the park and buried her just like Cal buried Haley. Just how he was planning to bury Dominique."

Gus and Brody walked out with another deputy. Brody's face was sheet white. "Mara," he said. "They found something in

Dominique's bedroom drawer. It's a clump of blonde hair stuck to duct tape. A lot of it."

The weight of it all threatened to pull me down. "I think you'll find it belonged to Talia Brewer. "

"He said we didn't know how crazy she was," Lance said. "He called her a psycho."

I winced at the word. "She's a very sick woman. Vinny was cheating on her with Talia. It triggered something in her. She hurt her in the same way she'd been hurt by Emmons."

"That's why Emmons didn't say anything about Talia," Gus said. "Son of a bitch. He was telling the truth. And now he gets what he wants. He gets to live. Talia Brewer wasn't his kill. "

"Not directly," I said. "But he broke that girl, Gus."

"Maybe," Sam said. "But he wasn't the only one. She'd known nothing but abuse her whole life."

His face fell. I think he saw the pain in mine. "Mara," he said. "Enough. I'm taking you to the hospital. Gus? Brody? You'll work with B.C.I. here. If you have any other questions for Mara, you know how to get a hold of her."

Detective Lance's phone went off. He held up a finger, asking us to wait. He stepped away for a moment.

"No arguments," Sam said to me. "You need to get that bone set if you ever want to use your left thumb again. She was going to kill you. She was playing out her own torture and abuse."

He looked at the river. It could have been my grave. I shuddered. The movement sent new pain shooting through me.

"Let's go," Sam said. "There's nothing else you can do here, Mara. Let's get you taken care of."

He was right. I let him put a gentle arm around me and lead me to his car. The Maumee River churned behind us. I couldn't help but wonder if it was also the last sound Talia Brewer heard.

48

One week later ...

When Peter Reilly walked into the courtroom at the start of Calvin Emmons's sentencing hearing, his face was flushed, his eyes glassed over. I thought he might be having a heart attack.

"Relax, Reilly," I said, as he approached me. "You're getting what you want today. This is just a formality. You barely even have to talk."

Over the last few days, the bodies of Catherine Simpson and Lindsay Goode had been conclusively identified. Their injuries matched what Cal had told me. Four days ago, the Wood County sheriffs found the body of Eliza Mattis. Further analysis in Emmons's barn turned up fragments of her DNA along with Lindsay's.

He'd told his last horrible truths. Though I couldn't lay Talia Brewer's murder directly at his feet, his confession would at least spare the families of three other women the nightmare of trial.

Even with all of that, I would have still gone forward on the death penalty. It was Cindy Chambers who begged me not to. "I can't have the loss of another life hanging over me," she said. "That man is a monster. I know in my heart he'll go to hell for what he did. He'll be in jail for the rest of his life. But I just can't bear knowing those two small children of his will have to grow up waiting for him to be put to death."

That, in the end, had been the hardest part of this for me to stomach. Carter and Bailey Emmons would carry the weight of their father's sins, and their mother's. They were truly Cal Emmons's last victims.

So I got to face Cal Emmons one last time. All swagger left him as they led him into the courtroom in chains. He looked meek. Docile. Thin. His new reality was starting to set in.

Judge Saul heard from both me and Peter Reilly. She put to paper the agreement we'd hammered out. Cal Emmons would spend the rest of his life in jail. No possibility of parole. He could never kill again, but he could still ruin lives. I had to fight not to let mine be one of them.

As they led him away a final time, Cal turned and looked at me. His eyes went down, resting on my bandaged thumb. I tried to conceal it behind my briefcase but wasn't quick enough. Cal gave me a curious look, then a smile lit his face.

My thumb began to throb. A four-hour microsurgery to install pins, plus a few months of physical therapy, and they told me it would be good as new. I was lucky.

Lucky.

Behind me, Sam walked up wearing a grim face. I gathered my things and went to join him. He walked me out of the building. We were two weeks away from Thanksgiving. I hadn't used any of my vacation days. After this hearing, Kenya insisted I take a few weeks off heading into the holidays. Though my first instinct was to protest ... there was too much to do ... who would manage my caseload ... I decided to take her advice and spend the time with Will.

"You know, I've never been disappointed not to go for the death penalty until now," I muttered.

"I know how you feel," Sam said. "But don't think Emmons's time will be easy. He's got enemies he doesn't even know about yet. At least, I hope."

Sam held the door for me as we walked into my building. Things were quiet today. Cal Emmons's now moot sentencing hearing had been the main event. As we passed by Kenya's office, she was on the phone. There would be another press conference. A million questions.

"Sheriff Clancy is already on his way over to greet the circus with Kenya," Sam said, echoing my thoughts. "Do you need to be here for this?"

"You know what?" I said. "No. Let me just grab my things. It's five o'clock somewhere. How about I buy you a beer?"

Sam smiled. "How about I buy you one, I'm still on duty for another four hours."

"You're on," I said. We got to my office. Things were starting to get decidedly less quiet out there as news of Cal's sentencing reached all corners. Someone had a television on. I could hear Reilly's voice as he spoke to reporters just outside the courtroom.

"Shut the door," I said. "I figure I've got about ten minutes before they realize I'm in here."

I sat behind my desk and put my feet up. Sam's eyes traveled to my heavily bandaged and splinted thumb. I saw sympathetic pain go through his face.

"It'll heal," I said.

"I just hope Dominique can," he said.

My heart darkened. "Vinny Meyer accepted a plea deal this morning. Twenty years."

"Sure, now he confesses," Sam said. "How the hell did he get that poor girl to go along with disposing of the body ..."

"She doesn't remember a lot of it, Sam. The psychologist working with her thinks she's disassociated. Like she's locked off that part of her brain that holds the memory of her worst trauma. The thing is, I buy it. On that riverbank, Sam, she was just gone. There was nothing behind her eyes. She was playing out something and going through the motions. Her defense attorney will claim she's not competent to stand trial. I think I'm going to try to sway Kenya to go along with it. That girl doesn't belong in prison, Sam. She belongs somewhere she can get help."

"Mara," Sam started.

"I'm thinking with a clear head. I promise. Vinny is another matter. I'll make it one of my life's missions to see him locked up too."

I pulled my hand down below my desk so Sam would stop staring at my bandaged thumb. So I would.

"So he gets Dominique to help him stage Talia to look like one of Cal Emmons's victims."

"That's what she said," I said. "I believe her Sam. I do."

"I just don't know that a jury ever will," he said.

I smiled. "They believed her before. Without her, Cal had a good shot at an acquittal. No matter what else happens, I know Dominique is the reason he'll never kill again."

Sam nodded. It was justice. It just came in a way neither of us could have expected.

Someone pounded on my door.

"So much for making a clean getaway," I said.

"We could still slip out the window?" Sam said.

"We're on the second floor," I countered.

He went around my desk and peered out the window. "I've never been one to shy away from a good caper," he teased. "That dumpster would probably break our fall."

"Rain check," I said. "Help me dodge this presser. Then I'll make good on my offer to buy you that drink."

He froze. The corners of his mouth lifted in a smile.

"You asking me out?" he said.

A flare of heat went through me. The words had just sort of spilled out. It felt natural. At the same time, I wasn't sure I was ready for the ramifications. I opened my mouth to answer, but never got the chance.

My door opened. One of the sheriff's deputies I barely knew stood there.

"Hey, Keller," Sam said, recognizing the guy. "Can it wait?"

"Uh ... hey, Lieutenant." Deputy Keller held a folded piece of paper in his hand. I recognized the color of it. It was a summons.

"For me?" I asked.

I reached for the paper. Deputy Keller had an odd look on his face. It made me look more closely at the summons. It was from the civil court. My name appeared at the top. My mind raced through the possibilities, settling on one.

"Skinner," I whispered. "Does he actually think he can sue me? Kenya never said a word ..." I braced myself before pulling the rest of the paperwork out of the envelope. What would it be? Wrongful discharge? Some bogus claim of workplace harassment?

"Mara?" Sam said, coming closer to me.

"Thank you, Deputy," I said. "Consider me served. You can go."

He excused himself with another apology and disappeared. Sam came to me, reading over my shoulder.

"Son of a ..."

We read the court caption together. Adam Skinner's name was nowhere on it. It got hard to breathe.

Jason.

"What the ..." Sam's question died on his lips.

"Jason's going after me for full custody of Will," I said. I quickly scanned the next page with his attached motion. "He wants to move him to D.C. with him."

I crumpled the paper and let it fall to the ground.

"He can't," Sam said. "You're not going to let him."

I couldn't yet find the words. Sam found them for me. He put his hands on my shoulders and waited until I met his eyes.

"We aren't going to let him," he said. "You, me, Kenya, Gus, even Hojo. We're family, Mara. Whatever it takes. Whatever you need."

I smiled. He was right. I wanted him to be right.

My door opened again. This time, Kenya stood there. She startled a bit, seeing Sam standing so close to me.

"I'm sorry to interrupt," she said. "But I can't put this off any longer. I need you out there. We need to talk to the press about Emmons. Are you ready?"

I straightened my back. It would have been a lot easier to just say no and find a dark corner to hide in. I wouldn't. I couldn't. Kenya needed me. Will needed me. Even Dominique and victims like her still needed me. As Sam put a steadying hand on my arm, I found the strength to walk outside and face the next battle head-on.

Up Next, Mara's personal and professional lives collide in her latest murder case. This time, the path to justice could reveal a dark family secret those close to her would do anything to protect. Don't miss Path of Justice.

Click the cover or copy into your browser to find out more ==> https://www.robinjamesbooks.com/pathback

UP NEXT FOR MARA BRENT...

Catch more of Mara Brent with her fifth book, Path of Justice.

https://www.
robinjamesbooks.com/pathback

NEWSLETTER SIGN UP

Sign up to get notified about Robin James's latest book releases, discounts, and author news. You'll also get *Crown of Thorne* an exclusive FREE ebook bonus prologue to the Cass Leary Legal Thriller Series just for joining.

Click to Sign Up

https://www.robinjamesbooks.com/marabrentsignup/

ABOUT THE AUTHOR

Robin James is an attorney and former law professor. She's worked on a wide range of civil, criminal and family law cases in her twenty-year legal career. She also spent over a decade as supervising attorney for a Michigan legal clinic assisting thousands of people who could not otherwise afford access to justice.

Robin now lives on a lake in southern Michigan with her husband, two children, and one lazy dog. Her favorite, pure Michigan writing spot is stretched out on the back of a pontoon watching the faster boats go by.

Sign up for Robin James's Legal Thriller Newsletter to get all the latest updates on her new releases and get a free digital bonus prologue to Cass Leary Legal Thriller series. http://www.robinjamesbooks.com/newsletter/

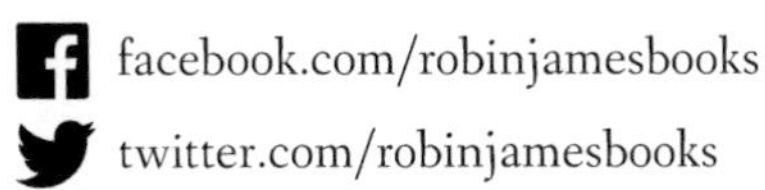

ALSO BY ROBIN JAMES

Mara Brent Legal Thriller Series

Time of Justice

Price of Justice

Hand of Justice

Mark of Justice

Path of Justice

With more to come…

Cass Leary Legal Thriller Series

Burden of Truth

Silent Witness

Devil's Bargain

Stolen Justice

Blood Evidence

Imminent Harm

First Degree

Mercy Kill

Guilty Acts

With more to come…

Made in the USA
Columbia, SC
24 August 2021

44169014R00233